Bookman Dead Style

"An exciting, intriguing plot. . . . I highly recommend *Bookman Dead Style* to anyone who enjoys . . . well-crafted mysteries."
                                        —Open Book Society

Comic Sans Murder

&

A Dangerous Type Mystery

PAIGE SHELTON

BERKLEY PRIME CRIME
New York

BERKLEY PRIME CRIME
Published by Berkley
An imprint of Penguin Random House LLC
375 Hudson Street, New York, New York 10014

ISBN: 9780425277270

First Edition: December 2017

Printed in the United States of America
1 3 5 7 9 10 8 6 4 2

Cover art by Brandon Dorman/Peter Lott Reps
Cover design by Lesley Worrell
Book design by Kelly Lipovich

For Phyllis A. Whitney

Acknowledgments

Thanks to:

Michelle Vega, Jen Monroe, and Leis Pederson. They make a great team.

My agent, Jessica Faust, for her continued support, and for laughing at all the right lines.

As always, Charlie and Tyler.

My readers are rock stars. Thank you for everything.

1

Larry Gerald might not have thought it too odd to find an abandoned ski boot on the Star City slopes, but it's what he found inside it that was most unexpected.

He spied the gray boot resting atop the still-solid snow base at the edge of a copse of pine trees, the branches currently green and not powdered with the white stuff. It was his first day on a snowboard, which might have contributed to his piqued curiosity about the boot. He'd taken a lesson but had spent more time on his behind than upright on the board. He welcomed an excuse for a moment's rest as he came to an awkward stop next to the boot and sat back onto the snow.

"Ouch," he said, realizing that even sitting was going to cause some pain for a little while. He was out of the way for a minute or two, he thought as he looked toward the run. Most of the boarders were at least ten years his junior and moved down the mountain or through the half pipe as if their snowboards were extensions of their legs, not something foreign buckled onto them.

He shook his head at himself and his inability to accept that even he, onetime star athlete, was destined to lose a little of his innate athletic ability once he reached thirty, never mind thirty-five. Besides, he'd been a swimmer, not a skier. Different muscles.

He smiled then, because none of that mattered. He was having a great time in Star City, Utah, taking a well-deserved vacation and enjoying the sights, the sounds, and the greatest snow on earth, according to the Utah tourism Web site he'd perused before booking the trip. He didn't have much to compare it to, but the snow did seem pretty great and Star City was spectacular. Even now he could look out and see the valley that held charming shops and even more snow-covered slopes alive with happy skiers and snowboarders. Life was good.

For the most part. Law school had been rough, the divorce rougher. Still plenty of time to make a good go of it, though.

He reached over for the boot, thinking that he could tuck it under one arm and drop it off at lost and found. He'd been so off-balance on the board that carrying a boot the rest of the way down couldn't possibly make the experience any worse.

Ski boots are naturally heavy, but there was something different about this one, something weirdly balanced, maybe. With the boot in his thick-gloved grip, he peered inside.

And then he screamed and tossed the boot away, sending it flying a short distance through the air, landing only a few feet from him on its side.

Though the inside of the boot had been filled mostly with what Larry would describe as "gore," he knew he'd seen the foot, ankle, and sock that had originally gone into the boot. When it had been attached to the rest of a body.

His breathing and heart rate sped up immediately, and though he'd never hyperventilated or had a panic attack, he knew that something like that was about to happen.

He noticed a snowboarder making her way toward him. She'd either heard his scream or noticed the flying ski boot and drops of blood that now fell across a small patch of the whitest snow ever, making it not so much the greatest snow anymore.

"Hey," she said as she took off her helmet and goggles, pieces of her curly blond hair escaping its ponytail. "You okay?"

"I know you," Larry said, oddly zoning in on the fact that he'd seen the girl before.

"You might have come into my great-grandfather's shop, The Rescued Word. I work there sometimes. I'm Marion."

He nodded and wished he could just keep his attention on her and that wonderful shop rather than what he'd seen a few moments before.

"Are you hurt?" she asked again. "The blood . . ."

"It's not my foot," Larry said.

"What?" Marion asked, but realization came over her features quickly. "Oh. In the boot. There's a foot?"

"Yes."

"Well, that . . . that just sucks."

"Big-time."

She didn't look into the boot, but she swooned for a beat or two. Larry tried to get up to help her, but his legs were spaghetti. Fortunately, she recovered quickly.

"I'm okay, and I can get help," she said, holding her hand up to stop him. He fell back onto his sore behind again.

Marion pulled out her phone and looked at the screen for a moment before she tapped it. She brought her eyebrows together as she inspected Larry. He was trying to look like he was okay, but he wasn't, not even close.

"Aunt Clare. Hey, will you call Jodie and tell her there's a problem up on Thor? Yeah, the half-pipe run. No, I'm not hurt. I'm up here with a man, though. Yeah, he found something that the police need to see. Okay, well, I'm not going to look in it, but I think it's a ski boot with a foot still inside. Only the foot."

Larry didn't bother to add "ankle and sock too," but the words rattled through his shaken and muddled thoughts.

"Right," Marion said. She ended the call and smiled stiffly at Larry. "The police will be here quickly. You sure you're going to be okay?"

Larry nodded, thinking that maybe law school and even the divorce hadn't been all that bad after all.

2

"Yep, that's what it was," Jodie said as she sucked on her straw. She'd hit bottom two pulls ago, but she wasn't one to let any drops of pineapple shake go to waste.

I shook my head, having lost interest in my own hot fudge sundae. But Jodie was a cop; she was used to these sorts of things.

"Where was the rest of the body?" I asked.

"That's the million-dollar question."

"No clues at all?"

"None. Not much evidence either. It wasn't as . . . messy as you might think. Frozen for the most part. It was beginning to thaw."

"Oh, Jodie. I don't want to think about that." I pushed up my glasses.

"I understand. Let's just say there are no clues yet. We're hoping something turns up soon."

"Could the person still be alive?"

"It's a possibility, but we don't think it's likely. As of about thirty minutes ago, no one missing a foot has checked into any hospital in the western United States. Even someone trying to hide that they were hurt would be hard-pressed to try to take care of that sort of wound on their own. Most people would seek help even if they were guilty of something and afraid of getting caught."

We sat across from each other in a booth composed of a Formica table and pink vinyl bench seats, inside the diner across the street from The Rescued Word.

Shortly after I'd called Jodie to send out the troops for my niece, Marion, and the man on the Thor snowboard run, Marion actually came into the shop to tell the tale of the afternoon's brief but jarring adventure.

She hadn't been too shaken up, but she'd been bothered in a semifrantic sort of way. It had taken two hot chocolates and one of Chester's stories to get her back to her normal bubbly self. Chester, my grandfather and Marion's great-grandfather, was the original owner of The Rescued Word. He frequently made up stories, some of his most famous being about the carved wooden doors over the middle shelves of the shop, a building that used to house the Star City Silver Mining Company. All of his stories were wild fabrications, but today he worked extra hard to direct Marion's thoughts away from spooky ski boots by inserting whiskey-addled fairies and magic silver from the old mines. I think she was more perplexed than entertained, but before long she was smiling and questioning the plot's logic. Of course, her father, my brother, Jimmy, a single parent, would probably want her to seek therapy just to make sure she was really okay. Jodie had said that Marion hadn't seen much but had made the call to Clare based solely on what Mr. Gerald had said. Jodie also said that Marion would be fine; she was young and would move on soon enough—unless she was the one to have separated the foot from the body, Jodie had added with a sly grin.

"What about a skiing accident? Maybe the body got flung to a place you guys couldn't spot right off," I said.

"We're looking. That's another possibility, but, again, it's unlikely. There are just too many weird things that would have had to happen for it to be something like that. Of course, weird things do happen, so we'll see."

"Foul play, you think?"

"Probably. But it sure is a strange one."

"I'd say."

"So, other than the boot, how's Marion doing?" Jodie said.

I thought a moment. "Oh, you mean the competition?"

"Yeah, sure. I'm worried about her."

"We all are, but she's moving past it."

Marion had been a part of the Olympic snowboard qualifying series of events this year. The Grand Prix had been held on our own Star City slopes. She'd aced the first two events, but then a heavy and sudden wave of self-doubt got in her head, and she couldn't finish, thus eliminating her chance to be invited onto the team this time around. She was so young, still only sixteen, so she'd have another shot. But it had most definitely been a rough time for her. I'd tried to comfort her. Chester had tried to explain that it was not a big deal, that her life would be long and she'd have lots more chances, and Jimmy had continually wondered how he'd failed his daughter.

"Good. She'll do great the next time around," Jodie said.

"I think so too. That is, if her family doesn't get in her head too much. We're trying to figure out the right balance. But she's still hitting the slopes every day, and her coach says she's still improving, that she hasn't reached her peak. Maybe something deep inside her knew she wasn't ready yet. Hard to understand subconscious motivations."

"She's amazing."

"I agree."

Jodie gave up on the shake, moving the cup to the other side of her clean plate. We'd both ordered cheeseburgers and fries, but most of my food was still in front of me.

"How's it going with the visiting celebrity?" Jodie asked.

"Nathan is working hard and driving poor Adal crazy."

Nathan Grimes, worldwide famous horror author, had made The Rescued Word his temporary place of business. He'd enjoyed time in Star City before, working on a couple of his most popular and bestselling novels: *Jump* and *Spark*. All of his titles were one word. I hadn't had the chance to ask him how that had happened, but he'd been working with Adal for only a little over a week, and only part-time, as they planned and prepped to print a book of Grimes's poetry on the replica Gutenberg press that Chester had built in our workshop. It stood amid old typewriters, typewriter parts, tools, and typeface boxes. Nathan had heard about the press when he was in the middle of *Spark*, and he hadn't been able to shake the idea of self-publishing his poetry. I didn't know how well the book would sell, but anyone who'd read his horror novels was sure to be surprised by his romantic way with words.

Adal was my apprentice. He'd come from Germany with the hope that I would teach him everything I knew about rescuing words: fixing typewriters, operating an old Gutenberg printing press, repairing books, even where to find the best paper products throughout the world. He and many of his family members, the male ones, had shown up in January for the Star City Film Festival. They'd stopped in the shop, and before I could even understand most of their names, Chester had offered the apprenticeship position to Adal. It had turned into one of Chester's best decisions ever. Someday Adal would take his skills back to Germany, but he was ours for a while. His full name was Adalwulf, but he'd told us to call him Adal. Later we wondered whether he made the request to avoid being called Wulf instead.

Adal had been a part of The Rescued Word family during the Grand Prix in February, and had become a surprising source of comfort for Marion. He was a stranger from another land who brought a perspective that she somehow tuned in to. He'd helped us all, but mostly Marion. It was time for Marion's job at the shop to take a backseat to her dreams. She could still work on personalizing stationery on her computer at home and at the shop when she wanted to, but Chester had made it clear that she got to choose the best way to accomplish her goals. He'd quit complaining when she couldn't be found or was late because she was on the slopes. It would have been only Chester and me at the shop if Adal hadn't come along, and we all preferred the idea of an apprentice over a new employee.

"I'm sure Adal is doing fine with the famous author," Jodie said. "How's he doing as an apprentice?"

"He's a pro, but why do you ask?" I said, though I suspected I knew the answer.

Jodie shrugged. "He's taking Latin from Anorkory. You know that, don't you?"

I laughed about his lessons with our resident Latin teacher. "I do know that. German, French, Spanish, and English just weren't enough for him."

"He's very into languages."

"He's very into you," I said as I picked up my mug of hot chocolate. I took a sip and then looked at her over the top of the cup.

"It's hard to take your disapproval seriously when you have whipped cream on the tip of your nose," Jodie said.

I wiped off the cream.

"Better?" I said.

"A little, but I still don't understand your disapproval."

"Well. It isn't disapproval so much. It's concern."

"I'm listening." She took a drink of her water.

As casual as she seemed, I knew she was paying attention. I took advantage of the moment. "You and Mutt broke up only a couple of weeks ago, and I'm not really sure you broke up all the way."

"Oh, we broke up all the way. No worries there," Jodie said bitterly.

"Well, you haven't told me what happened. That's weird. You tell me everything."

"I do not tell you everything. You don't tell me everything either."

"Actually, I do," I said, a tinge of hurt in my voice. "What won't you tell me?"

Jodie cleared her throat. "I don't want to tell you the details of the breakup yet, Clare, just like you didn't want to tell me the details of your breakup with Creighton soon after that happened. My breakup with Mutt is a sore spot that needs to fester a bit before I start picking at it and then finally letting it heal. That is how wounds work. They go through stages. Remember how you were with Creighton?"

"I do, but he's your brother. I was afraid . . . of your loyalty to him," I said.

Jodie laughed. "That's the most ridiculous thing I've ever heard. Not once since we were sixteen have I put my brother before you. I knew what he was when you started dating him. I wasn't surprised at all when he cheated on you. You needed time too."

"I'm sorry," I said. "I should have told you."

"No, that's not what I'm saying at all. I just want you to understand that I'm in no state to talk about my breakup with Mutt yet, even with you. But when I'm ready, you'll be the only one I'll want to talk to. I promise."

"Okay, but . . ."

"Right, it's too soon to start dating someone else. I've never had many dating options, and another one so soon after a pretty serious relationship is weird for me, but I like Adal. That's it—*like*. He likes me. We like each other and want to get to know each other. He invited me to take Latin with him. It's the weirdest thing anyone has ever asked me to do. I said yes, but I'm not going to fall in love so quickly this time. Okay?"

"Okay," I said, but then paused a beat. "You do know he has plans to go back to Germany, right?"

"Yes, I'm aware."

I paused again. "And, Jodie, I'm sorry for what happened with you and Mutt, whatever it was."

"It's okay. Really okay." She forced a sad smile.

"Mutt and Adal. You sure pick guys with strange names," I said with a grin.

"I know. Elmo's probably next." She laughed.

A loud rumble pulled our attention out toward The Rescued Word.

"Expecting anyone?" Jodie asked as a white panel truck came to a noisy stop and a young guy jumped out of the driver's side. He stood in front of the shop and took turns inspecting a clipboard he held and the front of the darkened windows.

"I'm not. I should check on Chester."

We got the bill taken care of quickly, and by the time we were across the street, Chester was in front of the store with what appeared to be a delivery guy. Chester wore a red silk robe that I'd never seen before, and held a sleepy-eyed Baskerville, our cat (well, the entire family's probably, but mostly his), in his arms. They were both in decidedly sour moods.

"What's up?" I said as we approached.

"This young man says we are expecting the items in his truck. I have explained to him that we are not, no matter what they are."

"What's in there?" I asked.

"Typewriters, I think," the delivery guy said. He was young and his face looked flustered and unsure in the glow from the old-fashioned streetlight.

"Little late for a delivery, don't you think?" Jodie said. I saw her hand go to the spot where her gun would be holstered if she was in uniform.

The kid shrugged. "Got caught in some snow up around Evanston. Sorry I'm late, but once I got here, I wasn't sure what to do except see if I could get these delivered. I'd like to get back on the road and back to Evanston tonight. It's gonna storm out this way tomorrow, and I came all the way from Nebraska."

"Where in Nebraska?" Jodie asked as she inspected the back license plate.

"Lincoln."

"That's a long way to bring some typewriters," Jodie said.

"Yeah, I was supposed to meet Lloyd here this afternoon. I've been calling him for hours, leaving messages that I'd be late. He was here today, right?"

Chester and I looked at each other.

"No one named Lloyd was here today as far as we remember," I said.

"Oh man, I was worried when I couldn't get ahold of him. I'm sure he'll call me back, but he told me specifically to meet him here this afternoon. He'll call me when he can. Must have gotten busy or something. He said there was a small reunion too, some meetings, I think. Maybe you can talk to him tomorrow?"

"I can't even think of someone I know named Lloyd," Chester said.

"Yeah, he said he knew you guys. Lloyd Gavin?" the young man said.

"Lloyd Gavin?" Jodie and I said together.

"We went to high school with him," Jodie said to me as I nodded.

"Wait a second," Chester said. "A gentleman called last week and asked for you, Clare. He wouldn't give me his name, but he said you and he knew each other when you were kids. I said you weren't in. He said he had some typewriters we should look at, but I told him we weren't interested. He mentioned he was coming out for some meetings and would stop by. I reiterated that we didn't want to buy any typewriters either for consignment or otherwise. He laughed. I remember being distinctly put off by his attitude. I told him to travel safely and that I had to go. Maybe that was him."

"That sounds like him," the kid said. "But they're not for sale. They're gifts."

"He was one of the really smart kids in school," Jodie said. "We always thought he'd go far, but Lincoln, Nebraska, wouldn't have been a destination I would have predicted."

"He did go far. He's a very successful businessman in Lincoln," the kid said.

"What's his business?" Jodie asked.

"Computer hardware and software development."

"Lloyd Gavin," I muttered, remembering his sweet and shy personality more than I remembered his smarts. He'd asked me to the junior high dance but had broken out in hives right before the event. His dad had come by my house to apologize for his son's nerves. I'd been heartbroken about missing all the fun, but I went back to Lloyd's house and we watched movies. He and I became friends after that. In fact, he'd been my best friend until Jodie came into my life at sixteen.

When Jodie and I became close, I'd tried to include Lloyd in our friendship, but he told me he could handle being friends with only one person at a time, that it was all just too much for him to hang out in a group. He told me it would be better for me to stick with Jodie than with him.

I'd thought that was pretty weird then and had no idea how to handle what at the time had seemed like an ultimatum, but now, years and life experience later, I knew that Lloyd was an introvert, perhaps as much of an introvert as someone could be—painfully shy. Somehow I'd managed to break into his world, and the ultimatum was actually an unusually mature kindness sent my way.

It was probably the kiss on his cheek I gave him when I went back to his house with his dad the night of the dance that cemented our friendship. I remembered my immature mind thinking that it was supposed to be my first date, so I deserved a kiss even if I was the only one to do it.

"Clare?" Jodie said. "You with us?"

"Oh, sorry. Yeah, I'm right here. I knew Lloyd in high school and we were pretty good friends when we were younger, but I don't understand what's going on with some typewriters that he wanted to give us."

"How about you open the back?" Jodie said to the delivery boy.

"Will do. Name's Dillon, by the way."

"Nice to meet you, Dillon," Jodie said, keeping a suspicious slant to her eyes. She placed herself in between me, Chester, Baskerville, and the back of the truck. No such thing as downtime for Jodie.

A few seconds later, Dillon swung open the back door and then turned on his phone's flashlight application.

"There ya go. They look like a mix between sewing machines and typewriters. Mr. Gavin said you'd know what they are, and he wanted you to have them. Made me promise not to wreck the truck."

We stepped closer and looked inside. Dillon had been correct; the three machines inside did look like a sewing machine/typewriter hybrid.

"Oh my," Chester said.

In tandem he and I adjusted our glasses.

"Hoovens," Chester said with a breathy sigh. Baskerville, not interested in the items in the truck, jumped out of his arms and trotted back to the shop's stoop, sitting and wrapping his tail around himself. His patience wouldn't last long, but he'd sensed that Chester and I might need a moment.

"That something good?" Jodie said.

"Yes," I said. "Very good. Very rare."

"Awesome," Jodie said. "All righty, then. Can we get these unloaded so Dillon can hit the road? I can call for help."

"Jodie, we can't just take these," I said. "They're too valuable."

"Let's see if we can get ahold of Lloyd. What's his number? Do you know where he was staying?" Jodie asked Dillon.

"Sure, but I've been trying to call him since last night. No answer."

"Like you said, maybe he's just been busy. Tell me the hotel too. We'll find him," Jodie said.

"I hope so," Dillon said. "He sure seems to be missing in action."

Jodie and I both froze for a moment before we shared a look.

"No, it couldn't be," I said.

"That would be a wild coincidence," she said.

"What?" Chester said.

I sent him a frown. I didn't want to say in front of Dillon what Jodie and I were thinking, but Chester would pick up on our thoughts in a second.

He did.

"Oooh," he said. "Well, that would be terrible."

"What's going on?" Dillon said.

"Come on, kid. Let's find a place for you and your truck to stay tonight," Jodie said. "Lock 'er up."

"Why? Why can't I just leave them and head back toward Evanston? I need to get home."

"We gotta find Lloyd before you can go. It's best that way," Jodie said.

Dillon scratched his head and shrugged, because he was too young to know what else to do. "Okay."

Chester and I did take a moment to jump inside the back of the truck and take a closer look at the Hoovens. More than anything we were shocked that we were even allowed to look at the rare old machines. They'd been secured with ropes and pulleys, so they weren't going anywhere easily. As much as we really wanted to inspect them, we didn't want to touch what was considered the first automatic typewriter machine; some even called them the first computers. Their mishmash of features—an old Underwood No. 5, a sewing machine table, and the player-piano-punched paper feed—were all antique elements that brought forth images of mad scientists and overflowing beakers, at least to our typewriter-driven minds. Owning them wasn't something either of us would ever be able to comprehend.

They were extraordinary, but I couldn't imagine they would ever be ours. They were just too valuable, probably worth between five and ten thousand dollars each, though I'd have to research to know for sure. Their place in history and their rarity made them museum pieces, not things that should be in our little shop in Star City, Utah. I was glad they weren't going inside The Rescued Word that night, but I was a little worried about their being in the open police station parking lot.

"I can take them down to Salt Lake to a secure facility if you think I should," Jodie said.

"Tonight?" It was already after eight.

"I could if you think it's best."

"You have officers on duty at the station all night, right?" I said.

"Yes."

"Just have them check on the truck throughout the night. Unless we were being spied on, we're the only ones who know about them. Besides, I'm probably overreacting; chances are that very few people know what they really are."

"Lloyd must know," Jodie said.

"Maybe," I said.

"I'll find him and we'll see."

She and I got Dillon set up at the same hotel our visiting author was staying at. It was conveniently located near the police station. I didn't knock on Nathan's door as I walked out of the hotel with Jodie, but I angled toward it and heard what I thought was the click-clack of typewriter keys. He hadn't mentioned that he wrote on a typewriter, but I'd ask him about it.

Jodie dropped me off at my house, affectionately named Little Blue, and left me with thought-provoking parting words: "Hope Lloyd still has both feet."

It was just her way.

3

"Hoovens. I've never heard of them," Seth said before he dug his fork into some pancakes. "Well, I might have heard of Hooven sewing machines, but not typewriters."

He'd been in southern Utah helping determine the safety of hiking through a specific slot canyon after a small earthquake had registered in the area the previous week. He'd gotten back late last night, so he went back to his apartment. We met for our morning breakfast date at a new place in town, the Pancake Joint. It was an immediate hit, popular with locals and tourists, and it was difficult to get a table, even early on a Wednesday morning. Fortunately, we'd had to wait only a few minutes before being seated.

"Yes, Hooven sewing machines. Their typewriters aren't that well known, but they were revolutionary, kind of the first computer."

"Really?"

"Yes. They were electric, having been put together with a manual and a modified Underwood No. 5, and—here's the original Hooven connection—a sewing machine stand. They used the same idea that player pianos used, the paper with the dots in them being sent through a feed and over a roll. You could print a bunch of the same thing. The first form letters, but not mimeographed. Each copy an original, so to speak."

"Really? When were they all the rage?"

"The early nineteen hundreds, but maybe not *all* the rage. They were expensive, so were only available to a select few."

"I had no idea."

"Crazy, huh?"

"Yeah."

"The remaining Hoovens are rare, hard to find, and each one can bring between five and ten thousand dollars. They belong in a museum."

"And Lloyd wants to give you three?"

"That's what Dillon says, but we need to talk to Lloyd, and as of this morning Jodie still hasn't."

"So, you think he might be the one missing a foot?"

"Not really, but it's all a strange set of circumstances."

"I'd say."

"How was your trip?" I said.

"Great. Busy, but great. I'm thoroughly enjoying living and working in Utah," he said with a smile.

"That's good to hear."

My relationship with Seth had gone the opposite direction of Mutt and Jodie's. My geologist and I were rock-solid, rocking and rolling, and completely digging each other. We worked on coming up with new puns all the time, but there were really only so many.

"I brought you something," Seth said as he put down his fork and reached into his pocket.

Seth frequently brought things to me from different parts of Utah. The items were mostly little things like rocks or sand—he'd brought me a small glass container full of sand from the Coral Pink Sand Dunes once. The sand was more orange than pink, but I liked the way he'd chosen to share his intrastate travels—with little souvenir-type items that I now kept in a glass bowl on my coffee table.

"Oh, it's a . . . I can't remember the name. I know it's not a scarab, but that's what it reminds me of," I said as I took the small fossil.

"Trilobite."

"That's right. The sea creatures, back when Utah was covered by a sea." I smiled. "From how long ago?"

"Cambrian Period, five hundred seventy to five hundred million years ago."

"How could I have forgotten?"

"No need to remember; I'm here to help regarding all things old and geological. I got it on the way home. I had to swing around to House Range and drop off some papers to a colleague. It made for a long trip."

"Well, I'm glad you're back. Thank you. I love it. I really do. Let's name him."

"Him? You sure?"

"Can I be sure?"

"I don't think so, but that's for someone else's PhD."

"Maple," I said as I glanced at the bottle of syrup on the edge of the table.

"That'll work."

I put the fossil in my bag just as my phone started to ring and vibrate from inside the outer pocket.

"Jodie?" I said as I answered.

"Where are you?" she asked.

"Pancakes with Seth."

"Come over to the station when you're done, as quickly as possible please," she said.

I was momentarily startled by her use of "please." It wasn't that she wasn't polite, but we'd known each other long enough that our requests to each other didn't usually require such formality.

"We're on the way," I said.

Seth didn't ask any questions, but put one more forkful of pancake in his mouth before he pulled out some cash and left it on the table to cover the tab.

"Let's go," he said.

e⁓

As we hurried in through the police station doors, two young women decked out in ski gear exited. One still had her ski boots on, which struck me as odd but only in a distant something's-off way. The two women spoke to each other in serious, concerned tones, which I also noticed only peripherally, again as something vaguely wonky. They were even less aware of us than we were of them, passing through the doors without a glance in our direction.

We hurried down the hallway. I hadn't been concerned that Jodie had called me into the station for any reason other than Lloyd, but as we approached her office I began to wonder if maybe something had happened to someone in my family. A wave of panic tightened in my chest and I took a deep, cleansing breath.

As we went through the doors and into the office Jodie shared with five other officers, her brother and my ex-fiancé, Creighton, was leaving the room. He'd become my ex a few years ago now, and we'd managed to learn a civility toward each other. Correction: I'd become less angry with his old cheating ways. He hadn't changed much from his quiet, sometimes brooding, sometimes less-than-polite self. I hated to admit it, but having Seth in my life had probably been the biggest catalyst to move me to a better place with Creighton. Surprisingly, he and Seth hadn't had much trouble being friendly to each other, which probably helped too.

"Seth, Clare," Creighton said as he stood to the side and held the door. "Jodie's waiting for you."

"Everything okay?" I said.

Creighton's eyebrows came together at my tone. "I think so. It's about the guy you guys knew in school."

"They find him?" I asked.

"Jodie's got the details."

"Thanks," Seth said before he nodded me inside.

"Hey," Jodie said as she looked up from her desk and signaled us over.

Jodie rubbed a tired eye with her fist, the childlike move endearing even though it was done by a tough policewoman. "It was him, Clare."

"Lloyd? The foot was Lloyd's?" I asked, my voice way too high-pitched.

"Have a seat," she said.

I sat.

"A body was found by a couple of backcountry skiers. In fact, they left as you were coming in. The body, identified as Lloyd's, was missing a foot, and . . . and he had been shot in the head. Although it's unlikely that there's more than one dismembered foot out there, we are having further tests done to confirm, but we think it's Lloyd's, and of course, it's murder."

"That's horrible," Seth said. He looked over at me as he swung a supportive hand onto my knee.

I put my hand over his. I'd heard Jodie's words, but they didn't want to register. "Not a skiing accident? But a bullet? Killed?"

Jodie shook her head slowly. "No, not an accident. He was shot with a gun, a wimpy .22, but they're not so wimpy at close range. We think he was shot at the top of a hill, a ledge, and then shoved off. The body fell about a hundred feet and . . . well, somehow the foot got detached and was moved over to the more populated area by a . . . we're still just guessing . . . by a wild animal."

"Oh, that's not good," I said. I cleared my throat, embarrassed at my simplistic take on the tragedy.

"No, it isn't," Jodie said.

"Good grief, Jodie, who would have killed Lloyd?" I said.

"Not one clue. Literally, not even one. All we know is what Dillon told us. He wanted you to have some Hoovers delivered to you."

"Hoovens," I said.

"Right. That, and Lloyd was coming here for some sort of small reunion or meetings. If it was some sort of class reunion, I didn't hear about it. You?"

I shook my head. "Do you think someone killed him for the typewriters?"

"We can't be sure of anything at this point, and since we don't have much of anything else to go on, we're looking more closely at every little thing. I need to inspect those machines and you need to be with me in case you see something that doesn't seem right. . . . I don't know, Clare—we just don't know anything. We need to look at everything."

"Sure."

The door swung open and banged against the wall. We all turned to see Dillon say, "Sorry" to Creighton as they came through together. Creighton just sent him a level but slightly sympathetic gaze.

Clearly, Dillon had heard the news; his nose was red and his eyes were puffy. I didn't know exactly how old he was, maybe in his early twenties. He was obviously upset, whether he truly cared about Lloyd or not. From my vantage point, it looked like he cared plenty.

Jodie stood. "Come on—let's go someplace more private. You're both invited."

We all went back through the door and to an interview room that smelled like Pine-Sol and old aftershave. I wondered who'd been in there before us. The space was cramped, but we each had a chair. Seth and I shared a brief look as we sat. We both probably wondered why he was there, or whether Jodie had truly thought through the fact that she'd invited him.

I also noticed another shared look, this one between Creighton and Jodie. He was higher up in rank than she was, though he wasn't her direct supervisor. However, it would be up to him to give her the nod of approval to conduct the questioning. He did exactly that, and with much less Creighton attitude than many of his nods.

Recently, Jodie had had suspicions about some of her brother's activities. She wasn't sure he was on the up-and-up, and she'd shared her concern with me, but of course she couldn't give me all the details. We'd talked about conducting our own private investigation, but I thought she was scared to find out the full truth about him, so our in-depth snooping was more talk than action. However, now every time I was around Creighton, I was extra tuned-in to his behavior.

"Dillon, we're so sorry about Lloyd," Jodie said. "It's tough news to hear, particularly when you're somewhere where you don't know anyone else. We want to let you go home, but we can't just yet. Do you understand that?"

"Sure." Dillon sniffed.

"All right. Dillon, you came here to deliver the Hoovens, right?" Jodie said.

"Yeah."

"What else did you know about Mr. Gavin's trip to Star City? Give me as many details as you can. You mentioned a reunion or some meetings."

Dillon looked at each face in the room. I didn't know whether he was stalling because he needed a moment or if it was his way of memorizing the people around him.

"Just what I said earlier," he finally said.

"Repeat for all of us to hear, please," Jodie said.

Dillon blinked and looked up at Creighton, who leveled another gaze at the younger man, this one unsympathetic.

"I was supposed to meet him here. He wanted to give the Hoovens to Clare and Chester Henry. He came out early to meet with some high school friends. He said there was a reunion—no, maybe he just said meetings. I'm just not sure. I totally thought that Clare was one of those high school friends, even though he didn't mention her when he talked about the meetings, just about the Hoovens."

"Did he say any specific names at all?" Jodie asked.

Dillon rubbed a finger under his nose as his eyebrows

came together. "Yeah, just one, though, and he didn't mean for me to hear him say it. He kind of muttered it like he wasn't saying nice things about the guy, and it was such a different name. Donte."

Donte Senot? I didn't say the words out loud, but that was the only Donte I could remember from our high school days. I hadn't seen him in years and I had no idea what he'd done with his life, but both Jodie and Creighton wrote in their small notebooks.

"Any other names?" Jodie asked. "Think about it."

"Not that I can remember right now. Lloyd's assistant, Brenda, will probably know everything though. She always does."

"All right. We'll call her. What was Lloyd's business, Dillon? Start with the name of the business and then tell us what he did, give us a history of it if you have one," Jodie said.

"I started working there only about six months ago, so I don't have much history. My parents were happy when I went to work for Gavin Enterprises, though. It's computer stuff—not the whole computers, just parts that make other computers better, and some software. Mr. Gavin's clients are companies that make computers. They buy our little parts, put them in their computers, and their computers are better. That's all I really understand. I'm just a gofer really, and I had my CDL from another job, so Lloyd asked me to drive the truck out, even though a CDL isn't needed to drive that size of truck." He paused as if his mind had to catch up with the words. "If you want to know more, just call his assistant. She'll know everything."

Jodie repeated her name and then asked for a phone number. After Dillon gave her the information, Creighton stood up and left the room.

"Dillon, tell me some other stuff about Lloyd. What was his house like? Did he have a pet? Did he date? I'd like to get to know the man."

Dillon sniffed and looked at Jodie like he couldn't quite believe the things he was being asked, but he continued. "Nice house, but not very big, not a mansion. He didn't have any pets. In fact, I remember him talking about wanting a dog but knowing he couldn't take care of it the way he wanted to. He worked too much. I have no idea if he dated; not something we ever talked about." He paused, but it was obvious he had more, so we waited silently. "He was a good guy, I think, not a bad guy."

"People liked working for him?" Jodie said.

Dillon shrugged. "I did. I can't speak for the others."

"How many employees?"

"Seventeen."

"Anything else you can think of that would help us understand your boss?"

Dillon's hand went up to the table and he started tapping with his fingers. He wasn't practiced at hiding his nerves.

"Am I a suspect?" he asked.

"Everybody is equally under suspicion right now. Dillon, we don't have enough to point at anyone more than everyone else."

"Okay," he said weakly. "That's all I can think of at the moment." His eyes brimmed with tears, suddenly glassy and bright. I felt a wave of sympathy, but I knew Jodie didn't. Sympathy could get in the way of an investigation.

"All right, Clare, your turn. You didn't know you were receiving the Hoovens?" Jodie said as she turned to me.

"No."

"When was the last time you talked to Lloyd?"

"Had to be high school, but I have no recollection of any conversation with Lloyd beyond the junior high dance we didn't go to because he broke out in hives. We had conversations in high school, but it would be impossible to remember any specifics."

"Oh yeah, you told me about that a long time ago. I forgot. He was sweet on you, wasn't he?"

I lifted an eyebrow. That was not a phrase she would normally use. I suddenly felt like I was being set up to answer something specific.

"A junior high sweet maybe, but that was a long time ago," I said.

"And he hadn't gotten in touch with you about any sort of meeting?"

"No."

"Did he get in touch with Chester, that you know of?"

"You were there last night when he said someone called that might have been Lloyd."

"Has that come up again?"

"I haven't seen Chester yet today. Call him."

"We will."

"Seth, have you heard from him?" Jodie asked.

"The man who was killed?" Seth said. "I don't know who he is, but I'm pretty sure I've never talked to him. I guess I'd have to see pictures."

"I didn't really think so, but I had to ask," Jodie said as she reached into her pocket and pulled out a piece of paper. "And your trip out of town has been confirmed. It looks like once again your job has kept you from becoming a serious suspect in a murder case, Seth. Not sure you're so lucky, Clare."

My eyebrows came together as both Seth and I sat

forward on our chairs. Jodie smoothed the small piece of paper. It had been torn out of a spiral notebook, its edges uneven and ragged.

"It seems that Lloyd knew about all you, Seth. And maybe he wanted to give Clare a call while he was in town," Jodie said. "Even if she hadn't been invited to the alleged meetings."

The note read "Clare Henry, still unmarried. Dating Seth Cassidy, local Star City geologist."

"That's completely creepy," I said. "I mean, no disrespect to Lloyd, and maybe it's only because he's dead, but that's a little unsettling. Where did you get this?"

"From Lloyd's pocket. His wallet was on him, lots of cash still inside it, and this was in his pocket."

"I'm sure I haven't talked to him in years," I said.

"Okay." Jodie twisted her mouth and then bit her bottom lip. "Dillon, another question about Lloyd. He liked to know things about people. Did he do research on people? Was he the extracurious sort?"

"I have no idea," Dillon said.

He was a horrible liar, but I didn't understand the lie completely. He knew more about Lloyd than he was admitting. I admired the kid's loyalty to his employer, no matter what the reason. Dillon stayed stubbornly silent, but he couldn't miss the three pairs of wide eyes and lifted eyebrows staring down his denial.

"Ask his assistant," Dillon finally continued sheepishly.

"We will." Jodie sat back in her chair. She'd gotten what she needed from us, which I silently and quickly concluded was first, knowing if Lloyd had contacted either me or Seth and second, learning what kind of guy Lloyd really was when it came to looking up old junior high dance dates. Of course I had no idea how the answers might contribute to the investigation. "Now talk to me, Clare. Anything weird happen lately, phone calls, a sense of anyone watching you or anything like that?"

"No, nothing, Jodie. I don't think Lloyd was stalking me, not in person at least."

Dillon shifted in his seat as Jodie's eyes landed back on him.

"He wasn't married ever? Lloyd, I mean," she said.

"No."

"Does he have any pictures in his office, personal things on his desk?"

Dillon's eyebrows came together. "Not that I'm aware of."

"Uh-huh. All right. Well, Clare, I want you to think about my question about anything weird. Will you do that? Don't discount anything. Let me do that. Even though Lloyd is dead, we're going to have to do some backtracking to find his killer. You know, learn what kind of man he'd turned into. This note could mean something or it could mean nothing at all, something he wrote down at the last minute as he was walking out the door. Or there's more, somewhere. When you've got nothing, you've got nothing to lose."

"Of course," I said, but I wondered if Jodie actually had more than she was fessing up to, that she was pretending to have nothing for a reason. I'd ask her about it later, but I doubted she'd give me a straight answer.

"Good. Dillon, make yourself comfortable at the hotel. Clare, you and I need to look over the Hoovens and then you can go," Jodie said.

"When can I go home?" Dillon asked.

"We'll let you know."

Dillon sighed and shook his head but didn't say anything else as he left the room.

I stood but gestured for Jodie and Seth to stay put.

"What?" they said together.

"Sarah McMasters?" I said to Jodie.

"Okay?" Jodie said.

"Who's Sarah McMasters?" Seth asked.

"Until just a few minutes ago I didn't put the pieces together, but you know that new bookstore?" Seth and Jodie nodded. "Well, Chester mentioned the owner's name to me just a few days ago. Sarah McMasters. If it's the Sarah McMasters we went to high school with, I know that at least at one time she was married to Donte Senot."

"I'll see if I can talk to her, and find Donte through her, or find her through him, or find them another way. I can't imagine Lloyd was talking about any other Donte. How many could there be?"

"You know, Sarah and I got along," I said.

Jodie crossed her arms in front of herself and sent me a smirk. She remembered that the two of them did not get along. In fact, they had disliked each other.

"Well, I'm not the only police officer in town," Jodie said. "And I do see what you're attempting, but remember, *we're* the police. I appreciate your interest in helping us, Clare, but let us take care of this one."

"Of course, but you didn't like her," I said.

"Neither did you." She turned to Seth. "Sarah was all about image, money, those sorts of things."

"Surely she's grown out of that," I said.

Seth and Jodie shared a look.

"Maybe. Let's go look at those Hoovens," Jodie said.

"Sounds good to me." I led the way.

4

Ultimately, we might have spent a total of five minutes looking at the Hoovens. Jodie didn't want to undo the ropes around them quite yet. I told her that I didn't see anything suspicious on or around them, but I'd never seen a Hooven in person before, so I couldn't be sure.

She sent Seth and me on our way. Seth had the rest of the day off, but I didn't. As he dropped me off in front of The Rescued Word, we told each other we'd meet up later. We'd progressed to not making many specific plans. We were always together, when we weren't working, at least. It was a good spot to be in, though I couldn't help being worried that I was taking him for granted. Chester had already lectured me—*"That's the spot you want to be in, Clare. I know you've never enjoyed an easy rela-tionship before [insert grumbled curse words about Creighton], but the ability to appreciate each other comes with the trust that you can sometimes take each other for granted."*

Seth still curled my toes with his good-bye kisses, though. Chester also made fun of my post-kiss twinkling eyes, adding that we were probably a long way off from truly taking each other for granted. Marion rolled her own eyes, and Adal pretended not to notice.

Post-kiss and nonspecific plans cemented, I stepped toward the landing to the shop and was surprised to see the metallic spool of a typewriter ribbon on the ground. The black ribbon was still attached, but unfurled and under the door leading into the shop. It was a trail of bread crumbs I thought appropriate to the store and I wondered if it was someone's promotional idea.

I picked up the spool and started rolling as I went inside.

I was greeted by a number of chattering voices, the loudest of which at the moment was Baskerville, who was meowing unhappily.

He sat on the end of the middle shelf, perched as if he'd been hoping someone would come in and either rescue him or be a willing audience to his complaints. I couldn't immediately figure out the reason for all the ruckus, but soon I realized I wanted to escape with him.

"I know, boy." I looked for ink on my fingertips before I petted him. "They are certainly noisy. I'll do what I can."

Satisfied I understood his plea, he let me pet his head, angled just right so I'd get the spot behind his left ear, for a few seconds before he jumped up to the east shelves to catch some sun, though he did send me one more pleading look.

As I turned toward the crowd by the counter, Chester's eyes caught mine. He barely restrained rolling them in front of our very vocal customers, a middle-aged couple I didn't recognize but who looked to be ski tourists in expensive ski gear. I turned again and looked out the front window. I hadn't noticed their Range Rover parked across the street before, but now I did. It was a newer model, but I couldn't see the plates from this vantage point.

"I don't understand," said the woman loudly as the man hefted up an old typewriter. "This is your job. I would like this typewriter fixed."

"Uh-oh," I muttered quietly. Chester didn't have much patience for demanding attitudes anymore. He'd admitted many times that he was long past thinking the customer was always right.

"Hi!" I said cheerily as I approached, still winding the ribbon along the way. I smiled. "Looks like you dropped something."

From up high, Baskerville meowed disapprovingly at my friendly tone. I ignored him.

"Oh," the man said as looked at the back of the machine he held. "I'll be. It sure does."

"An Olympia Spendid!" I said. "That's . . . splendid!"

Chester smiled, but the couple didn't.

"Is there something I can to do help?" I said.

"I hope so," the man said. "You fix typewriters, right?"

"That's correct."

"This man says you can't fix this one."

I smiled at "this man" as he ran his finger over his mustache. A smile pulled at the corner of his mouth before he spoke. "That's correct. But I've only started working here this week, so perhaps Clare can better assist you."

Chester might often fabricate stories for the customers, but it was rare that he didn't admit to being the owner and founder of The Rescued Word. These two must really have tested his patience.

"Good. Clare, then. We need this fixed. It's very important," the man said.

"Well," I said. I took the typewriter and placed it on the back counter. I wondered where Marion and Adal were but didn't ask. "This was a beauty once. I'm Clare Henry." I extended my hand to the man, but I checked again for inky fingers first.

"Oh, we're Janise and Evan Davenport," Janise said, her words clipped.

I suddenly realized that the raised voices had definitely been Evan's and Janise's, but they hadn't been raised toward Chester. Only Evan's had. In hindsight I realized that Janise's had been raised out of frustration, and her wide eyes and tight mouth told me the frustration had been at her husband, not at my grandfather. It was a worthwhile moment of clarification.

"Welcome. Your Olympia was a beautiful machine at one time." It was like all the other Splendids: squat and compact, portable with a snap-on top cover that made the housing a handy-dandy case. Spendids had come in different colors. This one was beige with maroon keys, the shift key a contrasting beige to match the case. The last Splendid I'd seen had been pink with beige keys, the shift key a bright red. They were cute. One of the Spendids' fiercest competitors and, frankly, one that was even more portable, was the Hermes Rocket. Those had smaller carriage return levers, though, which kept my recommendations toward the Spendids when someone asked about a good old portable.

"Right. Yes, it was my mother's," Evan said.

"Oh," I said as I better understood. I sensed Chester's change in attitude too. Emotional typewriters were special; we all knew that.

"So, what happened to it?" I asked.

"I dropped it!" Evan said.

"I see," I said as I looked inside at the key bars. They were bent at unnatural angles. The casing looked like it had been in a head-on collision with something much bigger. "You know, not all damage to typewriters can be repaired."

"But you *fix* them. It's what you do," Evan said.

I sent some tight eyebrows to Janise. She seemed to be a combination of flustered, embarrassed, and at a loss for words even though she'd said almost the exact thing he'd just said. The difference was she'd figured out how ridiculous the idea was that this typewriter could be repaired.

"I'm sorry, but like a car that's been in a bad accident, your typewriter is totaled," I said. I'd never seen someone so adamant about their typewriter, even one they had an emotional attachment to. I swallowed and decided to just ask the question that came to mind. "Why is it so important to have this put back into good condition?"

Janise put her hand on her husband's arm. "Honey, let me take care of this. Go on out to the car."

Evan blinked at her and opened his mouth to say something.

"I got this," Janise said. "Let me."

Evan shook his head and then abruptly turned and walked out of the store.

"His mother passed recently?" Chester asked as Evan paced back and forth in front of the shop's windows.

"Yes," Janise said. "It was particularly traumatic. Evan was driving the car. She was in the backseat, having insisted upon sitting back there with this." She tapped the typewriter. "She'd brought it over to our house, and Evan was taking her home. They were hit from behind. He didn't have a scratch on him. His mother wasn't so fortunate, and you can see what happened to the typewriter. We came up to Star City today for a book. The woman at the bookstore told us about this place. We've been carrying around the typewriter since the accident two months ago. He's obsessed with it, and when he heard you repaired them . . . well, his obsession took on a whole new meaning. We were at the bookstore, and the second the woman there told us about you, we were off. I need to go back and apologize and pick up the book she graciously found for us. My husband is one of the most levelheaded people I know. Or at least he was until all this happened. I think he'll be okay, eventually. I hope so."

"I'm so sorry," I said. "I could possibly find another typewriter like this one, but I wouldn't feel right about pretending it was this one that I'd fixed."

"No, thank you, but that wouldn't work," Janise said. "So there's absolutely nothing you can do for it?"

The three of us looked toward the mangled machine.

"No, of course there isn't," she said. "I'll just take it. I'm sorry we disturbed you."

"No problem. I'm sorry about everything you are both going through," I said.

"Ms. Davenport, may I ask a question?" Chester said.

"Of course," she said as she hefted the typewriter.

"What's the book you came to town for?"

She lifted her eyebrows a moment. "This won't surprise you, but it's titled *Speeches from the Dead*. A New Age thing that supposedly gives instructions on holding your own personal séances. I'm not a believer. Neither was Evan before the accident. We live in Boise and drove all the way down here mostly just to pick up the old, out-of-print book, and then we left the bookstore abruptly. I'm embarrassed."

"Starry Night Books?" I asked, thinking about the name of the shop I was just talking to Jodie and Seth about. "That's the used bookstore, right? The new one in town? I think it's owned by someone I went to high school with."

"I don't know how new the shop is, but yes, it's a used bookshop. The book is next to impossible to find, which I thought should tell Evan something about the validity of the information inside it, but it didn't. He wouldn't let her mail it. We had to drive down. I thought getting away from home might help, but it hasn't. Anyway, this is much more than you wanted to know. Clearly, I need to get my husband some professional help. In the meantime I hope you accept my apology for his bizarre behavior."

"No apology necessary," I said.

She looked at Chester. "Why did you want to know the title of the book?"

"I've been through some of what your husband is going through. I wondered . . . Well, I'm afraid I wasn't into anything metaphysical, but I do have some books I could . . . This is not my place, but would you like me to write down some titles of books I found helpful during my period of grieving?"

We glanced out the window at the still-pacing man. Chester ran his knuckle over his mustache. He'd known deep grief when my grandmother died. His current girl-friend, Ramona, had experienced it when her husband died. Chester's and Ramona's shared experiences had given their relationship an extra dimension, but I knew my grandfather had also done a lot of his own reading.

"That would be lovely," Janise said.

Chester grabbed a small piece of lavender paper and wrote a brief note, handing it to Janise.

"May I walk you out?" he asked.

"No, thank you." She smiled weakly. "It's probably better if I just go. He's really quite normal. When he isn't, I suppose."

"It's always rough," Chester said.

With one last nod, Janise turned and walked out of the shop.

"Clare," Chester said when no one but Baskerville, who'd hopped down and made his way over the center shelves after Janise left the building, was left to hear us.

"Yes."

"You know I don't believe in censorship in any form, don't you?"

"I do. If I may quote you, 'it's the slipperiest slope of all.' I believe that's what you've said."

"So when I ask you these next questions, please know that I'm not in any way supporting censorship. I'm also not asking to sound critical, because a used bookshop's gotta be a used bookshop after all, but tell me more about the woman who owns the shop. You went to high school with her?"

"We did. In fact, Jodie and I were just talking about her," I said.

"Some synchronicity."

"You have a problem with her selling a personal séance book?"

"No, not at all. Remember what I said about censorship. But I've heard . . . odd things about the owner. What's her name?"

"Odd, really? Sarah McMasters Senot. Jodie confirmed that she's still married to Donte Senot, who we also went to school with. They ran with the popular and pretty crowd, from what I remember. What have you heard?"

"Just that she's very into metaphysical stuff. That's not a bad thing, but I've heard it now from a few people. I was just wondering. I meant to introduce myself to her, but I haven't had the time."

"Interesting," I said. "I'll ask around. I can introduce you to her."

"We'll see. I'm not one for either censorship *or* gossip, but in this case, be discreet. At least for now."

"Okay," I said. Baskerville punctuated my doubtful tone with an equally doubtful meow. "Is Marion coming in?"

"Yes, I believe she is—momentarily, in fact. Just for a couple hours to look at orders. She's doing okay, our girl, isn't she?"

"I think so," I said.

As if on cue, Marion flew through the front door. She was fresh off the slopes, with red cheeks and a wide smile. She reported that she hadn't found any body parts today, which had made her practice time much more enjoyable than yesterday's. I gave her less-than-graphic details of what the police had discovered and then left the store to her care. Chester went to the back workshop to attend to some printing press repairs for Nathan and Adal, who were both scheduled to come in later to work on the poetry book.

I decided that since she'd come up twice in conversation in the last couple of hours, I'd been given a distinct sign that I was supposed to go talk to Sarah McMasters Senot. I hadn't talked to her since high school. She and I didn't really have much of a history at all, but it would not be weird to shop for a book, or just stop by and say hello.

I told Marion I'd be back shortly and ignored Baskerville's odd warning-like meow as I went through the front door.

5

Though I hadn't yet been inside Starry Nights Books, I'd walked past it many times. It was located right on Main, halfway between Bygone Alley and Little Blue. I'd peeked in through the front window a number of times, once finding a nicely done display of Phyllis A. Whitney books. My mom had been a big reader of Ms. Whitney's novels. I'd found her collection in a box in our garage when I was a teenager and I'd read them too. The contents were slightly dated, but the stories were still compelling, and she'd become a shared favorite author for Mom and me. As I thought about the time I'd spent engrossed in the books, I missed my parents and hoped they were almost done with their sunbird adventures in Arizona.

The narrow brick building that housed the bookstore had last been home to a young man who taught guitar.

Before the place was filled with books, I'd walk by and look in to see the music teacher and a student in the otherwise empty and stark space, with only their guitars, two folding chairs, and a music stand. The walls were all plain lath and plaster, and those in the know—Marion—told me that the acoustics were perfect and the teacher was "hot"; thus he had a steady stream of eager students who wanted to learn guitar, most of them female. His business was well suited to Star City, but he apparently decided to move down to Salt Lake City to find a bigger population to draw from. Marion had told me that he had the same success going on in his new digs and his student list had grown.

The guitar teacher's story was unlike that of our resident Latin teacher, Anorkory Levkin, who'd found, miraculously in my opinion, that Salt Lake folks had no problem driving up the canyon to learn an old dead language. And though Anorkory was a wonderful and friendly man, I'd never heard him described as "hot." It didn't seem to matter.

Once inside the bookshop, I felt an immediate sense of good claustrophobia: the kind that comes with close and jam-packed bookshelves that leave only *just* enough walking room. I spied a counter and a cash register about halfway down the long building, but didn't see anyone working.

"Hello?" I said.

"I'm in the back. Make yourself at home. Have a cup of whatever we've got. Shop or I'll look at whatever you brought in in a second," a woman's voice said from somewhere in the walled-off back depths.

Any reason to peruse a bookshop was a good enough

reason for me. A quick scan made me think that romance novels filled the front shelves, followed by mystery, and then science fiction toward the back. Though I could have found hours of reading enjoyment on those shelves, they weren't what I was looking for today. I zoned in on the shelf closest to the cash register; it was the least crowded and though it held some books, it had other things too, shiny things—crystals and rocks, the names of which I was sure Seth would know on sight. The few books there were clearly metaphysical; a couple of titles I was able to immediately read were *Living with the Dead* and *They Never Really Die*.

"Hi. Oh, you're . . . Clare! That's right. Hello." Sarah peered around a doorway to what must lead to a small room in the back corner. Her dark hair was pulled up and dusty and she wiped her hands on her dusty jeans as she came around and joined me out front. She didn't look much different than she had looked in high school—still pretty. I'd forgotten about her posture, but I suddenly remembered my high-school-aged curiosity about how she always managed to stand so straight. How had she never slouched? It looked like she'd kept up the good work, and I straightened my own shoulders as she approached. I suddenly felt bad about not stopping by earlier to say hello.

"Hey, Sarah, it's great to see you," I said.

"You too, Clare Henry. You look the same."

"You too. You and Donte moved back to Star City?"

"No, not really, just put the bookshop here. We still live in Salt Lake City. I love it here, but Donte's company is in Salt Lake. His company makes more money—lots more—than mine does, so we're down there until I outdo him." She laughed. "Not a real possibility. He's so darn successful, you know."

Aside from her posture, I remembered the reasons we hadn't been the closest of friends, and I was surprised that grown-up adults still said the types of things she'd just said. She'd spoken about her high school accomplishments (the specifics of which I couldn't recall at the moment) the same way she'd just talked about Donte's success. I didn't know what his company was or how it had become successful, but I was happy for them both. Jodie would have rolled her eyes and said something sarcastic, but I smiled and nodded.

"That's great," I said. The expression on my face and the pushing up of my glasses must not have hid my confusion.

"You don't know? Well, Donte has a successful textbook publishing company. He started with that proof he did at the U."

I was even more lost, but I tried to hide it better. I was still unsuccessful, but at least I knew "the U" meant the University of Utah.

"You don't know about Donte's success? Oh, that's right, you weren't part of that brainy crowd."

I wasn't, but neither was she, nor Donte, for that matter. I didn't point that out.

"Right," she said. "Well, he changed the entire world of mathematics with one simple equation. Then he printed a textbook and it sold millions. He's now working with other textbook writers to print and sell their books."

"That's really terrific, Sarah. I'm happy for you both."

"Thanks. You're still working with your grandfather?"

"I am. We're still rescuing words."

She sent me a smirky smile, and I began to doubt that she and I ever really did get along. "I guess we are rescuing them too, as a used bookstore would do."

"True. Hey, speaking of high school, I just heard some terrible news this morning. I wondered if you'd heard."

"What?"

"Remember Lloyd Gavin?"

"Of course. Well, I didn't until recently, but . . . why?"

"He was killed, murdered."

Sarah sat down hard, as if she collapsed more than sat. Fortunately, there was an old chair behind her that was unfolded and at the ready.

"Oh," I said as I hurried around the corner of the counter. "I'm so sorry. I shouldn't have . . . I'm sorry."

"It's okay. I'm just shocked," she said. She swallowed hard. The inside light was sallow anyway, but I wondered if she'd lost every ounce of blood from her face. "Donte was supposed to meet with him. I'd better call him."

She seemed to look around for her phone, toward the counter and cash register, and then she patted her pockets.

"Hang on. Let me get you some water or something," I said. "Is there anything in the back? A sink?"

She nodded distractedly. "Yes, there's a small bathroom, but there's a water tank right inside the back storage room. Water is a good idea. Thank you."

"You sure you won't fall out of the chair while I'm gone?"

"I'll be all right." She steadied herself by leaning on the counter's side wall. I wasn't sure that would help, and I hesitated a bit before I hurried away to get the water.

The storage room/office was so small and so packed with boxes of books that I thought the health department or the fire department or some such organization would close the place down if they saw it. I stood in the only small open floor space in the middle, and had to turn and reach to grab the cup from the dispenser and the lift the handle to get some water. Not only were the shelves and desks and other floor spaces packed with papers and boxes of books, but the garbage can next to the water tank was overflowing with paper cups and pieces of paper. I was sure she was overwhelmed, but the part of me that likes organization wondered if I should offer her some help. The thought flew away as I hurried back to her.

Fortunately, she was making a quick recovery. Her pallor became much more normal.

"Thank you," she said after she took a sip of the water. "That's not a normal reaction for me, but it did catch me off guard. Obviously, I hadn't heard. I do need to get ahold of Donte, though. Do you mind?" She'd found the phone and held it gripped tightly in her hand.

"Of course not."

"Can you tell me more? What happened?" she asked. She hadn't tried to loosen her grip to make the call yet.

I'd told her about Lloyd mostly to see her reaction or what she said about his connection to Donte. But I didn't know how much Jodie would want me sharing about the horror inside the ski boot or any of the other details, so I said, "I don't really know much more."

If word got out that Marion was the one to call about Lloyd's still-boot-clad foot, I'd think of something to tell Sarah.

"Goodness," she said before she finally opened her fingers and made the call.

I pretended to look at some nearby shelves as she spoke

to Donte. Her side of the conversation made me think that her husband didn't know about the murder either. I smiled to myself when she said, "Yes, Clare Henry, remember her? Well, we went to high school with her." As she ended the call, she seemed back to her old self. She even stood from the chair.

"I'm sorry if I surprised him too," I said.

She blinked at me as if she'd forgotten I was there. "Yes, he was surprised. Their meetings were supposed to start this evening. He hadn't heard a word from Lloyd, but he didn't really expect to until tonight. Donte's in Salt Lake City. If it's a murder, though, I'm sure the story will hit the news outlets there at some point."

"I'm sure. What was he meeting with Lloyd about?"

"I don't know. Donte wasn't sure. All I knew is that it was some sort of reunion of some successful graduates from our high school."

"How did he hear about the meetings? I mean a phone call, an e-mail?"

Sarah shrugged. "I just know there were some meetings or get-togethers or something like that."

"So, Lloyd, Donte, and who else?" I asked.

"Um. Well, there was Howard Craig, but that's all I remember Donte mentioning, and he only knew that because Howard called him to ask if Donte would be attending too. I think."

"Oh yeah, Howard's family had lots of money," I said, remembering a redheaded, aloof, well-dressed teenager whose crowd I was far too poor and poorly dressed to be a part of.

"That's nothing like the money he made on his own."

"Really?"

"Yeah, some oil thing up in Wyoming. Beaucoup bucks."

"I had no idea. Is Howard in town too?"

"I would guess he is." She nodded. "He never got married, but his parents and his siblings are still in and around Star City. I didn't think to ask Donte to track him down and let him know. I should call him back."

"It might be good for the police to let Howard know. Do you know where he might be staying?"

"His family's house or the Three Bells; that's where he's stayed before," she said.

"I'll have my friend Jodie track him down. She's a police officer."

"Sure. That's a good idea," she said distractedly.

"I had no idea about Howard's success, but good for him. And good for you and Donte too, Sarah. I'm happy for you all."

"Thanks," she said dubiously. For the first time since I'd come into the store, she looked a little older than her high school self. Still pretty but suddenly a little more human, though the amazing posture was still there. Maybe it was the doubt I heard in her tone. Like she wasn't used to people being happy for her.

"This is a great bookstore," I said.

"Well, I hope it will be. It's kind of a mess right now, but I certainly have plenty of inventory, and you'd be amazed by how many visitors stop by for something to read while they're here to ski. I think it will be all right."

"And that's interesting stuff," I said as I looked at the metaphysical shelf.

"Yeah, I think so," she said.

"You believe in talking to the dead?"

"Oh yes." She cleared her throat. "Well, I find the ideas behind it very interesting."

I remembered the title of the book Janise and Evan had mentioned. "Hmm, *Speeches from the Dead*. Sounds fascinating. . . ."

"It is. Unfortunately, that one's not for sale, Clare. Someone already purchased it. They just have to come pick it up."

So they hadn't come right back to the bookshop? There were probably many reasons, but I couldn't help wondering why.

I nodded. "That book looks old." I pointed to the only one on the top shelf. *Living with the Dead*'s hardback cover was bent and worn at the corners, its colors faded. "In case you ever have any books you want repaired, we can help."

"Hmm. I'm glad you brought that up. I might have some need for you and your skills," she said. "And that one *is* old. Not supervaluable, but about twenty years old and hard to find. It's got some pretty controversial ideas, but it doesn't need repairing."

"Like what? The controversial ideas?"

Sarah gave me the longest, deepest look I thought I'd ever had sent my direction. I pushed up my glasses and tried not to waver my return glance.

"If you're really curious you should come by some Thursday evening. I have a group of friends. We gather on Thursdays and talk about those sorts of things."

"Thank you for the invitation." I smiled, though I wasn't sure I was quite that interested.

"You know, I'll be honest with you, Clare. It's the biggest reason I wanted to have something back here in Star

City. There's something about this place, this town on the mountain. I feel like I'm much more in touch with the other side up here."

Even Elizabeth Owl, who owned the crystal shop, had never talked to me about such things. She was Seth's landlady, her shop below his apartment, and she also sold metaphysical books, but I didn't think her selection was so specific to communicating with the dead. If I remembered correctly, hers was more about self-improvement.

"That's interesting," I said. There was probably no one on this planet who felt less connected to the "other side" than me, but I kept that to myself because, frankly, I was open-minded enough to think that it was my disconnect that hadn't allowed those sorts of things into my life.

"It *is* interesting. I'm happy to share more. So are my friends. Come by some Thursday night."

"I'd probably enjoy that," I said. One more time, I pushed up my glasses, this time with the hope of distracting Sarah from my forced enthusiasm.

"Give your family my best," she said cheerily, and with a clear note of finality. She turned to make her way back to her office. "I know you and Creighton Wentworth are no longer together, but I hope your personal life is satisfying nonetheless."

I was caught off guard by her mention of Creighton. Why did she know he and I weren't together, how did she remember that we were, and why did she care enough to bring it up? I tamped down the defensiveness that wanted to make its way out of my mouth and just said, "Thanks so much, Sarah."

I liked her shop, but I wasn't sure she and I would ever get along enough for me to hang out inside it. I was curious about the metaphysical touch, mostly because after speaking with Janise and Evan, I expected more than a few shelves. Admittedly, I was also slightly curious about the Thursday night meetings, but, again, I didn't think she and I would get along well enough for me to attend one.

It was too cold to linger outside for long. I blew on my fingers, grabbed my phone out of my pocket, and hurried back toward The Rescued Word. I hit Jodie's number as I went.

"What's up, Clare?"

"Howard Craig was also invited to the meetings or reunion or whatever. He's at the Three Bells or his family's house."

"How do you know this?"

"I stopped by Starry Night Books to tell Sarah hello. I also mentioned that Lloyd had been killed. I can give you the other details in person."

"You shouldn't have done that, but I can't state the specific issues offhand—other than you just should have left it to us. I know, I know, we should have been there by now."

"Sorry if I did something wrong, but it's good information, huh?" I smiled.

She hesitated long enough that I could tell she was smiling too, but only briefly. "I'll talk to you later, Clare."

We disconnected the call and I hurried along. *I have work to do too, Sarah McMasters Senot.*

An old 1960 Facit typewriter (a series II with a pica typeface that was quite wonderful, by the way) had come in the day before and needed my undivided attention.

Unfortunately, it wasn't meant to be, and my plans to get to work were diverted by our visiting author and one of his complaints.

6

Chester had long ago perfected the cat-that-ate-the-canary pose. He was even better than Baskerville. Chester's eyes were the first ones mine found as I hurried into The Rescued Word. I stopped short, wondering if maybe I was being sent some sort of warning.

I surveyed. Marion was behind the counter but standing back a bit. She behaved as if she didn't notice me, her pensive attention fully on the group of three on the other side of the counter. Along with Chester were Adal and our visiting author, Nathan Grimes. They were not in the middle of a happy moment.

Baskerville, from his spot on the counter, leaned to the side, around Adal, and looked at me with the sort of wonderment I knew him to have when the agony of strife filled the air and disturbed his peace.

"Clare," Adal said. *"Guten Morgen."* He cleared his throat. "Good morning."

His German accent was light most of the time, sometimes even unnoticeable. But when he was upset, sometimes not only did his accent get heavier, but he used German words too, some familiar to everyone.

"Good morning, everyone," I said as I stepped closer to them. "How's everything?"

Chester raised one eyebrow as Adal cleared his throat again.

"I'm afraid I'm causing some difficulties this morning," Nathan said.

"Okay. What's up?" I said.

"I'm unhappy with the fact that Adal will not let me set the type myself. What I'm saying is that I'd like to put the type in the trays myself. I want this to be a completely self-published work, recto-verso if you know what I mean."

I looked at Adal. He'd apparently taught Nathan "right" and "left" when it came to the sides of a leaf of paper, though Nathan was stretching the meaning. Still, I liked that he was learning and Adal was teaching.

"He's chosen the Bridgnorth," Adal said.

"Oh. Nathan, that's one of our oldest types. I'm sorry but only Chester, Adal, and I are allowed to work with it."

"I'm not going to break it," Nathan said.

"No, that's not . . . Perhaps there's another font you could use. Truly, you picked the only one we are extra-extracareful with. It's become our endangered species. And besides, we're low on Bridgnorth *E*'s."

"I can work with that, use other *E*'s. I really need to use Bridgnorth," Nathan said.

When I first heard that Nathan Grimes was going to be spending some time with us, I was sort of excited and sort of not excited. The Rescued Word was a business and we were all busy, and though I loved all writers and almost every single book I'd ever read, I didn't know how much of a diva Nathan might prove to be. I'd told Chester that if Nathan didn't behave, I would kick him out, even if he was a bestselling author and one to whom Jodie had given her own five-star rating by calling him "a damn good writer." I'd been extra-alert to any diva behavior, but I hadn't seen much up to now.

What I liked most about Nathan, other than his wonderfully creepy prose, was that he wore a cap and scarf with an authentic flair that hadn't been carried off well since Sherlock Holmes. I'd heard he also smoked a pipe, but though I thought I'd smelled tobacco a time or two, I'd yet to see him smoking.

"I'm sorry, Nathan, but let me look over the type and confirm that we need to be as careful as I think we need to be. I'll do that this morning and let you know," I said.

"This isn't up for debate. I'm the customer and I'll use the font."

Chester sent me another smile, still kind of Cheshire. I was one millisecond away from telling Nathan that this just wasn't going to work, that either he'd follow the rules or he'd have to find someone else's Gutenberg replica, when Marion piped up.

"I have an idea," she said.

We all looked at her, even Baskerville.

"How about I search for something that's like Bridgnorth type? I've learned so much and have an eye for similarities." She laughed. "Maybe I'll even find another rare set that

Nathan could buy for himself. That would make the book even more self-published. It shouldn't take long, and our network of connections is vast. You have something else you could work on for a few days, right?"

Marion smiled and looked at Nathan. She kept her gaze level, but she'd been friendly in her tone, friendlier than where the rest of us were probably headed. We waited.

A long moment later, he said, "I think your idea is brilliant."

"So do I!" Chester said.

"I do too," I said. "Yes, please, Marion, see what you can find. Let us know."

"Even better for me to have time to work on Frank a little more. He's a bit out of shape and could use a few more tweaks," Chester said. "No time like the present to get to it." He grabbed Baskerville.

"I have a typewriter to work on. Marion, you okay up here?" I said.

"Fine. I can look for the type and help customers."

"All right, come on back, Adal and Nathan. You two can work on . . . something."

"How about I run across the street and grab some coffees for us all?" Nathan asked as if he hadn't been on the verge of an angry storm a few minutes earlier. Or maybe it was his way of apologizing.

Adal answered for us all. "That would be lovely. Thank you."

Nathan took off his scarf and placed it on the counter in three perfect folds. He placed his cap on top of the scarf and smiled before he walked out of the shop, a happy pep in his step.

"Huh," Marion said before she turned to her computer. "It's cold out there."

Adal and I sent each other small shrugs.

"Want to help me work on a Facit?" I said.

"Definitely," he said.

$\sim$

"No, it's one-hundred-percent true. An Olympia Splendid. That's the kind of typewriter I work on, at least for my first few drafts. I can transcribe onto a computer, but I simply cannot write on one. I have to have a typewriter and I have to hear it. The sounds, the keys, the bell, the return, they've all been a part of my writing since I was a child. There's no other way for me," Nathan said as he plopped his feet up on the other side of the large desk the Facit was sitting on. Adal and I looked at each other yet again.

"The portability?" I said.

"Yes, and the reliability. I love it. People at the airport look at me like I'm crazy, but I don't go anywhere without it."

"What color is it?" I asked.

"Red."

"The keys?"

"Black."

"A wonderful machine." I sighed.

Nathan laughed and sat up, thereby removing his feet from the desk. "I'll bring it in tomorrow for you to have a look."

I laughed too. "I sound a little starstruck, don't I?" I said.

"It's good. We're the same type of person, Clare. It's

why I was attracted to your shop and why I find all of you so appealing. You are my people."

Not far behind us, Chester dropped a tool and grumbled a complaint. It wasn't that we didn't like Nathan. We just hadn't really gotten to know him yet.

"We had a couple come in just this morning with one that had been ruined in a car crash. It broke my heart how much they were going to miss it," I said. "It's just a machine, of course, a thing, but when you use a thing to create other things . . . well, I sound a little ridiculous."

"Not at all. I would miss mine deeply if it broke. Oh, I don't even want to think about it."

"You know, even though this is the business I work in, I can't remember the last time the same old typewriter came up for discussion more than once in a day, let alone a few hours," I said, thinking about the bookshop also coming up twice in a short amount of time. "If someone brings it up a third time, we might have to wonder what the universe is telling us."

Nathan smiled and nodded. "So, what's wrong with the one you're working on? You called it a Facit?"

"Yes," I said. "It's actually unique. It's from Sweden." I pointed to a spot under the typewriter case's handle that had been stamped with "Sweden." "But the really cool part is its font. It's entirely cursive."

"I've never heard of such a thing," Nathan said.

"It's true. We're mostly just servicing and tuning up this one, but here, I can show you."

I grabbed a piece of paper from a stack on the corner of a nearby worktable. Chester had put the paper there the other day after he'd grown tired of seeing it out front and being mostly ignored. It was the worst possible shade of neon green you could imagine, and we'd purchased it after only seeing a picture of the color on an Internet site. Chester made a habit of never buying anything for the shop that he didn't first see and touch in person, but our normal salesperson had been ill and we didn't want to miss an order, so we worked online. The green looked good in the picture—fun, lively, different. As Chester had said, in person it was more like flat, pukey, and too different. We'd had it out front for a short time, but now we were using it only as scratch paper in the back.

I threaded the paper through the feed, rolled it up, and typed: *Now is the winter of our discontent.*

"That's the cutest thing I've ever seen," Nathan said. "I must have one. Do you think the owner of this one would be willing to sell? I'd pay a good price."

"I doubt it, but we can mention the idea when they come in to pick it up if you'd like," I said.

"I would, I definitely would," Nathan said.

"Nathan, did I hear that you have a cabin near Star City?" Chester asked as he joined us by the desk. His nose was smudged with ink, his perpetually tanned skin glowed, and his eyes twinkled. He loved working on Frank.

"No, I don't have one, but my friends do. They let me borrow it one summer."

"I bet you and your Splendid loved it," I said.

"We did. I hope to take advantage of their offer to use it whenever I want to again, but it's small and I can't work with others in my space. I need to be alone, and unfortunately they like to spend time there too. They would get in my way."

We all looked at him. He was smiling, but it was difficult to know how serious he was being.

Chester nodded. "Pesky friends."

"Exactly," Nathan said. "Oh, you can smell the monks from it. I mean, you can smell their wine or at least the grapes. I'm not much of a drinker, but that's pretty wonderful. There's also a narrow creek and lots of birds outside the window next to the table I worked from."

"Perfect," Chester said.

We'd closed the door between the front of the shop and the workshop and it suddenly slammed open.

"Oh, sorry about that," Jodie said as she shut the door only slightly more gently than she'd opened it.

She was in full work mode, which meant she was rarely gentle or quiet when she came into a room.

"Everything okay, Jodie?" Chester asked.

"I'd like to grab Clare for a few minutes," she said.

"About the disembodied foot?" Chester asked.

Jodie blinked. "Well, yes, I suppose."

"A disembodied foot?" Nathan asked.

"We'll tell you all about it," Chester said as I hurried back to the front with Jodie.

"So that's Nathan Grimes?" Jodie asked when the three of them were out of earshot. I'd caught the fleeting eye lock between her and Adal, but they probably thought no one noticed.

"That's Nathan Grimes," Marion said from her spot behind the counter.

"That's him, in the flesh," I said.

"He's very . . . authorly," Jodie said.

"He is," Marion said as she stood from her chair. "He's nice in a funny, demanding way." She looked at me. "I found some type. Want me to go back and show him some pictures and give him the purchase details?"

"That would be great. I'll be up here with Jodie for a second anyway, in case someone comes in."

"He's a damn good storyteller," Jodie added after Marion had gone into the workshop.

"He is," I said. "So, what's up?"

"First of all, tell me about your visit with Sarah. I sent an officer up there right after we spoke, but the shop was closed tight, no Sarah in sight."

I replayed the events of my time at Starry Night Books as Jodie took notes in her Jodie shorthand that she once told me only she knew how to interpret. I'd already mentioned Howard, but she still took notes as I told her again what Sarah had said. She gave me no indication of whether she'd tried to speak with him already. She liked to take note of everything, though.

"All right, Clare. Sounds like no harm was done, but seriously, let us do this."

"Okay," I said, though I wanted to point out that I was just being a friendly neighbor to Sarah. I figured I'd just ask for forgiveness again next time. "Did you talk to Howard?"

Jodie rubbed her finger under her nose after she put the notebook in her pocket, completely ignoring my question. "Lloyd was one weird duck."

"He was brilliant. Sometimes brilliant people are a little odd."

"Right. He liked you, you know? I remember a little of it. I think he was sad you wanted to be friends with me, not him."

"No, that wasn't it." Even so many years later I didn't want Jodie to think she'd come in between me and someone else. "We were kids. That's all."

"What would you make of the note in his pocket? And he gave you three of those Hoovens, Clare. Why would he do that?"

"I don't know," I said. "Maybe they were gifts from a rich man who had fond memories of our young friendship? Maybe he did want to come see me—to talk about typewriters. It's hard to know, Jodie."

"He cared for you, obviously, but in what way and why?"

"Why do you think the answer to this is important?"

She shook her head. "Don't know yet." She bit her bottom lip and looked out toward the front window.

"What?"

"I talked to his assistant, Brenda Phillips. She's on her way to Star City, should be here this afternoon. She's distraught and wants to get all the details in person. But after I told her the bad news, her first question knocked me for a loop. She asked if Lloyd had had a chance to talk to you yet. When I told her that he hadn't, she was more devastated about that than the fact that he'd been killed. Or at least that's what it seemed like."

"Well, that's definitely strange, but we still don't know why. Did she say more? He's never once tried to contact me, Jodie."

"She didn't say why, told me she'd tell me more when she got here. I got the impression that he was even weirder now than he used to be. Okay, so you're much kinder than I am and probably wouldn't call him weird, but he might have made you uncomfortable if he'd visited. I guess we'll never know. Anyway, the reason I'm here mostly is this, you available for dinner tonight with me and Brenda?"

"Sure. Will I be an official investigator?"

Jodie half smiled. "Closer than you've ever been

maybe. I could question Brenda just fine, but not only do I get the sense that she'd like to meet you. I think you might have more insight into Lloyd's personality, so you might have better questions, or get better answers out of her. We'll see, I suppose. I'm not deputizing you or anything."

"Of course not."

"All right. Gotta go. I'll pick you up at Little Blue at around six."

"I'll be ready," I said. "By the way, I think there's another reason you want me to go to dinner tonight. This invitation, while welcomed, is unlike you and goes against me staying out of your investigation."

"See you tonight," she said as she turned to leave.

"I'll be ready," I said as she went out the front door.

Jodie revved her Bronco's engine, backed away from the curb, and then screeched the tires as she pulled away, but only enough to let everyone know she meant business.

7

It took less than one second inside the restaurant to realize what Jodie had been keeping from me. We met Brenda at a barbecue joint halfway to Salt Lake City, down Parley's Canyon. The Pig Stuff had been around a long time. On a good day and when the breeze was just right, you could catch a whiff of their hickory smoke up in Star City. Their food lived up to their tantalizing aromas.

As we walked into the restaurant, I spotted Brenda immediately, even though we'd never met before. And she spotted me.

She and I could have been twins. We were, unquestionably, doppelgangers.

"You must be Officer Wentworth. And of course you're Clare. I'm Brenda," she said soberly but with a firm handshake. She'd been crying and her nose and eyes were red underneath the glasses she wore, with frames that almost matched mine. My nose and eyes even got red in the same way hers did when I was upset.

Jodie shook her hand first. I was second and I lingered.

"You see this, don't you?" I said. "We could be sisters."

"Absolutely," she said. "It's as I told Officer Wentworth on the phone earlier today; I had the job the second I walked into Lloyd's office because I look so much like you. Though I didn't know about our shared looks right away."

I looked at Jodie. She shrugged and said, "I'm still pretty surprised. It's uncanny, that's for sure. Come on, let's sit down."

A young server dressed in black pants, a white dress shirt, and a pink apron adorned with a very happy smiling pig on the front guided us to a booth in a back corner. Jodie had flashed her badge and requested the most private seats possible. The place was so crowded that we wouldn't have any real privacy, but it was the best available option.

We all got through a few awkward stares at each other as we perused the menu, but then finally got down to business after we placed our orders.

"Like I said, I didn't know about you at first," Brenda said to me. "One day . . . This wasn't as creepy as it might sound, by the way—I need you to know that Lloyd and I never had a personal relationship, but we worked very well together. I have . . . had immense respect for him and his genius. I loved working so close to someone so smart." Her voice caught and she took a moment. "Anyway, one day he asked if I'd consider wearing different glasses. If I hadn't known him so well by then, I would have thought much less of him, been scared by him maybe, but it was more an offhand comment than anything. I laughed and asked why he had such a request. He became embarrassed and then told me all about you. I need to stress here that he never pressured me into any sort of relationship but a professional one, but when he talked about you, Clare, he made it clear how much I looked like his first love. Clare Henry."

Jodie whistled and said, "Sorry, Brenda, there's no way to make that story not sound creepy, but whatever."

"Okay, well, right," she said, not becoming defensive, which was the best way to handle things when talking to Jodie, or any police officer maybe. "Anyway, after he told me about the crazy coincidence of us looking so much alike, he told me the kind of glasses you wore. When the ones I had broke a couple weeks later, I bought these."

"How long ago was that?" Jodie asked.

"About three years ago," Brenda said.

"How long have you worn that style of glasses, Clare?" Jodie turned to me.

"For about five years," I said, seeing where she was going with this.

"And you haven't seen Lloyd in just over ten. He must have seen you, though. You're not on any social media sites, so he must have seen you in person."

"Well, he's from Star City, Jodie. He might easily have seen me on a visit and I just didn't notice."

"Would you like to see a recent picture?" Brenda asked.

Jodie and I both nodded.

Brenda reached into her bag and brought out her wallet. "This is the most recent picture I have of Lloyd."

Jodie and I were both struck silent at the handsome man on the cover of the brochure Brenda had extracted from the inside of her bag. Gone were Lloyd's greasy combed-over hair and skinny face and sallow skin, replaced by a filled-out friendly smile and shampooed hair with a natural wave that was appealing even in its short cut.

"No way," Jodie said.

Brenda laughed. Her smile was a stark contrast to her reddened nose and eyes. We even had similar teeth. Had she worn braces too? The idea of asking the question was too uncomfortable.

"He said you were going to be surprised when you saw him, Clare," Brenda said. "He really wanted you to see him, know about his success, see that he'd left the geeky guy behind."

"You haven't ever seen this version of Lloyd?" Jodie said.

"If I'd seen that guy over the last five years, I would never have recognized him as Lloyd, but I don't think I have," I said.

Jodie's eyebrows came together in a doubtful glare as she zoned in on Brenda. "And you two never . . . you know?"

"I do know. And never. No. We were strictly professional and knew that we would make the company better by not becoming more than that."

"But you had a crush on him, right?" Jodie said.

"No. And here's the part you really won't believe. He didn't have a crush on me either. He adored Clare. At first I was someone to keep that reminder fresh, but I'm smart and definitely my own woman. We moved past it all pretty quickly."

"After you got the glasses," Jodie said as she reached for a sauce-covered rib.

Brenda just shrugged.

"His company was successful?" I said.

"Very successful. He started out by writing a computer program that changed the way medical personnel get their X-ray and scan imaging. Much quicker and more accurate. Then he improved the machinery used to see the images. The improvements went from there and turned into other things, mostly in the computer and medical fields. He loved that world, made him feel like he was saving lives, and he probably was. 'Better, faster, stronger' was his personal slogan. He was very good."

Dillon hadn't had so many specifics regarding Lloyd's business, but he had also been quick to say that Lloyd had been successful.

"What were the duties of his assistant? What did you do specifically?" Jodie asked.

"We worked together constantly." Her voice cracked again. She cleared her throat. "He wasn't into what he called the dirty work. He worked the ideas, made the decisions regarding who would follow through with his ideas, but then got bored quickly after that. I did the follow-through. I made sure everyone else was getting things done, the dirty work. I was also Lloyd's sounding board. I've never been shy about my opinions, and I have strong ones. I'm sure I helped him to help create better things, but only in small ways. The business was mostly him."

"You were his Girl Friday, his Right-Hand Gal?" Jodie said.

"Those sound pretty sexist to me, but I suppose in a way they're accurate," Brenda said. "I was also the one who kept a close eye on things so I could report to him and we could catch problems before they became too big. He listened to my ideas, and though he always improved upon them, the core of some of the things the company did began with me."

Jodie nodded. She was the least sexist woman I knew and had, in fact, set me straight a time or two. She'd just been trying to either get a reaction out of Brenda or see just how she handled the question.

"Where did he find the Hoovens?" I said after they spent more than a long moment staring at each other.

"Oh, those! They were found in the basement of a building he bought at auction. He tried to research them, maybe find their owners or relatives of the owners, but to no avail. In fact, it was my idea to give them to you, not his," Brenda said to me.

"Really?"

"Yes. It didn't take much to convince him, though, and when he got the invitation to the meeting, he thought the timing was meant to be."

"So the meeting wasn't his idea?" Jodie said as she put down a rib and wiped her fingers on a napkin.

"No, what made you think that?"

"I guess Dillon did, but not in so many words," Jodie said. "So, Lloyd got a real invitation?"

"Yes," Brenda said. She fell into thought. "Well, he said he was invited. Maybe I'm guessing on the formal invitation part." She thought again. "But why do I think there was a real invitation?" She shook her head. "I'm sorry, I can't be sure. I'll try to remember and I'll have some people check his office. Have you gone through the things in his hotel room?"

"We have. No invite. In fact, no mention of the meeting on his laptop calendar or anything," Jodie said.

"He didn't give me access to his calendar, so I'm not

sure what to tell you about that. I do know he kept most things in his head. He liked memorizing events, times, addresses," Brenda said.

"Any mention from him at all regarding where the invitation, formal or not, came from, or who?" Jodie said.

"No, but . . . hang on. I remember the day he told me about being invited and I spotted an open envelope in the trash. For whatever reason I spotted the Star City postmark on it and maybe I just assumed it had contained an invitation. Lloyd told me that he and three others were invited to some meetings, but he didn't mention the other names, and I didn't ask. I wouldn't have known the people anyway, unless Clare had been involved, and he would have mentioned that first thing."

"No idea who the other three are?"

"No. None."

I wondered if she was being truthful. She seemed to be, but even Dillon had known about Donte, though he said he'd only heard Lloyd mutter the name accidentally. I'd told Jodie what Sarah had said about Howard. It was interesting to watch Jodie play dumb to get the answers. It didn't seem like a difficult technique, but it was definitely fascinating. One more name and she'd have the entire group.

"What was so compelling to convince Lloyd to come back to Star City for meetings with three people he went to high school with? Three people he probably didn't get along with, because he was very much a loner, and I don't think he really had any friends beyond Clare back in junior high," Jodie said.

"I asked him that." She fell silent and into thought again. She wiped her fingers and then put the napkin on the table next to her plate. "Despite his brilliance and kindness, Lloyd had a major fault. His ego. He loved his success, and I was under the impression that he was ready to rub in that success with some people who hadn't been so kind to him in high school. I tried not to let it bother me, his ego, but it did sometimes. I think he had the whole scene planned out in his head. He'd make a grand return to his hometown. Everyone would envy him, and you"—she looked at me—"would fall in love with him."

"That wasn't going to happen," Jodie said. "Did he know that Clare wouldn't be interested in him or was he off his rocker? That's a real question, Brenda. Was Lloyd nutty weird or brilliant weird, or just weird weird?"

"Brilliant weird. I think he knew what was real and what was fantasy, but he was probably pretty close to buying into that fantasy world."

Jodie nodded. "I need that invitation, or the names that were on it if there was one. Can you help with that?"

"I don't know. I'll have someone search his office. I'll try to remember if there was more I saw or heard that day, but it wasn't an important conversation. There were bigger things, business things on our plates back then."

"Anyone you can think of who he might have mentioned other than Clare over the years, someone from here he either liked or didn't like, someone who didn't like him maybe?"

"He never spoke with fondness about Clare's boyfriend," she said with an embarrassed smile. "Which is another way of saying he had a few bad things to say about him."

"Seth?" I said.

"Yes, but some other guy too . . . Creighton. Sound right?" Brenda said.

"Oh yeah, that sounds about right," Jodie answered.

"It wasn't a big thing," Brenda said. "Please understand that Clare and her boyfriends, whoever they were, didn't come up in conversation all that much. I'm just trying to remember things, and those things are bigger in my mind right now."

It was like focusing in on a color or a number and you see it everywhere. Made sense. But I wondered if Jodie was thinking the same thing I was—had Creighton seen or talked to Lloyd recently? She'd questioned Seth, but not Creighton, at least not in front of me.

I was sure we'd . . . I mean *she'd* find out.

The rest of the dinner was filled with silent and small-talk moments. I didn't know this woman who looked like me, and when we didn't have specific things to discuss, it was weird. The conclusion I came to was that Brenda was all about her job. She had little to no social life, but that might just have been what she wanted us to think because she probably thought dinner with the twin she'd never met before was just as weird as I did. Jodie never did much small talk. She'd had her questions answered and fell into mostly silence as she worked through the new information she'd learned.

She stayed silent as she drove up the hill to Little Blue and finally spoke after I got out of the Bronco. She rolled down the passenger window. "I have an idea. . . . Well, I'll call you tomorrow," she said quickly before she turned the truck around and retreated down the hill.

I watched and smiled at the taillights. I always liked it when she had ideas for tomorrow that I got to be a part of.

8

"Clare, please tell me more about the disembodied foot. I mean, the mere use of the word 'disembodied' makes the entire set of events interesting to me. Chester only had the highlights. Your best friend is an officer of the law. I'm sure you know more." Nathan Grimes wore his scarf and cap as he leaned on the corner of one of the workshop tables. His nose was still red, making me think he'd just come in from the cold. "You must share."

"Good morning, Nathan," I said. "You here by yourself?"

"I am. Momentarily at least. Your charming grandfather said he'd be back later and Adal had to run to the post office. He said it's just around the back but that he had to go out the front to get there. He'll return soon too. I expect my new type to arrive today; the sellers overnighted it, and even though it's early I didn't want to chance missing the delivery."

"Where's the type coming from?"

"A collector in Boston. He and I spoke on the phone for about half an hour, and I feel I paid him well. I hope it's in as good a shape as he claimed it to be. Marion had him send us some pictures that Chester and Adal inspected with critical eyes. They seemed satisfied. It's not Bridgnorth, but it's similar. It's old and expensive. I think the best part is that no one, including the owner, knows the name of the font. It's a mystery." He held out a picture for me to look at.

"It could be Bridgnorth . . . no, the *C*'s and *E*'s are missing the middle parts."

"I know." Nathan smiled.

"Marion did good work."

"She did."

Even though I wouldn't be the one to use the type, there was always something exciting about getting a new box in. Reflexively, I looked out toward the front of the store, but no one was headed this way with a delivery.

"I'm so excited I could barely sleep. Oh!" He stood and stepped back from the desk, waving his hand toward its top. "I brought my Splendid."

"Ooh," I said as I stepped around.

The snap-on case was off the typewriter, so I could immediately appreciate its full beauty.

"Here," Nathan said as he grabbed a piece of the green paper from the scrap stack. "Give it a try."

I typed a line or two from Hamlet. The keys had the perfect give and snap.

"This is comfortable," I said.

"It's perfection. I have it tuned up by a guy back home. I take it to him once a month for a general once-over. If I lived close by Star City, of course I'd bring it here."

"It's a piece of art," I said as I ran my finger over its rounded edges and good-sized keys. As I got to the top, I said, "Oh, a slightly loose paper finger. Want me to tighten it up?"

"Let me see." Nathan moved behind me as I gently jiggled the metal paper finger, one of the two parts that kept the paper against the front of the platen.

"It's not bad. Just a little," I said.

"Yes, please. Thanks!"

"It's an easy fix." I reached behind me, grabbed a small screwdriver, and made the quick and easy repair in seconds. "Good as new. Really, almost literally. You take very good care of your typewriter."

"Thank you. Does that earn me any disembodied foot points? Tell me what you know, and I admit fully that I will probably use the details in a book. I will change names to protect the innocent, though I've found that no one is truly innocent."

"I'm not sure I can tell you much, except that Marion came upon the gentleman who found it on the slopes and I went to school with the gentleman who lost the foot and whose body was also found later. It was murder."

Nathan blinked at me. "How spectacular. Except for the poor victim, of course. Was the cutting off of the foot the cause of death?"

"I'd better not say more. Details will come out soon, I'm sure."

"So tragic. Do you know of any clues?"

"No." I didn't think the things I knew were really clues anyway.

"You're not sure how much you are at liberty to say. I understand that."

I laughed. "Not only am I not at liberty. I'm not qualified. Whatever I know is only because I've wormed my way into Jodie's business or overheard something because I was in close proximity to her. Plus, Marion called me when she found the man who'd found the boot."

"I see."

"Uh, Nathan, Marion doesn't know anything either."

"I understand."

But I could see the disappointment in his eyes.

Baskerville hadn't made an appearance until that moment. He meowed from a spot at the bottom of the stairs that led up to Chester's apartment.

"Good morning, Baskerville," Nathan said. "Come on over."

"He's not . . ." I was going to say that the cat wasn't friendly and would probably ignore the author, but I would have been wrong. Baskerville trotted to Nathan and rubbed his head on Nathan's ankle. "That's a first, Nathan."

"I have a way," Nathan said as he bent over and scratched behind the cat's ears.

"I'd say." I smiled. "Tell me more about your book of poetry. I know about the love poems, but do you have any gruesome and scary ones?"

Nathan laughed. "No, they're love poems only. I tried writing horror poems, but I just can't. I do, however, love writing love poems, and I've got a knack for it, if I do say so myself."

"That's going to surprise your readers."

"Something tells me that most of my regular readers won't be interested. I understand that. I like love poems and I liked the idea of creating my own book. You can see I'm not in this one for money."

"I've heard that no writer should write for money," I said.

"True, that, my dear, but then, every once in a blue moon, one of us strikes gold and it all quickly becomes about the money, or purposefully not about the money, like this book of poetry is for me."

"I see. You're one who struck gold?"

"I did. Big gold," he said, but with no tone of arrogance. "It doesn't happen often, but it happened to me. I'm glad about it now, but I went through some terrible growing pains. Didn't know what to do with myself for quite some time. I've figured it out. I used to always think it so irritating when someone said sudden success and money could take some big adjustment, thinking that it was one adjustment I wanted to try. Well, it is worth it, don't misunderstand, but it's . . . discombobulating too."

His honesty was refreshing.

"Interesting," I said. I didn't admit that I'd never had big money ambitions, that working in The Rescued Word was exactly what I wanted to do and where I wanted to be. I never wanted to leave Star City, unless it was for a quick ride down to Salt Lake City.

Adal pushed through the door and into the workshop. He muttered something in German I suspected was a string of curse words.

"Busy at the post office?" I said.

"Yes," he said after taking a calming breath. "They need more employees, or faster ones maybe."

He was back to English, but it was sprinkled with a light German accent.

"It's been an issue for a number of years," I said. For whatever reason the Star City Post Office is always training new employees. No one seemed to stick around for long. Maybe the workload had grown to be too much as the town had expanded and no other post office had been added to assist the population. Jodie thought it was because the building was so small that the workers became claustrophobic quickly and had to get out of there, so they found other jobs.

"I'm sorry." Adal shook his head and then smiled. "I was in a hurry. I need to slow down."

There was more, I could tell. "Adal? What happened?"

Adal smiled weakly as his eyes moved from Nathan to me and back to Nathan again.

"Would you like some privacy?" Nathan said as he stood.

Adal put his hand up. "No, I'm sorry. It was nothing. I ran into someone at the post office, and I was left unsettled. I apologize." He took another deep breath and let it out.

Nathan and I looked at each other, and it became clear that he didn't want to leave if he wasn't asked to.

"Adal?" I said. "What happened?"

"I saw Jodie's brother, Creighton," Adal said.

It took me approximately two seconds to understand what must have happened. Creighton was less than friendly to Adal, maybe even downright rude.

"What'd he say?" I said.

"He just reminded me that I'm here temporarily and Jodie lives here, and that it would be a good idea to put an end to our friendship before it went too far."

"Ah," Nathan said. "You and the lovely police woman are dating?"

I looked at Adal. This was the first he'd said anything

around me regarding any sort of relationship with Jodie. I didn't want to interject something that might cause him to remember he was keeping mum.

"We are close friends," Adal said. "I'm sorry if I'm causing any strife with her family, though."

"Oh, dear man," Nathan said. "We need to read some of my poems together. Do not let anyone get in the way of something that is made of real love. No one!"

I wanted to add, *Especially Creighton!*, but that would have been immature to the point that I would have had to apologize. Instead I said, "Creighton's a bunch of hot air, Adal. If Jodie knew her brother said something to you, she'd set him straight."

"Oh, please don't tell her," Adal said. "I didn't back down, but I should have told him more than just to mind his own business."

"Next time, slug him in the jaw," Nathan said.

"He's a cop; he carries a gun," I said.

"Oh. Well, say something dreadful to him in German, then," Nathan said.

We all laughed.

"I can do that," Adal said.

"Creighton sometimes likes to be tough just because he can, Adal. Don't let him bother you too much," I added. "Jodie doesn't."

Adal nodded, but the blush that spread on his cheeks told me he was either embarrassed or angry. He'd work it out.

"Okay, well, let's get to work," I said.

But, as seemed to be the case lately, my phone buzzed with someone who was sure to cause another delay.

9

"Sorry. Go ahead and get started without me. Excuse me," I said.

I moved to the still-empty front part of the shop to answer Jodie's call. Baskerville stayed close on my heels.

"What's up?" I said.

"Wanna come with me to talk to Donte?"

"Of course," I said, but I cringed. I knew Adal could take care of the store and Nathan, but I would be neglecting my real duties.

"Be out in front in three point five minutes," she said.

"Will do."

Fortunately, Chester reappeared at the two-point-five-minutes mark. I told him about Jodie's invitation, and Adal and Nathan had come out front, overhearing my conversation with Chester. Nathan encouraged me to come back with details, and Adal walked me out to the Bronco.

I didn't miss the smile between him and Jodie. Gone were any signs of post office or Creighton annoyance.

"So, you guys trying to keep your relationship a secret for a while?" I asked when we were on the way.

"It seems like the right thing to do," Jodie said with a shrug.

"Okay, but just an FYI, I don't think it's much of a secret."

"Yeah, I know, but work with me here."

"Will do." I took a sip from the coffee she'd brought and then set it back into the cup holder. "So, we're going to question Donte?"

"We're going to go talk to him, try to get some information out of him without making him feel like he's being grilled or questioned. He's not a suspect, yet at least, so the casual approach is our only real option anyway."

"I can do casual."

"Yes, you can, and let's face it, Clare—you were more liked than I was back in high school. I think you'll be an asset to my plan."

"Always glad to be an asset. So, any new clues at all?"

"None. I did go talk to Lloyd's parents. That was rough."

"Oh! I can't believe I haven't given them my condolences. I didn't even think about it."

"We've all been a little stunned."

"I'll go by and see them today or tomorrow. Do they still live in the same spot?"

"Yes."

We fell silent for most of the rest of the trip down the canyon. We'd made the trip to Salt Lake City more times than we'd ever be able to remember, and the mountain views and curves in the road were familiar. After you took the last curve and the cityscape came into view, there was always a moment of appreciation. It was good to make it down the canyon in one piece, of course, but the appreciation was for the beauty that we were fortunate to live around. The city was different from our small mountain town, but they were both stunning.

Donte Senot's textbook publishing company was on the west side of the city, south of the airport and surrounded by warehouse-style buildings similar to his: nondescript, large, and rectangle shaped. Donte's boring beige building stood out only because of the sign adorning the spot above the front door.

"Senot Textbook Publishing," Jodie quoted the funky and flashing neon.

"The neon book is cool," I said.

"And the numbers. Oh yeah, Donte wrote a math textbook. Who woulda thunk it, huh?"

"Some of us obviously don't reach our potential until after high school."

"Yeah, I'm still headed toward my peak," Jodie said. "Come on, Donte's expecting us."

We were greeted by an empty receptionist's desk in the small, stark entryway.

"It's freezing in here," I said.

"Maybe books and ink need cold temperatures," Jodie said as she inspected the few plaques on the side wall proclaiming that Senot Textbook Publishing had done some awesome things. She turned away from the wall and peered down a corner. "Hello?"

"Actually, it's best to keep the environment dry. Not

too hot or too cold. Not too much light either. But those are more preservation techniques than mass printing, so maybe there're things I don't know," I said.

"I think you told me that once before, the stuff about the dry."

"Hello?" a gentleman said as he leaned out from a doorway halfway down the hall.

"Hi, we're here to see Donte," Jodie said.

"Jodie?" the man said as he stepped out from the office. "I should have known. You haven't changed a bit." He joined us and took her hand, shaking it using both of his as a big smile spread across his face. "And Clare! This is a treat." He turned to me and repeated the friendly greeting.

"Hi, Donte," I said. He didn't look a thing like he had looked in high school. He looked much better. He'd gotten a little taller, filled out more through his shoulders, and though his brown hair was short, his face had aged nicely, in an appealing way that made me think of cowboys and rugged things. He didn't look younger than his about-thirty years, but he carried the years very well.

"Well, come on back to my office. We don't really have a receptionist because we don't get many visitors. When we do have special guests, Sarah comes in and hosts us all. She's still the hostess with the mostess," he said with a laugh as he led us back down the hallway.

Jodie sent me a half eye roll, but I tried not to react. I didn't remember Sarah being much of a host, but since Jodie and I weren't part of their crowd, we didn't get many chances to be her guests.

Inside the office, there was no sense that Donte had become successful. Like everything else except for the sign out front, it was boring and beige. His desk was covered in spreadsheets, and the back of his laptop was clean. There were no pictures of children or Sarah anywhere.

"Have a seat. I'll give you a quick tour of the press when we're done in here, but I'm too curious about your reasons for coming to talk to me to do that first. Sarah told me what you told her about Lloyd, Clare. I'm still in a state of shock. I assume that's why you're here?"

"It is why we're here," Jodie said.

"Ask me anything." He half smiled. "I'm an open book."

"Right," Jodie said. "What can you tell me about the meeting or meetings you were supposed to attend or were invited to attend with Lloyd? Start by telling me about the invitation itself. When did you receive it?"

I wanted to interrupt when she got out her notebook and pen and remind her we were just there casually, but that would have been a mistake, of course, particularly if I wanted to be invited to go with her again.

"Oh, I . . . I think about two months ago," he said. He opened the front drawer to his desk. "I searched for the invitation this morning after we spoke, Jodie, but I couldn't find it. I'll keep looking. You can have it the second I find it."

"And it was supposed to be meetings about business, entrepreneurship, et cetera?"

"Well, not totally. It was worded something like 'A meeting of the minds. Successful friends coming together again to share ideas.' Something like that, but that wasn't it exactly."

"That sounds like it was definitely something for businesspeople to discuss business things," Jodie said.

"Right. Well, for Lloyd, Howard, and myself, that would be an easy assumption. But how to explain Creighton?" Donte said.

It was rare that Jodie was stunned. This was one of those rare moments, but she recovered.

"Creighton?" she said. "Creighton was invited?"

"Yeah, he was invited. I thought you knew." Donte looked at me. "Sarah said she talked to you."

I cleared my throat. This had gone from casual to formal quickly. "She told me about Howard being invited, but she couldn't remember the fourth person." I looked at Jodie so my eyes could tell her that I would have absolutely told her about Creighton's being invited if Sarah had mentioned him.

"Okay." She nodded quickly at me and then turned back to Donte. "So you, Lloyd, Howard Craig, and Creighton?" Jodie said.

"Yes, those four," Donte said. His eyebrows had come together sharply. I could read his mind. He'd moved past the part where his wife had forgotten that Creighton had been invited, and had come quickly to the conclusion that something was weird if at this point Jodie didn't know that her brother, another police officer, had been part of the group.

"Who sent the invitation?" Jodie asked.

"No idea. It wasn't clear, but there was a Star City postmark. For a short time I assumed Creighton, but then I realized that the others also still have ties to Star City. Anyone could have sent it."

"I'd sure like to see that invitation," Jodie said.

"I'd love to give it to you. I was bowled over by the news of Lloyd's death yesterday and felt compelled to look for it. I wonder if I absently picked it up and put it in a file or something. I'll get it to you the second it turns up. I'll bring it up to Star City or have Sarah take it to you."

"That would be great. Thanks," Jodie said. "Donte, have you been in contact with Lloyd, Howard, or Creighton over these last ten or so years?"

"Not really. I had a beer with Howard when he came back to Star City a time or two, but I haven't seen Lloyd since high school and I don't remember ever really knowing Creighton at all. He was older than us and traveled in different circles."

"Did anything in high school, or later for that matter, happen that would make you think the four of you should get together ten years later for a reunion?"

Donte laughed once. "Nothing at all. Apparently Sarah knew Lloyd, had a class or two with him, but she had to tell me who he was when I got the invitation. I had no memory of him. When I saw Creighton's name I had one of those 'uh-oh, a cop' moments, but I quickly realized that was kind of dumb of me. Howard and I were friends, so that didn't seem out of place, but the invitation was a complete surprise."

Jodie nodded twice slowly and asked, "How's the bookstore going?"

"Fine so far, but Sarah can't get caught up. Too soon to know much of anything regarding its success or failure. All I really know is that her inventory is huge, and I'm thankful that it's not in my garage."

"I understand. She's got some woo-woo stuff going on too, huh?" Jodie asked.

Donte blinked. "Oh, her life-after-death metaphysical stuff. Yeah, that stuff is weird." He straightened his crinkled forehead. "It's her thing, not mine at all. I don't understand any of that stuff. It's weird for sure, though." He cleared his throat and blanched momentarily before he brought his features back in line again. If the meta-physical stuff was a wedge between the two of them, he didn't want us to know, but too late.

"Yeah, I agree," Jodie said.

"You guys live in Salt Lake?" I asked when the beat of silence went on a bit too long. If I read her correctly, Jodie was okay with me jumping in.

"Yes, in Sugarhouse. It's a great place to live and Par-ley's Canyon is close, so Sarah can get to work up in Star City in less than half an hour most days. She gets to her work much more quickly than I get to mine."

"Any kids?" I said.

"No, not our thing. You two have any kids?"

"Not yet," we replied in tandem.

"Plenty of time," he said with a polite wave.

"Yep," Jodie said.

"So, what happened to Lloyd? I mean, can you share the details of his murder? Or, maybe you can tell me what he did after high school? Sarah wasn't clear on that part," Donte said.

"He moved to Nebraska and used his smarts to start a computer-something company. We've determined that he was killed but something happened to his body afterward. I can't go into detail. He'd been in town for less than forty-eight hours according to his parents and his check-in time at the hotel," Jodie said.

Donte shook his head slowly. "Terrible."

"Very. Where were you two days ago, day and night, Donte?"

The surprise in Donte's eyes lit genuinely. "Oh. Well, here and then I was at home, I guess. That's where I usually am at night. Can't think of anywhere else I might have been."

"Can anyone but Sarah confirm that?"

He thought a moment. "Well, one of my print folks can tell you I was here during the day, but I'm afraid no one but Sarah could tell you I was home at night."

"When did she get home two nights ago?"

He frowned. "Late, I suppose, but she was working, trying to get that bookshop straightened up." He sat up and shook out his tense shoulders. "Jodie, I didn't kill Lloyd. Neither did Sarah, if that's where your mind is going."

"Good." Jodie smiled as if she was trying to let him know she might have been kidding about asking him, but only *might* have.

"Want to see the printing part of the facility?" Donte said.

"Yes," I said enthusiastically.

Donte led the way out of his office and the other direction down the hallway. Once out of the stress-riddled air in the office and back in control, Donte seemed to relax.

"We do the whole books here, from soup to nuts, or from text to shipping, I suppose. I know you and Chester do printing, but yours is unquestionably much more personal and artistic, even in the simplest ways. I remember going into The Rescued Word when I was a kid. Even back then, it was a great place, and Chester let me watch him work on the printing press. It was a life-changing moment probably, but I didn't realize it at the time. Anyway, our press is much different, much bigger."

Donte walked us through a tour of the rest of the facility. The press was big, long and intimidating. Mechanical.

There were no print runs scheduled and we didn't see any other employees, though Donte mentioned a couple were on their breaks and would be setting up the press later if we wanted to stick around. Jodie said that we didn't have time, but we hoped for a rain check.

Even on such a grand scale, the place smelled just like The Rescued Word, but with less coffee scent. It felt like home, but a more palatial home that could afford house-keepers. As I'd already noted to myself earlier, I had no ambition to see Chester's business become anything like Donte's, and neither would Chester, but it was good to see modern technology in action, if only to appreciate my timeworn skills and those customers who needed them.

As Donte saw us to Jodie's Bronco, Jodie told him to be on his toes.

"You think the killer set up the meetings and is planning to kill us all?"

"I just don't know, Donte. But a murder has occurred. It's always good to be careful."

Donte swallowed hard before he said, "Will do."

He watched us and waved until we were all the way out of the parking lot. I'd had no sense that he was anything but friendly, but Jodie might have thought differently. She grumbled a noise in the back of her throat.

"What? Oh! Creighton? I asked.

"Yes, but there's more. Donte's hiding something," she said.

"I didn't pick up on that at all."

She sent me a sideways glance but didn't try to point out what I'd missed.

"Let's head home. I need to talk to my brother," she finally said.

"Can I come with?"

"No, not on this one, Clare. Besides, I might not want any witnesses."

"Got it."

"Oh, by the way, when we get back up to Star City, I'm having the Hoovens delivered to The Rescued Word."

"Jodie, they aren't ours. I mean, we can't accept them."

"They are legally yours, Clare. There are some weird dynamics regarding us keeping them in a truck in our parking lot. There are even weird things about us putting them in a storage shed. The cold temperatures might not be good for them."

"They were in a basement in Nebraska for who knows how long. They'd be fine in a storage shed."

"But Lloyd wanted you to have them. It's clear that was his intention. They're in this limbo that makes for too many people not responsible enough for them. We have to bring them up to The Rescued Word."

I didn't know what to say. I was nervous about the responsibility of something so valuable, but excited to have them too. How could I not be? I was sure Chester and I would donate them to some sort of museum if they ultimately proved to be ours, but we would have to keep them secure until then.

"Okay," I said, still working out logistics in my mind. "Okay."

The roads got us from place to place, but leaving the city and moving through the canyon usually released the stress that came with city traffic. Today, not so much. The stress of the city, along with the stress of the murder, stayed with us for every curving mile.

10

I took a deep breath of the cold night air and let it out slowly. What a day.

Almost immediately after Jodie dropped me off, her partner, Omar, and two other officers brought the truck up with the Hoovens. Chester was fit to be tied, for about thirty seconds. And then his eyes took in the machines, and he was put under their spell. Once they were in the workshop, crowding the space far too much, he couldn't stop inspecting them in a way that was almost fawning.

We all liked looking at them, and we all wanted to spend more time with them, but that didn't take away the fact that we probably had over twenty thousand dollars' worth of rare typewriters sitting in our workshop, and none of us would accept the fact that they were ours. Chester promised to move a cot into the room if it would ease my concerns over the machines' safety. I told him his sleep was worth more than the typewriters, and we had to remember that an ad hadn't been put out announcing what we had. Not many people knew, and most people wouldn't even know what they were looking at if they came upon them.

I was glad the day was over as I enjoyed the night air. It was somehow sweeter when I breathed it in as I stood outside the shop on Bygone Alley. It had been a good winter and I'd seen my fair share of time on the slopes, but I suddenly craved more. Cold, fresh air did that to me. I didn't see that happening this week, though.

It was dark outside but hadn't been for long. I glanced at the time on my phone. Seth had been called to a late meeting, so I was on my own for a while. Home, some soup, and a good book sounded like the right combination.

"My goodness, the air smells better up here than anywhere I've ever been," Nathan said from behind me. He'd been leaning against the wall next to the shop's front window. He bounced himself away from it and moved next to me.

"I was just thinking the same thing," I said as I jumped in my skin a tiny bit. "I didn't see you over there."

"We writers of things scary like to lurk in the shadows," he said.

I laughed. "For a writer of things scary, you aren't very scary yourself."

He sent me a half smile. "Well, when I came out of the shop, I was taken by the view. The alley is as charming as London during Jack the Ripper's time. I wanted to soak it in."

"Back when they threw their waste out onto the streets?"

"Well, sans waste, I suppose. It's quaint and very perfect."

"Oh no, you're not going to use it in one of your novels, are you, turn it into a place with monsters and such?" I said with my own smile.

"I just might."

I laughed. He was an interesting man. A perfectionist, diva-ish (sometimes), pleasant sometimes, and not creepy at all. Earlier I'd thought the sideways slant he sometimes did with his eyes might be creepy, but now I saw it as something more playful. He liked to have fun, but his fun was a little different than for the rest of us.

"Actually, that might be kind of cool," I said.

"You'll be the first to know. Can I interest you in dinner? We can invite your gentleman friend," he said.

"Dinner sounds great. Seth is busy, but I'm available." I paused. "Are you . . . I mean, aren't you pretty well-known? Can you eat in public and not be bothered?"

"Watch this." He took off his scarf and hat, something I'd seen him do a few times now. "I don't look like Nathan Grimes any longer, do I?"

"Huh. I wondered why you did that. You're right, though, not as much like the famous author. Nice trick."

"It's been very helpful. I'll take them off when we get to the restaurant. It's too cold right now," he said as he rewrapped. "Where to?"

"Follow me," I said.

For an instant I debated crossing the street and eating at the diner, but I changed my mind and led us out of Bygone Alley toward a small taco place that had been a Star City landmark as far back as I could remember. They'd named the restaurant the Taco Place, and they sold nothing but tacos. Not today's designer tacos, but hard-shell-only tacos with all sorts of stuffing options. As he said he'd do, Nathan took off his scarf and hat before we entered. No one gave us a second look as we were shown to a table in a dark corner.

"See?" he said when we were seated.

"You are your own disguise."

"I didn't do it on purpose. I really do like this scarf and hat. They became my trademark, and when it became difficult to go out and about without being approached all the time, I came up with this idea. It's been a real sanity saver."

"You're kind of a rock star, aren't you?"

"Kind of," he said sincerely as he looked at his menu. "Lots of people like horror."

I smiled and pushed up my glasses. Though he'd almost become 'just Nathan' to me, I was having dinner with a famous author. I needed to enjoy the moment.

"Have you always wanted to be a writer?" I asked after we'd ordered.

"No, not until I was thirteen and I met a famous author."

"Who?"

"Phyllis A. Whitney."

"Oh, my mom loved her books so much. Probably still does. The bookstore up the hill recently had a window display of her books. It brought back good memories." The third time in a few days that store had come up. The universe was telling me to pay attention.

"My mother loved her too. I was with Mom one day at a restaurant in North Carolina. She gasped and tried not to point as she told me that Ms. Whitney was at the next table. Mom wasn't sure what to do with herself."

I laughed. "I bet you get that a lot now too."

"Only when I wear the scarf and hat. Anyway, I got up and went to talk to her. I said my mom loved her books so much. I don't have any idea where I got the guts. I think I'd just never seen my mother in such a state before. I wanted to do something to make it an even better day for her. Ms. Whitney invited us to her table, where she and my mother talked for at least an hour. They talked about writing and the discipline needed and joy involved with putting a story down on paper. The way Ms. Whitney spoke . . . well, I think I got caught up in my mom's dreams, if that makes any sense at all."

"It does."

He took a sip of his water. "She traveled to every single place she wrote about. Ms. Whitney and her assistant went to each and every place, Clare. Now we have computer maps and pictures and the Internet, but she refused to write a story without seeing the location first. I think I just wanted to be so much like this intelligent, impressive woman that I abandoned any other idea and decided to become a writer because only writers could be so wonderful, or that's how my youthful mind worked through the day at the restaurant."

"That's very cool. Chester would love to hear the story about Ms. Whitney. He collects author stories."

"Oh yeah? I'll tell him."

Our plates of tacos were delivered and I was satisfied with the happy, surprised expression on Nathan's face. I'd hoped he wasn't immune to their charms.

"Would you share something with me?" he said after we'd both taken a few silent bites.

"About the foot?" I said after I swallowed.

"Yes," he said with a smile. "And the rest of the body

that had once been attached to it. I might be able to help. I do a lot of research."

I laughed. "I think this is more mystery than horror."

"Still." He shrugged.

"So, this is okay dinner conversation?"

"I think it is. If it upsets your sensibilities, we can wait until dessert." He smiled again.

I told him a skimmed-over, halfway-true version of everything I knew, except for the part about Creighton. That seemed like something I should keep to myself. In fact, I probably shouldn't even know about that part myself.

"Well, of course whoever sent the invitation is the killer," he said. "The other invitees should be on alert."

"Jodie told Donte to keep on his toes. I'm sure she or one of the officers did the same with Howard and Creighton. Do you really think the other invitees are in danger?"

"There's a chance of it, and that's good enough for an armed guard in my opinion."

"Really?"

"Sure, but I'm probably a bit more paranoid than the rest."

"I don't know. I don't think the police have any real feel for it at all."

"Your friend Jodie did go talk to Donte."

"True." Though I didn't know what Jodie was really thinking, and I knew she wouldn't tell me. "I hope the killer isn't someone we know, which sounds horrible, of course."

Nathan nodded. "I get that, though. I hope they figure it out quickly. Tell me about Lloyd when he was a kid. What was he like?"

"A really smart, shy, nerdy guy, with seemingly very few friends."

"Well, we've all heard that story before. The nerdy outcast makes good, makes millions. But I'm sure he also made some people mad on the way up the ladder. It's impossible not to. Surely, the police are looking at that too."

"Oh yeah," I said. But I wasn't sure at all. I suddenly wondered how Jodie would react to me making real suggestions regarding her investigation, or asking probing questions. We had our boundaries. I wasn't an officer of the law, and though I might tease her about it sometimes, when it came down to police business, I had no business there whatsoever.

We were also good enough friends that maybe I could push the envelope, and she'd never allowed me to be so involved before.

"It's a deeply curious and sad set of circumstances," Nathan said.

"Very much so. Lloyd and I were friends a long, long time ago, when we were kids. As we got older I found I was comfortable around other people, but Lloyd, not so much. It's like I went into the water a little deeper, but he didn't."

"Oh, that's good. Mind if I use that someday?" Nathan said as he pulled a small notebook out of his coat pocket.

"What'd I say?"

He laughed and wrote down the words he told me he'd someday use in a book. Considering the genre he wrote in, I was already anxious to see the context he created.

"Not bad for a typewriter repair person," he said. "And you and your grandfather are so much more. You both know that, don't you?"

"Well, we have other services we offer."

"Yes, but the printing press. The stationery. The building. The history. The Rescued Word is a gem."

"Well, thank you," I said.

"You're welcome, and I'm glad to be a part of it, if only for a short time."

"Us too. I'm sorry, but I don't collect author stories like my grandfather, so while I know your writing, I don't know whether you're married or have kids. May I pry?"

"Not prying at all. Never married, no kids. I've been romantically involved a time or two, but I'm not an easy man to live with, Clare." He sent me a wry smile. "I keep the strangest hours and I'm not good at letting people have their way. I want to write, eat, sleep, watch television only when I want to do those things. If someone else gets in the way of my choices, I get grumpy. I decided a long time ago that I'm better off living by myself, and so are those who might, even briefly, think they want to live with me. Don't look at me that way. I'm not lonely and I have friends—patient ones who know I can be unavailable for weeks at a time and then desperately need to see them, so I don't lose contact with the human world. I travel quite a bit too. It's a lovely life, and many authors enjoy their solitary time."

"Sounds like it," I said.

I remembered my first impression of Nathan and how it had changed, would probably change some more. I thought it might have changed from Adal's perspective too, and if it hadn't I thought it would eventually.

Nathan informed me that he never skipped dessert, so after too many tacos we ordered two pieces of cheesecake, one plain, one topped with strawberries, and shared them.

I hadn't eaten so much taco and cheesecake since the last time I'd been in the Taco Place with Seth a few weeks earlier.

Nathan slipped on his hat and scarf and we walked back to The Rescued Word. I couldn't convince him to let me drive him down the hill to his hotel. As I turned to go up the hill to Little Blue, I glanced at my rearview mirror.

I had enjoyed the evening with the horror author, and it would have been impossible for me to know that that moment would be the last time ever I'd ever see that adorable hat and scarf.

11

The house, located just past Star City's city limits, was only a short distance away from Interstate 80. A cute house that had been modern twenty years ago, it still looked well taken care of. It fit well with the cozy neighborhood that had, over the years, filled out with lots of trees.

I was immediately taken back in time. I was unsettled anyway because of the task at hand, but the memories the small house evoked took me right back to that night when Lloyd couldn't bring himself to attend the dance, the night his dad brought me there so we could watch movies and have a junior high date anyway.

I hadn't been back since then. I hadn't had occasion to even drive by. There was no real reason for me to feel bad about that, but I did. I climbed the few stairs to the front porch and knocked. I pushed up my glasses and told myself not to cry, that crying wouldn't do Lloyd's parents a bit of good.

Footsteps approached and then the door opened slowly.

"Mr. Gavin?" I said.

He pushed open the screen door. "Yes?"

"I'm . . . well, I went to school with Lloyd. I'm so sorry for your loss." I held out the flowers and card I'd brought with me.

He blinked, his eyes not all the way dry from his last cry.

"You're that Henry girl," he said.

"I am. Clare Henry."

"I remember you. Please come in. I'll grab Sylvie." He pushed the door open wider.

While I wanted to offer my condolences, I had been hoping I wouldn't be invited inside. Even more firmly I told myself not to cry.

The front room overflowed with flowers, and I realized I hadn't paid attention to the news. What had been said about Lloyd's murder?

"Please have a seat," he said as he motioned toward a floral-print couch.

"Who's here, Samuel?" a voice came from another part of the house.

"Clare Henry, Sylvie. Come out a minute."

A few seconds later we were sitting together in the aromatic front room. Clearly, both of Lloyd's parents had been dealing with a lot of emotion and I was surprised by their attempts to act strong in front of me. I wondered if they had any other friends or family around to help them with things.

"I remember you," Samuel said. "You came over and

watched movies with Lloyd when he broke out in a rash at the mere thought of going out on a date with you."

"Oh! That's you," Sylvie said as a small smile tried to pull at her lips.

"That's me," I said. I cleared my throat. "I'm so terribly sorry for your loss."

Sylvie and Samuel looked at each other. Each of them seemed to gain some strength from the other one before they turned back to me.

"Thank you," Sylvie said. "It's so . . . shocking, I suppose. He came to town, we had a short visit, and now he's gone."

I saw the shock that mixed with their emotion. Their wide, glassy eyes made me think they had been experiencing moments of lag, when their bodies kept going, but everything else couldn't quite catch up.

"When's the last time you talked to Lloyd?" Samuel said.

"Oh, it's been at least since high school," I said. "We didn't stay in touch, I'm afraid."

"Really?" Sylvie said. "He mentioned you a time or two since then, I'm sure."

I didn't know what to say, so I just nodded.

"Yes, in fact, he was back visiting us a couple of years ago and I know he mentioned that he was going to meet you for dinner," Sylvie said.

"I, uh, I don't think that was me," I said. "I'm sorry. Perhaps another friend from our younger days."

Sylvie cocked her head as surprised concentration took away the sadness and shock for an instant.

"I must be remembering wrong," she said. "I'm sure the details will come back to me later."

"Did you know who he was meeting, or seeing on this trip?" I asked.

"He told us he was here for some skiing only, that he didn't have plans to do anything more than rest, relax, and ski," Samuel said. "Why? Were you going to see him on this trip?"

"I didn't know he was coming into town, but . . . well, he sent me and my grandfather some generous gifts, some very valuable typewriters."

"That's right, your grandfather owns The Rescued Word," Sylvie said. "Well, Lloyd was always fond of you. I'm not surprised he sent them, but he didn't share that with us."

"This is terrible timing, but I think you two should have them. They're larger than your typical typewriter, so I'll have them in safekeeping until you're ready."

Sylvie and Samuel blinked at me a few times, processing my words. No one could have expected to be talking about typewriters in the middle of such a tragedy.

"We couldn't take them. Lloyd apparently wanted you to have them," Samuel finally said.

It seemed way too crass to bring up their value at this moment, so I just said, "You know, I should have talked to you about this later. We'll talk again in a few weeks. For now, what can I do for you two?"

"Nothing at all, thank you, though," Samuel said. "The funeral will be the day after tomorrow."

"I'll be there," I said.

"Thank you," Samuel said. "You know he was murdered? Killed."

"I do." My throat tightened and I swallowed hard. "I'm sorry."

"The police don't have any clues at all," Sylvie said. "But I know who did it."

"You do?" I said.

"Now, Sylvie," Samuel said. "Don't go spreading rumors. That's not fair."

I homed in on Sylvie. "Who do you think killed Lloyd?"

"One of his competitors, of course. He was so successful, Clare. He even said when he first got home this time that he'd just caused shock waves through the entire computer technology world. I told the police. They're going to check it out."

I didn't remember Jodie asking Brenda about Lloyd's business competitors, but maybe she did that without me present. My list of questions for her was growing.

"Any specific competitor?" I said.

"No," Samuel said too firmly. "No, no one specific. We'll let the police do their jobs."

"Of course," I said.

Sylvie didn't seem bothered by her husband's firm tone, but she did switch her focus. She concentrated on me.

"I remember now," she said a second later. "He did mention his fondness for you frequently, but the last time he was in town he had dinner with someone named Senot . . . or something like that. He said he was meeting an acquaintance from high school, and since he'd mentioned you a few times over the years, I guess I thought it was you. Do you know someone by that name?"

"Yes, we went to high school with Donte Senot, and he married another high school classmate, Sarah. He must have had dinner with them."

"That must be it," she said. "There was something more, but I can't remember it right now."

I nodded again. "If you do remember it, just give the police a call. I doubt the Senots had anything to do with the tragedy, but it wouldn't hurt to tell the police every single thing you can."

"You're right," Samuel said.

Sylvie's eyes saddened again. She'd had a respite from the grief briefly as her mind was engaged with other things, but the pain was coming back now. I wished I could be of help, but I sensed it was time to go.

I stood. "Well, I'm sorry to have just dropped by, but I did want to tell you how sorry I was."

They saw me to the door. I doubted they had any financial problems, but the typewriters might be a help to them down the road.

I got into my car and took a deep breath. That hadn't been the easiest of duties, but I had no way of knowing that that wasn't even going to be close to the most difficult part of my day.

12

"Hey, Clare," Chester said as I walked through the front door.

"Good morning," I said as I noticed his worried expression. Adal stood back by the counter, looking grim. I glanced at the time on my phone.

"I'm not late for something, am I?" I said.

Baskerville sat on the end of a middle shelf. He stood up and meowed woefully at me.

"What's up, boy?" I asked as I scratched behind his ear.

"No, you're not late," Chester said. "Nathan is."

"What time did you expect him?" I asked.

"An hour ago," Adal said.

"He and I had dinner last night. I got home about nine. Maybe he slept in." I remembered what he'd said about his schedule and how he needed the space to do what he wanted to do when he wanted to do it. "Or maybe he's writing. If he's in the middle of something, he might have lost track of time."

"He's not answering his phone," Adal said.

"Did you call the hotel?" I asked.

"I did," Chester said. "They knocked on his door, but he didn't answer."

"Maybe he's in the shower?" I said.

"Maybe," Adal said as he shrugged.

"He really does like to keep his own schedule. He told me as much. I'm sure he's fine," I said. "I could run down there," I offered, thinking they would both tell me it wasn't necessary.

"It wouldn't hurt," Chester said.

"I'll go with you," Adal said as he looked at Chester.

I didn't understand their concern, but I respected their instincts enough to make the trip.

The hotel receptionist didn't receive an answer when she dialed Nathan's room from the front desk.

"Is there any way you could check on him?" I asked.

"Unlock the door?" she said. "No! There's no real cause for alarm just because someone isn't answering their phone. I'd get in trouble."

She brought her eyebrows together as she looked at Adal and me. "Do you really think something's wrong?"

Adal looked at me. "I know you said he likes to keep his own hours, but he's been exceedingly polite since he arrived. He's texted me if he's running only a few minutes behind. He's texted me thank-yous every evening, but not last night. I didn't think anything of it until he didn't answer the phone this morning."

I wondered whether I needed to call Jodie; however,

even though a small amount of worry was working through my gut, I wasn't too concerned.

Fortunately, the girl behind the desk jumped in as she reached for something under the counter.

"You have to stay back," she said as she held up what I thought must be a master key.

"We will," Adal said.

Once we were outside room 154, Adal and I stepped back as she knocked. "Mr. Grimes, sir, are you in there?"

"Anything?" Adal asked.

She sent us an impatient look, and I put my hand on Adal's arm.

"Please stay out here as I go in," she said.

We nodded. I was impressed by her cool demeanor. She couldn't have been much more than twenty.

Using the master lock card, she unlocked the door and went inside. "Sir. Mr. Grimes?"

We stepped closer and peered inside.

"He's not here," she said after she checked all the reasonable spots. "But there are wet towels in the bathroom. He's probably just out for breakfast somewhere."

I leaned in more than she would have liked, judging by the frown on her face, and tried to digest the scene in the brief seconds before she closed the door again.

The bed was unmade. There were no food wrappers, but I spied a coffee mug and two clear plastic cups, both with a thin layer of liquid at their bottoms, on the nightstand.

I saw the Splendid, and stacks of paper on the small table next to the window. A piece of paper was threaded through the machine and I wished I could hurry over and see the words he'd put on the page.

The receptionist closed the door before I could snoop further. "Can I give him a message?" she said.

"Sure," I said. "Have him call Clare and Adal."

"Will do," she said with a brief eyebrow lift at my compadre's name.

She stepped quickly around us and back to her post at the front desk as Adal and I moved more slowly toward the exit. The mention of "wet towels" was enough to ease most of our concerns.

"He's just at breakfast," Adal said hopefully. "Not checking his phone."

"I think so," I said. "He'll be in when he's ready. We'll ask him to call us from here on if he's going to be late."

"Good idea," Adal said.

Whether or not it was a "stereotypical" German trait, Adal was nothing if not extraordinarily prompt, and he resented it when others weren't, took it personally. He had about a seven-and-a-half-minute window of forgiveness, but that was it. I'd never been an hour late to something we'd scheduled, but I imagined Adal might not forgive Nathan for this affront.

Our trip back up the hill was hurried. We both hoped we'd find Nathan at the shop with Chester and Baskerville, but we were disappointed.

When another two hours passed and we all (even Baskerville) became both irritated and worried, I did the only thing I thought was appropriate. I called Jodie.

She was at the shop in record time, bringing with her heavy bags under her eyes and an even more grim expression on her face than Adal's.

"You look rough," I said. "You okay?"

She shook her head. "What's going on with Nathan Grimes?"

I gave her a brief rundown, after which she relayed some orders into the mouthpiece of the radio that was attached at the shoulder of her uniform. She sent officers to investigate the hotel room and the surrounding restaurants.

"He walks up here from the hotel?" she said.

"Yes."

"I'll walk his route."

"I'll come with you," I said.

Adal had figured out what might happen and he suddenly appeared next to me with my coat.

"You'll need this," he said.

"Thank you."

"Call as soon as you know something," he said to Jodie. "You'll find him, I know."

She nodded, and even in the middle of moments so full of stress that I could feel the tension in the air, I saw her spirit lighten a little, the bags under her eyes become less heavy. I knew I'd just witnessed something I should take note of, something wonderful for my best friend. Now wasn't the time, though.

"We'll call," she said.

I tried to keep up with her typically heavy steps, but she was even quicker today, like a gazelle in army boots.

"Other than the fact that we're looking for Nathan, what's going on? Did you talk to Creighton?" I asked. "You look like you didn't sleep."

"I didn't sleep. I talked to Creighton. Then I couldn't sleep well." She didn't look at me as she spoke. She looked all around, at the people on the sidewalks, and into the shop windows. She even looked up a time or two toward second stories of buildings, but I couldn't figure out why.

"What did he say?"

"Not much of anything. He told me that my question to him about the invitation was the only thing that made him remember that he'd received one. He said he'd thrown it away, not interested in the least about going to a gathering with any people from high school, particularly ones he wasn't friends with. I believe him about that part, since he's a couple years older."

"You don't believe him about not remembering it and then throwing it away?"

"I'm not sure, Clare. Can you think of anyone less interested in high school friends than you, me, and Creighton? We all kind of followed the beat of our own drummers. I can see me just throwing something away if I wasn't interested."

"But if I got an invitation like that I'd remember it and I'd talk to you about it," I said.

"Right, but Creighton doesn't talk to me about anything. He's a cop, Clare. He's naturally observant. I would think that the murder would spark a memory of the invitation."

"What's going on with him, Jodie?"

"I don't know, but I'm going to find out. Help me look for Nathan."

"Nathan might have his scarf and hat on or he might not, and, bizarrely, he looks very different without them."

"Good to know."

We walked the route, twice. The second time we went into almost every shop, restaurant, and bar we came to. Other than the restaurants, most places were just opening for business. No one whom we talked to had seen Nathan that morning, but he'd had breakfast at one of the restaurants the day before. The picture of Nathan that Jodie held out for identification was the picture on the back of his most recent novel, displayed on the screen of her phone. In it he wore both the scarf and hat. Each time Jodie showed it, we received raised eyebrows and exclamations of how exciting it was that he was in town, but other than the waiter at the restaurant, no one had seen him in person. They were sure they would have remembered him.

"You were almost the last person to see him, Clare, but the man working at the hotel desk last night remembered him coming in."

"But the person working this morning doesn't remember him going out?"

"No, but she has her hands full in the mornings taking care of the front desk and making sure the breakfast bar is set up. He could have—and must have—walked right by her without her noticing. Don't know if the security cameras got anything, but we'll look."

"Wet towels?" I said.

"Yes, wet enough to think he cleaned up this morning, but where would he go after that?" She put her hands on her hips and looked back up the hill. We'd gone the full distance down again.

"The only places I can think of are a restaurant or The Rescued Word," I said.

"Did he mention any other things that might interest him? Does he ski?"

I thought back. "I'm pretty sure he mentioned that he'd never gotten into winter sports. No, it was that he'd never gotten into any sports, not winter specifically. He says that he only writes and reads and sometimes watches television. I bet he likes to go to movies, but it didn't come up and it's too early for a movie."

She nodded and bit her bottom lip, a habit she did so often and with so much conviction that I was always surprised she didn't draw blood.

She looked at me. "Clare, is there any chance at all that he's a flaky author who doesn't mind inconveniencing others because he's an arrogant jerk who doesn't care about other people's schedules?"

I took a deep breath. "No, I don't think so. I mean, he likes to stick to his own schedule, but he knows that about himself, so he's purposefully isolated himself. In a way at least. But he's been very aware of our schedules, enough to make me think that he doesn't want to be annoying. No, I don't think so."

"You sure?"

"Yes."

"Well, we didn't go up the hill past Bygone, and there's a bookstore up there. I think it's worth a quick check. He's a writer and a reader, so it might not be a long shot. I'll go up and see if Sarah is there and if she's seen him."

"I'll come with," I said.

We hurried back up the hill. I was in my winter shape, which was better than my summer shape, but I was breathing heavily when we reached the bookstore. Tourists liked to blame the altitude for their heavy breathing. My excuse was Jodie's weird ability to out-good-shape everyone else.

Side by side, we peered in the front window, but Jodi stepped back a second later to get out of the way of the person exiting the store.

"Jodie!" the man said. "You've been looking for me, I hear. I stopped by the station this morning, but you weren't there. How are you? I mean, this is a terrible time, and . . . well, I don't quite know what to say, but here I am if you want to talk to me."

"Name please?" Jodie said.

"It's Howard. Howard Craig. Do I really look that different?"

"Yes, you do, Howard," Jodie said. "You wore button-down collars and khakis in high school, not jeans and denim jackets. You had red hair. And the cowboy hat?"

She wasn't trying to be funny, but Howard laughed.

"I was pretty uptight back then and the red already went gray. Hey, we shouldn't be blamed for our high school selves, or some premature aging."

"No, probably not," Jodie said.

"And that's Clare behind you. You two are still hanging out together. Always good to see some things never change."

"Hi, Howard," I said as I extended my hand for a shake because it seemed like the right thing to do. It was as awkward as I'd thought it would be. The entire moment was awkward, and I just wanted to find Nathan, not talk about high school.

"Well, I'da known you two from a mile away. It's good to see you both," he said. "Even though something terrible has happened and it's probably the reason . . . well, I'm sure you wanted to talk to me because of Lloyd, right?"

"Yes," she said. "How about we go down to the station?"

"Can't we just talk here? I've got nothing to hide, so this would save us some time." He nudged the hat a little farther back on his head and brought his eyebrows together as he put his hands on his hips.

"Yeah, okay, let's just grab one of those tables so we're not in the way of pedestrians." She pointed across the street at the tables outside in front of a bar that hadn't opened yet. It wasn't warm outside and those tables were in the shade, but at least we wouldn't be standing in the middle of the sidewalk and we could still keep the bookstore in sight.

"Anybody else in the bookstore?" she asked as she peered in.

"Just Sarah. No one else. Who are you looking for?"

Jodie didn't answer but signaled us to cross the street.

Before I tagged along, I should have asked if I was invited, but I didn't. We each took a seat on a metal chair. Howard stretched his neck to look inside the bar, but the window was dark.

"Should I go get us some coffee from somewhere?" he said.

"No, that's okay," Jodie said. "We won't be long."

"Okay." He tipped his hat back again.

Jodie didn't rush. "Howard, what did you think you were invited to? Meetings or a reunion?"

"Oh. Well, the invitation didn't feel like a party. It felt like business was going to be discussed."

"Do you know who sent it?"

"Someone from Star City, according to the postmark."

"Did you talk to any of the people invited before coming to town?"

"I did. Donte and Sarah are friends and we talk every now and then. But, honestly, I don't think there was much more than a brief mention of the meetings. We all thought the whole thing was odd, but then we talked about something else."

"Then why did you come to town?" Jodie said. "Sounds weird. I understand Sarah and Donte, but you had to travel from Wyoming, and Creighton threw away his invitation."

"I didn't come to town for the meetings. I was coming anyway to visit family, so I told Sarah and Donte we could see what was going on together."

"Did you remember that Creighton was on the invitation?"

"Absolutely. Creighton, the big man on campus, a couple years older, football guy, dad a cop. Of course I knew who Creighton was."

"Were you surprised he was included?"

Howard thought a moment. "Probably, but I don't remember exactly."

"Did you talk about Creighton to Donte and Sarah?"

"Huh. I don't think I did. I think we got stuck on Lloyd and then moved on to something else. Really, Jodie, we didn't think much of it, but I know we put it on our calendars, mostly so the three of us could make plans to get together."

It was all plausible, but I understood what Jodie was trying to find out: did Sarah really not remember that Creighton was listed on the invitation or was she lying? And why would she?

As far as I could tell, the answer wasn't clear.

"Do you have your invitation?" Jodie said.

"No, it's at home," he said.

"I see. Can you have someone send it here?" she asked.

"I live alone, but I have a secretary I might be willing to tell where I keep the hidden key. I can tell you what it said. I have a photographic memory. I never forget anything."

"All right."

He recited the invitation with the same information everyone else had given. The names were the same, the times, the location.

"Lloyd was staying at the same hotel you are staying at. Did you see him?"

"Not once. I had no idea he was there. Why didn't he stay home? Are his folks still alive?"

"Yes. Why didn't you stay with yours?" Jodie asked.

"Good point. There does come a time when we'd all rather not stay with our parents, even if we like them."

"Did you and Lloyd get along in high school?" Jodie asked.

"Lloyd and I didn't know each other, Jodie. I can't remember ever having one conversation with him, or even one class. I didn't know him at all. Sarah did." He nodded toward the bookstore. "She told me we'd definitely gone to high school with a Lloyd Gavin; that's what I meant about getting stuck talking about him. When I got the invite I thought about pulling out my yearbooks to see what he looked like, but I never got around to it."

"Why would you four be invited to anything together?"

"I have no idea. Like I said, I didn't know Lloyd. I didn't even know you and Creighton had followed in your dad's footsteps and were cops. Sarah told me. As far as I can tell, the four of us had nothing in common, except maybe that we were all relatively successful."

"Right, but while I do give my brother credit for succeeding in his career, he doesn't make much money. The rest of you do. And you and Donte, and Sarah for that matter, were friends back then. Not Lloyd or Creighton. I feel like I'm missing something."

Howard shrugged. "Did you ask Creighton?"

"Of course, but he can't find a connection either."

"I don't know, Jodie, I really don't."

She nodded and squinted over toward the bookstore. "Howard, have you ever heard of the author Nathan Grimes?"

"Sure. One of the best horror writers of our time."

"He is," she said. "Have you seen him this morning, maybe in the bookstore?"

"No." Howard looked toward Starry Night. "Is he here, maybe doing a signing? Sarah didn't say anything to me."

"No, not a signing. So, you in town for a day or so?" Jodie asked.

"I guess. The meetings are off, of course, but I bet you'd like me to stick around."

"Yes, I would. Going to remain at the Three Bells?"

"Yep."

"Good." She handed him her card and told him to call her if he had any new thoughts regarding Lloyd or the rest of the group.

He said he would and then tipped the cowboy hat at us before he strode down the hill, walking much more bowlegged than he did in high school.

"Why did you ask him about Nathan?" I said.

"We've got another missing man, Clare. Coincidence? On the outside it seems like it, though truthfully I don't think Nathan's missing. Come on, let's go see if Sarah's in. Let's go see if she's talked to any visiting authors recently."

"I hope she has."

"I hope someone has."

Her eyes went toward Howard walking down the hill. I looked too. "Think he's up to something?"

"I don't know," she said. "I can't quite understand what might be behind these meetings. It would be immature for Lloyd to want to rub in his success. We're grown-ups, and Lloyd had a business to run. There's also the Hoovens. Howard seems like the least important piece of the puzzle, but I've done this long enough to make sure I take another look at all the links that seem unimportant."

"You think someone might have killed Lloyd for the Hoovens?"

She shook her head. "Money's always a possible motive. I'd like to follow it, but I can't even find a starting point."

We watched as Howard's figure disappeared into a small crowd.

"Something will come clear," I said.

"Right. Come on, let's talk to Sarah." She led the way back across the street and, silently, we hurried to the shop.

13

"No, I don't think I've seen Nathan Grimes," Sarah said with her eyebrows pressed tightly together. "I'm sure I would remember if one of the greatest horror novelists of our time came into my bookstore."

"He might not have been wearing his scarf and hat," I said.

Sarah and Jodie both looked at me.

"It's a trick he does. It's uncanny how he doesn't look like himself when he isn't wearing the scarf and hat. Maybe someone that reminded you of him?"

"This morning?" Sarah said.

"Anytime, sure, but yes, this morning specifically."

"I think I would have recognized him anyway and I'm sure I haven't seen him, particularly this morning. Howard Craig from high school was in, and the gentleman who ordered that book we talked about, Clare"—she nodded toward the metaphysical shelf—"came in for it, but no one else."

"Evan Davenport came in?" I said.

They looked at me again.

"Yes," Sarah said a second later. "You know him?"

"He and his wife stopped by The Rescued Word," I said.

"Who are they?" Jodie said.

"No one. I mean," I said, "just some people who came to town for a book and wanted to know if I could repair a typewriter. It was beyond repair. They told me about the book."

Jodie nodded, and Sarah looked at me with still-tight eyebrows.

"Will you call me if Nathan comes in?" Jodie handed Sarah her card.

"Of course," Sarah said as she looked at the card.

"Mind if I ask a question that might seem rude?" Jodie said.

"Not at all," Sarah said as though the idea of Jodie sounding rude wasn't unexpected.

"What's with all the candles at the end of the counter? They look like they've been lit, so they aren't for sale. It's hard to believe you would light candles in here; all the paper and stuff."

"Oh. Well, when I light them tonight I'll put them up front. I'll move a couple of the shelves out of the way and put a table up there. I'll be careful. That's not really a rude question, Jodie. It's very observant."

"Well, thank you, but why will you be lighting them tonight?"

I could tell that Sarah wished Jodie hadn't continued

asking. Her shoulder twitched and her fingers flitted weirdly as she put her hands on the counter.

"Thursday is our metaphysical meeting night, but we're having a séance here tonight instead. We're going to try to talk to Lloyd."

"That's . . . interesting," Jodie said.

"Want to come? Both of you knew Lloyd. It might be a good thing," Sarah said in a tone that made me think she didn't really want us to come, she was just being polite. Perhaps she really was the hostess with the mostess.

"I'll come," I said.

"We would both love to be here. Thanks for the invite, Sarah," Jodie said.

"Great," Sarah said. She cleared her throat. "It can't hurt, can it?"

"Not at all," Jodie said. "Hey, speaking of observant, what happened back there?"

I stepped forward to look over the front counter. Jodie had noticed not only the candles, but also a mess on the floor behind the counter. A pile of books filled up almost the entire space, leaving barely enough room for Sarah to stand. She looked like she was drowning in a quicksand of books.

"I knocked over a box of books that was on the counter," she said. "I can't get ahead of my inventory. People love bringing me their books."

"People from Star City?"

"From everywhere around here. Lots from Salt Lake City."

"Want some help?" Jodie said.

"Straightening books? No, it's my job. I just have to get organized. And stop taking boxes of books from people."

"Well, Clare and I are here to help if you need us," Jodie said.

I forced a quick smile, hoping to look like I agreed with Jodie's offer of help.

"That's very kind. I might take you up on your offer in a day or two. Let me get a little more organized."

"Sure. So, why are you trying to contact Lloyd?" Jodie asked.

"To find out what happened! He was murdered. Perhaps he can tell us about his killer. That would help, wouldn't it?"

"Definitely. I hope he shows up," Jodie said.

Only I, her best friend, would know she was working harder than she ever had done to sound sincere. Yes, she'd like to talk to Lloyd, but she didn't believe in any sort of communication from the dead.

"I do too!" Sarah said.

"What time should we be here?"

"The magical hour tonight is nine p.m. Don't be late."

"Not a chance. Thanks so much, Sarah," Jodie said before she turned to leave.

"See you later," I said to Sarah before I followed Jodie.

"Yes. Later," Sarah said with an uncomfortable smile as she leaned her arms on the front counter.

"We're going to a séance tonight?" I said when we were completely out of the view of Sarah's store's window.

"Yes, we are," Jodie said as we crossed the street. "I hope we get a chance to talk to Lloyd, and that Nathan doesn't show."

"Ugh. That sounds gruesome."

"Well, they aren't real. You know that, don't you? Séances, I mean."

"Sure," I said with a shrug.

Jodie looked at me. "There was something weird about the books behind the desk."

"The mess?"

"Yeah."

"I saw her small back office and storage area, and it was really messy. Maybe it's just the way she does things."

"But she said she hadn't seen but a few people today, and I take a gander at the store every time I drive by. I never see much activity and I've never seen anyone with a box of books."

"Maybe she just already had so many books herself."

"Maybe."

"What?"

"I'd like to spritz a little luminol back there to see if there's any evidence of blood."

"What? Just because of a messy pile of books? Remind me not to let you in the workshop anymore."

She shook her head. "It wasn't a normal mess, and the way she stood there so normally was weird, like she didn't want us to know the mess was there. I've seen that sort of behavior before, and it sometimes means someone is covering something up. If a box of books fell to the floor there, it would seem only normal to get it picked up right away, or even as she was talking to us. Her feet were buried in books."

"Cop instincts perking up?"

"Yeah, something like that. I'll try to get a look tonight."

"You're going to spray luminol back there tonight?"

"Probably not. But I'd like to see if something is still covering the floor, books or something else."

"What can I do to help?"

"I don't know. We'll see. Just watch me for signals."

"What are the signals?"

"You'll know them."

I nodded and hoped I would. "What about Nathan?"

"I'm going to walk down the hill and then back up again, but you get back to work. If he doesn't show up somewhere, I'll get him written up as a missing person when it's a legal option. Until then let's just hope he's being a flake. Famous people irritate me to no end."

"I know they do. Okay, I'll get back to work, but it's not going to be easy to stay focused."

"Yeah. I do think we should bank on the fact that he's just being a flake at this point, though. Seriously, he's a grown man in good enough shape to fend off most threats."

"Maybe a fan saw him and lost his mind. Took him."

"I doubt that happened. Let's hold off worrying a little longer."

"I'll try."

"See you tonight?"

"Definitely."

We parted ways at Bygone Alley. For a long time, I watched her walk down the hill. I wished I'd insisted on giving Nathan a ride last night. Jodie would be fine. She was a cop, and it was daylight.

But still.

❧

We were a somber bunch. Chester, Adal, and I didn't get one bit of work done in the workshop because none of us could bear leaving the front where we could look out the window and watch the door as if we could will Nathan to open it. Jodie stuck her head in to tell us she still hadn't found him before she took the Bronco back down to the station. She said she'd meet me at the evening's activities, about which both Chester and Adal were curious until I told them we were going to a séance. I was momentarily impressed by their almost matching scowls.

"See, what I heard is true. She's an odd one," Chester said.

We helped customers, but none of us had our best game faces on, and even Baskerville seemed morose. As the minutes ticked by, our concern only grew. I was sure Chester's and Adal's imaginations had concocted the same horrible scenarios that mine had, bad things we didn't want to come into complete focus, so none of us shared them aloud.

Seth came through the front door around four o'clock and paused inside it when we all turned our hopeful eyes his way. "What's up?"

I gave him the rundown, and he offered to go grab us all dinner. Chester and Adal weren't hungry, but Chester told Seth and me to go on our own, that he would call the second he had any news and I was to do the same if I heard from Jodie.

We didn't go far anyway, just across the street to the diner and a pink booth. Just as we got cheeseburgers and fries ordered, we were joined by someone who I thought might be going to the séance too.

"Haven't seen you for years, and now it's twice in one day, Clare Henry," Howard said as he stood from his seat at the counter and came to our table, his coffee cup in hand.

"Howard. Hi again. Seth, Howard and I went to high

school together. He was one of the folks invited to the same meetings as Lloyd."

"Oh," Seth said. "Well, nice to meet you. Join us?"

"I don't want to interrupt," he said.

"We'd love to have you join us," Seth said.

"Well, all right," Howard said as he sat next to me, keeping hold of the mug with both hands.

Seth and I shared a quick smile. It was the polite thing to do, but maybe not exactly what we wanted to do.

"Clare, how's the shop? Your family? I didn't get much of a chance to catch up earlier."

"Very well, thank you. How about you, Howard? You've become quite the success. Seth, Howard has an oil company in Wyoming."

"Really? I'm a geologist," Seth said.

For about the next half hour and while Seth and I ate dinner, but Howard only drank coffee, I watched a friendship form. Apparently, oil folks and geologists have many things in common. They tried to keep it nontechnical for me, but they slipped a couple of times and I just pretended I got it when they used terms like jug hustler.

"Clare and I weren't close in high school, but I was kind of a jerk; the now me wouldn't have liked the then me. I promise I'm not a jerk now. Not as much at least." He looked at me. "It's good to see you again, even if the circumstances are rough."

"Good to see you too, Howard. I wish I had stayed in better touch with everyone, with Lloyd. He was a good guy."

"I recently read about all his success. He must have been really smart, even if maybe he'd turned into less of a good guy."

"What does that mean?" I asked.

"His employees didn't like him, I heard," Howard said sheepishly before he took a sip of coffee.

"That's something you should tell Jodie," I said. "And how did you know that? Why didn't you mention that to her earlier?"

"I don't know. I was . . . I don't know. I read some articles about him, though. They're easy to find. I bet Jodie and the other officers have found them."

"What did they say?"

"That he was a taskmaster. Hang on—let me find them. You're probably right, though. Jodie should know. I was too focused on just answering her questions and how cold that chair was to have thought about the articles."

He grabbed his phone from a holster on his waist and started sliding his finger through Internet sites.

"I can e-mail her some links," he said. "You have her e-mail?"

"Send them to me. I'll pass them on to her. I hate to give out her e-mail without asking first." Besides, I wanted to read the articles too.

A moment later, I had the e-mail in my in-box, and then forwarded it to Jodie.

"I'll read the articles later," I said. "But what else can you tell me right now?"

"The thing I remember the most is that there was a small uprising at his company about a year ago. The employees all threatened to walk out if Lloyd didn't tell them the status of some of the projects they'd been working on. Apparently, he and one other person there were spending a lot of time behind closed doors, taking the work everyone else had done, putting it together and making money without sharing the details. Sounds somewhat petty the way I'm telling it, but the way it sounded in the articles, it was a strange way for a company owner to behave."

"The name of the other employee he was working closely with?" I said.

"I don't know. A woman."

"Brenda maybe?"

"Maybe. Yeah, that sounds about right."

I couldn't wait to dig into the articles and tell Jodie she should too.

We left the diner together, and when Howard confirmed that he was also headed to the séance, I took it upon myself to invite Seth and we walked up the hill together.

The night was cold and dark as the three of us marched up the hill to try to talk to the dead. The setting was perfect for an authentic séance.

But I still hoped they were fake.

14

I determined immediately that there would be no way
for Jodie to check the floor behind the desk tonight.
However, by the studied look on her face and her frequent
scowls that direction, I knew she was still trying to devise
a plan.

The séance was going to be weird, which didn't surprise me. Even if there hadn't been a séance thrown into
the mix, the night was bound to be weird just because of
the people in attendance. Besides myself, Seth, Howard,
Jodie, and Sarah, Donte was there too, and so was Creighton. I couldn't tell if Jodie hadn't known he was going to
attend or if she'd brought him along. Either way, the
brother and sister didn't behave as if they knew each other;
they took seats opposite each other at the round table that
had been placed at the front of the shop, right next to the
black velvet that now covered the front window. The table

was small and we were crowded together, all of our knees touching.

The shelves and stacks of books that had previously been where the table was now had been shoved back, creating precarious towers of books and things that lined up from the counter all the way back into the murky darkness toward the back room. The fire hazard that Jodie had been worried about hadn't lessened much.

The only light was from two candles in the middle of the table that flickered as we stirred the air when we took our seats.

Howard, Seth, and I had been the last to arrive and I wanted to kick myself for not being early like I was sure Jodie and Creighton had been. I wondered what I'd missed. We were greeted and told to take our seats quickly, that "the hour was upon us," and if we didn't get started soon we'd miss the window that offered the clearest communication with the other side.

"All right," Sarah said after we'd all been seated. "Thank you all for coming tonight. I know this is probably weird to most of you, and the circumstances of us coming together were unpredictable at best, deeply tragic at worst, but I believe firmly that the people who are here tonight are exactly the people who were supposed to be here tonight. Not that Lloyd's murder was fated, but this group coming together was, in ways I can't explain. Donte, of course, is required to be here, but please don't allow yourself to be in discomfort. Feel free to leave at any time. I don't even care if a departure disturbs the spirits. While I believe in all this, my priority is most definitely the living and their well-being."

I didn't think any of us would leave the table by ourselves, no matter what she said and no matter how uncomfortable we might end up feeling. Jodie and I shared a look of doubt mixed with acceptance. She almost rolled her eyes, but she didn't.

Sarah wore jeans and an old sweatshirt, which surprised me. I hadn't given it much thought beforehand, but I'd been disappointed she wasn't in a flowing long dress with big sleeves, something Gypsy-like.

Everyone else was dressed in street clothes too, including Creighton. Even though it had been a few years now and even though I didn't look back fondly, seeing him in something other than his uniform always took me back to when we were together, and sometimes a small fuse of anger lit at the back of my throat. Not tonight, though. In fact, I didn't have even one tiny spark of anger toward Creighton, which was happening a lot more lately.

After Sarah's welcome words, Donte smiled awkwardly and nodded at Howard. I could guess what was behind the smile—a mocked patience—but would've liked to know for sure.

Howard seemed to be enjoying the moment. He was interested and engaged, his eyes alert as they watched Sarah and took in everyone around the table. I was sure Creighton, Jodie, and Seth were all taking in the same things I was, but I'd ask later.

"All right," Sarah continued, "specifically, what I'm going to do is summon spirits. Invite them to communicate with us. I will ask for Lloyd, but it doesn't always work that way." She sighed. "I've tried to reach him on my own, but he doesn't seem to want to answer. I think there's a chance he doesn't really know who I am, though. Everyone, just send out welcoming thoughts and if you're afraid at all, try to let go of that fear. Fear doesn't work well here. Sometimes bad spirits feed on fear."

I wasn't feeling fear until she mentioned bad spirits feeding on it. Then I felt a small twinge of it, but I willed it away as I took a deep breath and reminded myself that I didn't believe in this stuff.

Sarah had behaved oddly when I quickly introduced her to Seth, but only briefly. She covered her lifted eyebrows with a quick and easy smile.

"Let's hold hands," she said. We did as instructed. "The circle is complete if we hold hands. I won't go into all the reasons why, but a completed circle is very important. If you need to remove yourself from the table, please try to remember to join the two hands on either side of you as you let go."

Donte shifted uncomfortably in his seat before his wife continued; I chalked that up to the fact that his knees were probably as uncomfortable as mine. Sarah took a deep breath and let it out slowly as she closed her eyes. "You don't have to close your eyes, but it helps."

Donte and Howard closed their eyes, but no one else did.

No matter what, whether or not I "believed" in what was happening, goose bumps rose on my arms and expectation swirled around in my chest. The setting, though messy, was perfect. The blacked-out windows, the candles, the old building smells of tired lath and plaster that mixed with the ink and paper scents of the books. Chester would have liked it and probably would have commented about how some coffee smells would make a nice addition.

However, Chester would have not stuck around for this next part. He would have had none of her "shenanigans."

"Spirits that have crossed over, we invite and welcome you to join us. We are a friendly group and seek friendly company," Sarah said. She neither moaned nor swayed, but her voice was loud and certain. "Please join us. Lloyd Gavin, we seek your company. Please come talk to us."

The candles flickered in the wintery draft that blew through the old building, and I thought I heard a buzz begin in my head. It was faint, but definitely there. I looked at Seth. I wanted to ask if anyone else was hearing it, but Sarah hadn't explained the rules about talking. Seth seemed unbothered. He squeezed my hand and then turned his attention back to Sarah.

"Lloyd, are you there?" Sarah said.

"There's a noise in my head," Howard said.

"What do you hear?" Sarah asked as she opened her eyes.

"It's like a low voice. I can barely make it out, but I think there's a hum or a buzz there. Can any of you hear it?"

"I hear a buzz," I said. "But not a voice."

Everyone else shook their heads.

"I don't like this," Howard said, his seeming good humor now gone.

"It's okay," Sarah said. "They can't hurt you. It sounds like you and Clare might be our conduits tonight. Howard, will you accept the spirit who wants to talk to you?"

I really hoped he said yes, because if I was second choice my answer was going to be a huge disappointment. There was no way I was willing to be a spirit conduit. I'd thought that if we heard any voices they'd come from Sarah or unspecific locations, certainly not from me.

"I don't know," Howard said nervously.

"It's okay," Donte said. "I'm starting to hear it too."

Phew, I wanted to say, but I didn't.

"Focus, Donte. Tell us what they're saying. Ask who they are," Sarah said.

It seemed like a long time passed as we all waited, but it was probably less than a minute before Donte took on a different pose. It was startling, and I wasn't the only one to sit up straighter and take notice as Donte's right shoulder bent deeper than his left and he hung his head so his chin almost touched his chest. It had to be an uncomfortable position.

"I'm looking for Creighton Wentworth," Donte said. It was his voice, but slightly different, maybe higher, but certainly twanged a little with an accent.

Creighton didn't answer.

"Who are you?" Sarah asked. "Are you Lloyd?"

"No! Who's Lloyd?" Donte said, his shoulder and head still in awkward positions.

"We're searching for the recently crossed spirit of Lloyd Gavin. Would you help us find him?"

"No, I want to talk to Creighton Wentworth!"

"Creighton, are you willing to speak to this spirit?" Sarah asked.

I knew him well enough to know that he was pulling together as much patience and acting ability as he could muster. Talking to spirits would not be something Creighton would ever buy into if there weren't a police investigation involved. His description of what was happening would include stronger words than "shenanigans."

"Depends on who it is, I guess," he said. His gaze was locked on Sarah. He didn't once look over at Donte.

I wondered what he was looking at or for, so I kept my eyes on her too.

"Who are you, spirit?" Sarah said. "We need your name."

"My name is Eloise MacPherson."

"I don't know who that is," Creighton said to Sarah.

"How do you know Creighton Wentworth?" Sarah said.

"He killed me," Donte's body but the twangy voice said.

"I don't understand," Sarah said, her voice too high-pitched. If she'd wanted to gasp, she swallowed it away. Suddenly, I was barely breathing.

"Creighton?" Sarah said.

"I've never killed anyone," Creighton said. "I've drawn my weapon, but I've never fired it in the line of duty."

I looked at Jodie. I thought she might be angry, but mostly I saw deep curiosity at the corner of her eyes.

"Details," Donte said with a twangy sarcasm. "Okay, so you had me killed. You took my stash and they killed me."

"This is about drugs?" Creighton said.

"What else would it be about?"

"I don't remember you, Eloise, but I have arrested drug dealers and have taken their contraband into custody. That's part of my job."

"That's not what I mean, Creighton Wentworth, and I think you know it."

"No, I'm afraid I don't know what you mean."

"You didn't arrest me. Now do you remember?"

"No," he said sincerely.

I looked at Jodie again. She was even more curious.

"I don't know what you're up to, Creighton Wentworth, but you got me killed and I'll do what I can to haunt your existence."

"That's not possible," Sarah said. "You're incapable of haunting anyone. You were invited into the body you're speaking from, and when you're uninvited you'll have no choice but to leave."

"We'll see."

Suddenly, three things happened at once. The front door swung open, slamming against the wall; the candles flickered out; and a groan came from Donte, but the groan didn't sound the same as Eloise's voice, nor did it sound how I would expect Donte to sound. The groan was distinctly masculine and lined with what sounded like the word "Help!"

Sarah had jumped up from the table, the first one to break the circle, I thought. I saw her next as she stood by a light switch on the wall. She flipped it up and the old fluorescents above came to life.

Both Jodie and Creighton had gotten to their feet and made a move like they were going to try to sprint toward the counter. Sarah had flipped the switch too quickly for them to go anywhere.

"Everyone okay?" Sarah said. "Donte, how are you?"

"I'm fine."

"Anybody else hear that groan come from Donte?" Sarah asked.

We all said we did.

"Donte, hon, was that Lloyd there at the end?" Sarah asked.

"I have no idea. The last thing I remember is saying I was beginning to hear a voice. Did someone speak through me? I don't remember inviting anyone specifically."

"Yes, but it was just one of Creighton's criminals coming back to threaten him," Sarah said as if it was no big deal. "That happens a lot. I should have thought about that when we started. I would have disinvited anyone who you or Jodie might have come in contact with through your police work. My bad."

"Donte, man, you sure you're okay?" Howard asked, his eyes saucerlike and shadowy from the harsh light above.

"Oh yeah. That's happened before. I must be set up to be a conduit and I must be easy for them, since they sometimes don't wait for my verbal invite. What did Creighton's criminal want?"

"Same old same old," Sarah said. "Threatened to haunt him. Happens all the time, Creighton. I'm sorry. You know you have nothing to worry about, don't you?"

"Of course I know," Creighton said.

Time froze for a second and I held my breath. I knew that tone. I'd never had Creighton's anger directed toward me, but I'd definitely seen it, and it was a loud, ferocious thing.

"Creighton," Jodie said.

He sent her a brief glare before he turned his attention back to Sarah. Though he didn't believe in séances, for all intents and purposes he'd just been accused of murder.

"What?" Sarah said. "Oh, I'm sorry, Creighton. There's no way to control the spirits, but when such accusations are made we don't believe them. Of course not. When it comes to police officers, we all expect such things." She blinked at Creighton, then at Jodie. "I should have prepared you all better. I take it for granted that everyone knows what I know. No, please don't take any of that personally."

Howard jumped in. "That last voice, though. That was different. Who was that who said 'Help'? Lloyd?"

"I don't know," Donte said.

Sarah shrugged. "Impossible to know for sure unless they tell us."

"Lloyd asking for help?" Howard offered.

"I wish I could answer. I wish I'd gotten more," Donte said.

"Well, I'm sorry, but that's all there is for tonight," Sarah said. "Sometimes the spirits get so wound up that they cause things like doors slamming open and other physical world stuff, but they really are mostly harmless. And police officers in attendance often get accused of things." She added the last part too emphatically.

I decided she'd gone from harmless to *mostly* harmless. No matter what had happened, there was more behind this séance than just trying to contact Lloyd. Though I couldn't quite figure out the true motivations.

"Where is everyone else?" I asked.

"Who?" Sarah asked.

"You said there was a group. A Thursday night group."

"I asked everyone else not to come tonight. This was just for us."

I nodded.

Sarah continued. "Sometimes the spirits scare everyone else from the other side away, so if that was Lloyd coming through at the end, I'm sure he's gone back to wherever he was because Eloise thought she had to make such a statement. We might try again later, but things need to settle first. I'll let you all know."

"We'd appreciate anything you have to offer us, Sarah. We've got nothing on this case yet. Nothing," Jodie said. "That's why both Creighton and I came tonight. If you can give us anything at all, we'd take it."

"It's so terrible about Lloyd. I'm sorry. Of course I'll let you know right away if I get anything that might help," Sarah said. "That's why we came together tonight. If only it were as easy as simply asking once. Maybe there's more work to be done. I'll think about it."

"Anyone able to round up that invitation for us yet?" Jodie said to the group.

"Where's Creighton's?" Howard asked.

"I threw it away," he said. "I wasn't interested in the meetings."

"Not your style, huh, Creighton?" Sarah said with a sly smile.

I was suddenly embarrassed for her, but I couldn't pinpoint why. If she'd been flirting, it was a small attempt, nothing that should bother anyone, but I couldn't help thinking she had overstepped some boundary.

"Not really," Creighton said.

"I've put in a call to have mine rounded up and mailed to me if they can find it," Howard said.

"Thanks. Let me know when you have it," Jodie said. "I will."

"Any luck finding Nathan Grimes?" Sarah asked.

"Not yet, but we're working on it," Jodie said. "If you see him, please have him call."

"Of course."

"Nathan Grimes is missing?" Howard said.

"Yes," Jodie said, admitting what she hadn't when we talked to him earlier.

"Wait a second. I just put it together. I might have seen him," Howard said. "I'm staying at the Three Bells, and I thought I saw him this morning, leaving the hotel. You asked me specifically about the bookstore earlier. I didn't remember . . ."

"What time?" Jodie said as she reached for the pocket that would be on the shirt of her police uniform. Since she was in civilian clothes, she had to pull a pen out of her jeans pocket instead. She didn't have any paper handy, so she wrote what Howard had said on her hand.

"Early. About six. He was carrying a stack of books. I wasn't sure it was him, but that hat and scarf were so familiar. I'll be. That must have been him."

"You see which direction he went after he left the hotel?" Jodie said.

"No, I barely saw him leave. It was just a quick glance. I'd gone to get some coffee from the vending machine and was coming back to my room. I don't even know which room he came out of."

"If you see him at all, call us. And tell him to call us too. That goes for everyone here," Jodie said.

"Of course," Howard said.

We filed out of the bookshop. Creighton, without saying anything, got into his car, Howard walked down the hill, and Jodie walked Seth and me up toward Little Blue.

The cold air and the now wide-open starry sky above were even more welcome than normal. I hadn't realized I'd been so tense inside the bookshop until my shoulders unknotted as we made our way.

Once well out of earshot and view of anyone still in the shop, Jodie said, "What the hell was that show about?"

"You think it was all a show?" I said.

"Of course. They staged it, but I have no idea why," Jodie said.

"Yeah, the fact that Donte jumped in to be the conduit gave it away for me," Seth said.

"I heard buzzing," I said.

"We all did. I just didn't want to say that out loud," Seth said. "I'm sure it came from something they were in control of, a machine somewhere."

"Actually, I didn't hear the buzzing, but yeah, I thought it was iffy when Donte volunteered to be a conduit," Jodie said. "I will most definitely look into Creighton's involvement with someone named Eloise MacPherson, but setting up a communication with a police officer was a safe bet, and it was easy to find someone who is dead now but had legal trouble when they were alive. It was sure to impress, unless you didn't fall for it. I know Creighton didn't. I didn't either."

"Did they know he was coming beforehand?" I asked.

"I didn't tell them," she said.

"That's . . . slightly unsettling."

Jodie grumbled.

"Why would they do that? Maybe so we'd spread the word about her 'abilities'?" I said.

"That doesn't seem quite right, but it's a possibility. I can't help thinking they're setting up something," Jodie said.

"You think they had something to do with Lloyd's death?" I said.

"I don't know. It's difficult not to suspect them. Hell, it's difficult not to suspect Creighton a little bit of something even if I don't want to. Something's up."

"I sent you an e-mail with some articles that Howard

told Seth and me about at dinner. We ran into him at the diner. Apparently, there was some strife at Lloyd's company, and that strife might have included Brenda."

"Your twin?" Jodie said.

"Twin?" Seth said.

"I haven't had a chance to tell you, but I will. Yeah, that Brenda, I think," I said.

"I'll read them right away," Jodie said.

"No word about Nathan Grimes, huh?" I said.

"No, none," Jodie said. "I will file a missing person's report when it's time. I've got some guys working on tracking his phone, but he can't be a priority until he's officially missing."

"I keep calling him and it's still not going directly to voice mail yet, so I think the phone still has battery life," I said.

"I do too," Jodie said.

It was the first time I heard a thread of real concern in her voice.

"But there's still a chance he's just being a flake," she continued when she caught me looking at her.

"I hope so. What did you guys think when Donte said 'Help'?"

"Part of the act," Jodie said.

Seth scoffed.

"It didn't sound like either Eloise or Donte," I said.

"More trickery, I'm sure," Jodie said.

I hated to say something I wasn't one hundred percent sure of, but it needed to be said. "Jodie . . . there's a chance that voice sounded like Nathan's."

At once, we all stopped walking. Jodie and Seth looked

at me. I had an urge to keep talking, but I didn't know what else to say. I knew that we'd only heard that voice briefly, and there was a chance my imagination was taking over my common sense, but I hadn't lied. To me, the voice had sounded like Nathan's.

"That's good to know, Clare," Jodie said. "I hope you're mistaken, or something."

"You're worried," Seth said. "I'm not discounting what you heard, but perhaps you wanted to because you're worried."

"Maybe, but . . . still."

"I got you," Jodie said.

Seth nodded and we resumed walking.

"I think I'll just have to go back in tomorrow and ask what Sarah was up to. Lots of weirdness, but it might not be important," Jodie said.

"Or it might," Seth said. "That was an interesting group of people. I didn't sense anything murderous, but they all seemed like they were afraid someone might tell the truth about something. Probably the truth about their success. It's rare that someone is as successful as they brag to be."

"Except Lloyd maybe. I think he was," Jodie said.

She'd done some research, had probably seen the articles already.

"He did well?" Seth said.

"Very," Jodie said. She looked at her watch. "Gotta go. Good night, you two." She turned and headed back down the hill to her Bronco. "You two behave, now."

"So, what'd you think of all that?" I asked Seth when Jodie was out of earshot.

"It was kind of laughable, but I appreciated that they didn't try too hard. No hokey music, no incense. It was the least woo-woo séance I could have expected."

"The whole thing was weird," I said as we climbed the stairs up to my front porch.

"It was, but I'm with Jodie—they are up to something. It's hard to know what, though."

"Yeah."

I pushed the door open and signaled for Seth to go in first. I looked down toward the bookshop as I followed behind. All was quiet on Main. I agreed with Jodie and Seth that the whole thing had been a show. Except for one part. That last uttered groan and "Help!" had come from somewhere other than someone's imagination. I didn't necessarily think it had come from a disembodied spirit, but it wasn't something that had been a part of the script.

For whatever reason and even though I'd been startled by the door slamming open, I'd kept my eyes on Sarah before the candles flickered out. The surprise on her face had been real, and it was directed toward Donte and that voice. I thought.

I just might have to stop by the bookstore again myself.

15

"Good grief!" Chester said as he flipped the newspaper down again and looked at me over its top. "Did she have to tell the world all these details? What is wrong with her?"

The "she" and "her" he was talking about was Jodie. As she'd predicted, Nathan's missing-in-action status had made it to the media, though I had a sense that she was glad about that, because more people would be looking for our missing author. The front-page, top-of-the-fold story was all about Nathan Grimes, his possible disappearance, and his visit to The Rescued Word to create his own book of poetry, a work of art. Chester's phone had been ringing off the hook since the first papers hit the street at about five that morning. Jodie had obviously answered some questions and supplied lots of details, and I couldn't argue with Chester that it might have been better to just state that Nathan was in town and some people had become concerned about his whereabouts. Be on the lookout!

Chester had read the article twice, just since I'd come into the shop and as he sat perched on a stool by the counter. Each reading had been fraught with *good grief*s, *oh my*s, *that woman*s, and the snapping and rattling of the newspaper itself.

"We won't be able to keep up today, Clare," he said. "Call Marion and see if she can help us out. Olympics be damned, we're going to be swamped and it will be for all the wrong reasons!"

He was probably right about not being able to keep up with the customers; I'd had to excuse my way through the gathering crowd outside the front door just to get in, and it would probably only grow by the time we opened. Everyone wanted to see where Nathan Grimes had been working on a book. Never mind that it wasn't destined to be one of his horror masterpieces. Even a thin self-published book of poetry by Nathan Grimes was going to be something sought after. But I kind of thought Chester was overreacting.

"Everyone will want to help search for clues to find him; they'll come in here and ask a bunch of questions and want to look around, but not for paper or pens. Oh, good grief!" Chester said again. "We'll have to offer tours of the workshop. Everyone's going to want to see the press again. I went through this back when I first built it. I built it to use it, not because I thought people would want to look at it. We don't even know for sure that he's missing yet! Gaa!"

He made some good points. "Well, of course they want

to look at it. Gutenbergs are rare, even replicas," I said. "We'll get through it." I hoped. "To confirm, though, no one really has heard any word about Nathan?"

Chester lowered the paper. "No, none. I called the hotel this morning and they haven't seen him. I assumed that if the police found him they'd give us a ring. It's not good news, but we must remain positive and hope for the best."

"We have to hope that he's an inconsiderate, arrogant author who doesn't mind worrying the people who've let him use their printing press, but I think it's almost been long enough that he can be officially listed as a missing person," I said.

The paper snapped again.

"We'll see, I suppose. I'll call Marion."

❧

"Oh, please, may I look inside that box?" the girl said. She couldn't have been more than fourteen or fifteen.

I held the heavy segmented box of typefaces on my forearm, but I moved it to my desk. There were only three people on my current tour of the workshop. The crowds hadn't been awful, but they'd certainly been curious and had distracted us all from our real work. At one point, Chester wanted to shut down the shop, tell everyone to go away. I told him that we'd be patient for one day, but if the crowds showed up again tomorrow, we'd lock the doors and not let anyone in.

"What font is this?" she asked as I handed her a Z.

"It's called Midnight Show. See how it looks like something that might be on a vintage poster for a theatrical production?"

"I do," she said, seemingly in awe of the small piece of type. The *Z* had two pointy triangle shapes sticking out from each side of the long, angled connecting line. "It's amazing how just a little difference in the design can change a whole font." She looked inside the box. "Where did you get these?"

"I believe my grandfather bought them from someone in Virginia, but you can ask him on the way out."

The girl's mother (or so I assumed, since they looked so much alike) became curious. She'd been behaving as if she'd only come in because her daughter was interested in printing as well as in being a horror writer one day, but now she looked over the girl's shoulder.

"You have to put those in one at a time?" she said as she peered through glasses she stuck on her nose.

I pushed up my own glasses. "Yes, onto this print plate." I reached to the shelf and grabbed a plate. "One at a time."

"Sounds tedious."

"It is. It's also very satisfying to see your efforts printed onto the page," I said.

"Any chance you have any Epique?" the girl asked.

"Ah, very Victorian. You know your fonts," I said.

"You have no idea," her mother said.

"I do have Epique." I reached and gathered again. "Go ahead and pick one up, but just by the back part, if you can."

"Look at the detail on this, Mom. Each letter has a hooked line running along next to part of it."

"How in the world can you get that detail without blobbing the ink?" the mom asked.

"Lots of practice, and some good luck," I said.

"What font was Nathan Grimes using?" the girl asked.

"I can't tell," I said. "It's his secret for now."

"But he's probably dead," the woman said. "And probably missing a foot if he's keeping with our latest trend."

"I doubt it," I said with a smile to the girl and hopefully a neutral look on my face. "I think we'll find him soon."

"Uh-huh, we'll see, I suppose," the woman said.

"Oh, I hope so. He writes such perfectly scary stuff," the girl said.

I was reading everything by her age too, but I wondered whether her mother had paid attention to exactly how perfectly scary Nathan's stories were and whether the two of them ever discussed some of the scenes.

"Well, come on, sweetheart, I need lunch before we hit the slopes this afternoon."

The girl looked longingly at the box full of Epique and then at the shelves filled with other boxes of type.

"Feel free to come back anytime," I said to her. "I might put you to work."

"Really?" she said.

"Absolutely."

They and the third person who was with them, the girl's quiet and disinterested brother, I assumed, turned and left the workshop. I sent my own longing look at the sealed box we'd received with the almost-Bridgnorth type. We'd decided not to open it and look until Nathan was back with us, safe and sound.

The most popular font of the day had been Snakehead, probably for its name, but it *was* an awesome type, handcrafted-looking letters, something older and not seen much these days. The type box with Snakehead was open on my desk. Since there was a break in the action, I picked it up to put it back on the shelf. I knew where Chester had gotten that box of typefaces: a back alley in a small town in Colorado. He'd had to knock a code on the back of a shut-down newspaper office and meet a kid who could give him the sealed box of typefaces only if Chester gave him money first. Cash. Nothing else would do. The kid took the money and ran, only dropping the box of type before he disappeared from the alley and onto the street. Chester had run after him, but stopped to pick up the box and lost sight of the kid. He'd tried to knock on the back and front doors again, but no one answered.

Or that was the story he told. Chances were pretty good that someone had brought it into the shop one day and Chester had grabbed some money out of the cash register to pay for it.

I stepped from around my desk and looked at the three Hoovens. For the most part our morning visitors had thought they were just a bunch of typewriters on old wooden stands that reminded them of sewing machines. No one behaved as if they knew we had three stupidly expensive typewriter contraptions in the workshop. And that was what they were: contraptions put together with the same idea the Frankenstein monster had been created from: some of this, some of that. I'd named the printing press Frank, and now we had three Frank Jrs. Maybe it was fitting that the author who'd gone missing was a horror writer. I shivered and tried to hold on to the hope we'd find Nathan alive, but that hope was definitely beginning to wane.

I wished for the time it would be appropriate to give the Hoovens to Lloyd's parents. I wished the machines were out of the shop, and away from my responsibility. I wanted to look at each of them closely, grab my tools, and tighten down a few things. But I didn't dare touch them. They weren't mine. At least, I couldn't think of them as mine.

Had Lloyd been killed in some way because of them? Would I have more readily accepted them if he'd given them to me in person? I sighed.

A murder and a disappearance. It was not a banner week in the small mountain town I called home.

The rush was over, it seemed. A few customers shopped out front, but no requests for press tours sounded as I joined Chester, Adal, and Marion.

"That was fun," I said.

The three of them, all a bit harried, looked at me like they weren't sure they'd heard correctly.

"No, really, I enjoyed talking about the press and type-writer repair. I think it was good for business too. Maybe we should publicize tours every now and then?"

"Yay for the Olympics," Marion said.

Adal tried to look cooperative.

From high atop the front ledge, Baskerville growled.

Chester looked up at the cat and then back at me. "I'll head to Salt Lake City on those days. I'm sure I can bother Ken every now and then."

Ken Sanders, rare book dealer in Salt Lake City, had become one of Chester's favorite people to visit. Always a gracious host, Ken had a shop downtown with comfortable seating wherein Chester could relax and ask him all sorts of book questions, and probably make up stories to share, even if Ken could always tell a real story from a fictional one.

I'd bring up my idea again later, once everyone had recovered.

"I guess it's back to normal unless we get any curious late-afternoon visitors," I said.

"I have a few orders to fill," Marion said. Adal had taken over most of her duties in our personalization department, but when she was in the shop, she liked to create her masterpieces. Talk about someone who was good with fonts. Marion's eye was impeccable, and she could take an order from a customer and turn it into something more than the person ever expected. Adal was good too, but not as good as Marion.

"I'll work in the back. I might go ahead and set up a print tray just to give things a try. But I won't open the box. I'll use something we have," Adal said.

"Good idea," I said. "Hey, go ahead and use our Bridgnorth if you want."

Adal's mouth pinched and he nodded. Chester and Marion were silent, but I knew they agreed with me. I hoped we'd all just get to be angry at Nathan for being a flake, but as the minutes ticked by, it was becoming more and more difficult to think he was okay.

"I'm going to go see Ramona," Chester said as he stood from the stool. "And then I might go skiing. I need some time on the slopes."

"Have fun and tell Ramona we all say hello," I said.

Once Chester was out of the shop and Adal was in the back, I stepped behind the counter toward Marion and her computer.

"I know you're busy, but I have a quick request," I said.

"Sure. I've got the rest of the day to work, and these orders won't take too long. Whatever you need."

"My computer in the back is terrible and slow. I know yours is better, and you spend lots more time in the Internet world than I ever would. Could you look up a couple of things for me?"

"Sure." She punched a few keys. "I'm ready."

"Howard Craig, oil guy up in Wyoming. Can you find anything on him, specifically how his business is doing?"

A few moments later her lightning fingers slowed.

"Right, I think I found him," she said as she pointed to a picture. "This look like him?"

"Yes."

"Successful oil man strikes it rich again," she quoted.

"Okay. I was hoping for more dirt on him if there's any to be had."

"That was from 2012, so it's pretty dated. Give me a minute."

More typing ensued.

"Ah, this is what you're looking for," she said almost a full minute later.

"What'd you find?"

"His business was, and I quote, sinking faster than oil into dirt, unquote. Terrible analogy, but they tried, I guess."

"Let me see."

In fact, Howard had been supremely successful at one time, an oil industry leader. He'd been described as a cowboy, a pioneer, an entrepreneur's entrepreneur, among other such accolades. But then his wells ran dry. Literally. After that, he faked it for way too long and ended up in a lot of debt, with a number of enemies.

"Seth would understand all the oil terminology, but the other stuff is loud and clear. Could you print that out for me, and one for Jodie too? I want to give her a hard copy, not put it in her e-mail yet."

"Sure, but how did you know?"

"I didn't. I guessed. Something felt off. Something still feels off. There's more going on, but maybe this information will lead us to more. I'd like you to look up Donte Senot and Lloyd Gavin next. I mean, look for any bad stuff about them, particularly regarding their businesses."

"Will do."

I'd read the articles that Howard had sent me, and they had painted a much less flattering picture of Lloyd's company than I'd gotten from either Dillon or Brenda. However, I hadn't found anything that made me think the business was having financial difficulties. An earlier quick search found nothing more, but if there was something out there, I hoped Marion's search would track it down.

Turned out that Donte's business was struggling too, at least according to an article from the middle of last year. It wasn't quite the bust that Howard's had become, but he would be closing the business's doors if a few more book orders didn't come in soon. True, he had created a new mathematical equation and formula, but it had been vastly improved upon since then, and he wasn't going to get any credit for the improvements, meaning no money or royalties if that was how those things were measured. He was struggling and the new textbook writers didn't find his publishing company nearly as appealing any longer.

Lloyd, however much discontent might have been rumbling around with his employees, seemed to have been doing fine financially. Better than fine. He had genuinely become one of the most successful men in the country. I was enormously happy and deeply sad for him. I wished we'd kept in touch, if only so I could tell him how proud of him I was. I was sure he had been pleased with that success, but didn't everyone enjoy it when that sort of recognition shone in their direction? And didn't competitors dislike that sort of success and recognition? Professional jealousy must have been a part of his life.

"Print them all out, please," I said to Marion as I pulled out my phone.

"You got it."

"Jodie, hi. Yes. Can I come see you? You're where? Really? Okay, I'll be right there."

I closed my phone, grabbed the copies, and hurried out of the shop.

16

"Stay up there, Clare. I'll come up in a second," Jodie said from the ditch.

I pulled my coat tighter around my neck. The narrow canyon road wasn't too snowy, but a strong wind blew through all the time and was bitingly frigid in the winter.

"In fact, go to my Bronco. It's too dangerous to have you standing out there on the road," Jodie continued.

I didn't have to be told twice.

From inside the cold but mostly wind-free cab of the Bronco, I could still observe Jodie, her partner, Omar, and one other officer I didn't recognize working in the ditch.

She plucked up a light green object that had been hidden by a small snow-covered boulder and put it in a plastic bag.

Suddenly, the color set off recognition bells in me. Was

that part of Nathan's scarf? I put my hand on the door again, ready to leap out and run back to Jodie.

But she, bag in hand, made her way toward the Bronco instead, seemingly giving orders for the other two officers to continue looking in the ditch, which was filled with snow, rocks, and dead weeds.

By the time she got inside the truck, my panic had grown.

"Is that . . ?" I said. I couldn't finish the words. Saying them aloud would make them too real.

"This is a part of a scarf," Jodie said. "Does it look like Nathan's scarf?"

I clenched my teeth to keep the tears at bay. I nodded once. "It might be."

"That's what I thought," Jodie said, followed by a string of imaginative expletives. Just when I thought I'd heard her twist them all, she came up with something new.

"Officer Marks was driving up the canyon when he saw the flutter of color over there. He called it in. We came out."

"Is there . . . anything else over there?"

"No body, if that's what you're asking. No other personal effects either. Found a couple of old beer bottles, but that happens everywhere. This fabric is dirty but barely worn, making me think it landed out there fairly recently."

"This isn't good," I said.

"Well, it's not bad either, Clare. It's a clue, though, and we needed one of those pretty badly. Without a body it's difficult to predict what might have happened, and it's important not to make any sort of rash assumptions."

I nodded once again and looked out the windshield, up the canyon.

"Annie Wilkes!" I exclaimed.

"Pardon me?"

I started speaking quickly, almost incoherently, but it was Jodie and she knew my verbal shorthand. "A character in a horror novel that steals an author away to her house in the woods and keeps him captive. I mean, well, that's not what I mean here. What I'm trying to say is that Nathan mentioned to me that he's been to Star City before, to a friend's cabin where he could write. He didn't say where it was, but there are cabins out this way, right? Right, yes. Maybe he came out to the cabin and maybe his friends kidnapped him or maybe he hurt himself. You know where this road leads? To cabins. Or maybe the scarf flew out of someone else's car as his body was being taken to the woods to be hidden forever. Because he didn't drive a car up to the shop, Jodie. He must have been kidnapped. He didn't have a car."

"I think the first option might be the best." She pushed the button on her microphone, and commanded that someone at the station try to figure out which cabin Nathan might have stayed in at one time. She asked for backup, telling the person on the other end that she and Omar were going to search the cabins up this particular canyon.

"Go home, or go back to work, Clare," Jodie said.

"You're joking, right?" I said. I buckled myself in to make the point that I wasn't leaving.

"You can't come up there with me," Jodie said.

"I'm not leaving this Bronco," I said.

Jodie rolled down the window and told Omar she and I were traveling a little farther up the canyon and to direct the other officers who were on their way to join us.

He waved us on and then turned his attention back to the gully to search for more clues. I hoped he didn't find any.

"All right," Jodie said as she rolled up the window. "You will do as I command, okay?"

"Of course," I said as I searched ahead of us and then down off the side of the road, into the woods opposite where Jodie and Omar had found the piece of fabric.

"Clare."

"I hear you."

"What do you remember about the cabin he mentioned?"

"I don't remember any more than that. Wait, he said the cabin was small and that he would have loved to spend some time there on this trip but he thought the owners might have been staying there. The monks! He could smell the wine production, and this would be the right area for that."

"Right, but this area is summer only," Jodie said.

"I know, but he might not have known that. We could also be on a wild-goose chase."

Jodie pushed the button on her microphone again. "Yeah, check Grimes's cell phone records again. If you didn't ask about any of the people he called having a cabin, call them back and ask. Tell me exactly where it is. I need this information right away. Got it?"

They got it.

We moved slowly around the narrow, winding road. We were lucky in that it was mostly clear of snow, which was unusual for this time of year. However, we'd both driven these sorts of roads enough to know about black ice that could send a car in the wrong direction quickly.

"It gets cold enough up here at night for black ice," I said.

"Yeah, and it's not getting warm enough during the day yet to melt it all," Jodie said.

"Oh jeez," I said as I caught sight of a cabin not too far off the road. "Its roof still has a couple feet of snow, and getting to the doorway would be impossible."

"That's a good sign. If Nathan came out here and saw the conditions, he knew he couldn't try to get inside the cabin. Oh man, I hope that was the case. People who aren't used to these conditions . . ."

"Drive you crazy, I know."

"Right, well, let's remain positive."

The road continued to wind and the cabins we spotted continued to be topped with snow, with no footsteps leading toward their front door.

"Jodie!" I said as we came around another curve and passed a car going slowly the other direction. "What's that?" I pointed.

"Looks like some of the same fabric." She slowed the Bronco and pulled it to the side of the road. "Be care—"

But I was out of the truck and quick-stepping my way to the edge of the road before she could finish. She joined me in record time.

"Oh no!" I said as we looked down a slope. Not as steep as some, this one was probably less than a hundred feet to the bottom. A car had gone off the road and was on its side below. "Nathan! Nathan!"

Jodie grabbed the fabric that had become stuck on the bark of a tree that had fallen sometime over the last hundred years or so. "The ripped-off part looks like the other piece was attached." She pushed the microphone button again and spoke emergency words and codes, ending with the command that they all hurry to get to the scene.

"I'm going to get a rope. Stay here," she said to me. "Do not try to go down there or I will have two people I have to rescue. I'm going to need your help, do you understand? Stay here a second and wait for me."

I nodded.

"Clare?"

"I will! Get the rope!"

She jogged back to the Bronco and came back with the rope. She tied it around her waist and then wrapped the other end twice around a tree. "I'm going to climb down there, but you will have to be in charge of the rope. Put on your gloves. The rope is around the tree so you won't have to deal with all my weight, but I really need you to stay focused and not let me fall. I can't help Nathan if I fall, got it?"

I nodded again and took hold of my end of the rope.

"Please be careful," I said to her.

"I will. Watch the rope."

She maneuvered herself to the lip of the downward drop and, like the pro she was, backed over the edge and started rappelling down, though it wasn't exactly like rappelling. The edge wasn't straight—it was sloped and covered in snow. So it was more like she was trudging through the snow at a weird angle, but the rope kept her from rolling down the side.

I lost sight of her.

"You okay?" I yelled.

"Almost there."

The rope suddenly slipped. I grabbed it, but the force of her weight mixed with gravity and I lost hold. For the longest second of my life, I watched the rope come un-coiled from around the tree, the end of it flying through the air and then disappearing over the edge.

I ran to the edge and stopped myself just in time to keep from falling over.

"Jodie!"

Another long second later she answered, "I'm okay, Clare. I was down before you let go. I'm on the other side of the car. Look for my hand."

I saw her hand come up over the car as she waved.

"I'm sorry, I didn't mean to let go." I wanted to cry. Fear for Jodie and Nathan had only multiplied.

"It's okay. I'm okay. The guys will get me out when they get here."

I couldn't see her, but I could hear her.

"Nathan?" I said.

The seconds had turned into things that took longer than they should, minutes, hours. Though it felt like forever before she answered again, it was probably only a couple of beats later.

"He's here, Clare. He's alive, but maybe barely. We need an ambulance."

"Don't you die, Nathan. Don't die!" I yelled.

The tears fell down my cheeks. I wanted to figure out a way to go help them, but I knew the best thing was for me was to wait for help up here.

"His eyelids are fluttering, Clare. He'll be okay," Jodie said again, probably because she heard my sobs.

I was without words by then, and the time that it took for help to come seemed like a millennium. Later I would figure out the timing and realize that it took only about five minutes for the many rescuers to arrive. I waved them down even though they couldn't have missed the Bronco and the hysterical blonde by the side of the road.

It was all I could do not to chastise them for taking so long.

17

"He's going to be okay," Jodie said as she put her hand on my shoulder. "It was only about twenty-four hours. It was cold, but he had the shelter of the car and his coat."

The wave of relief that washed over me with her assurance was welcomed.

Nathan and Jodie had both been rescued quickly. All it took was a few guys and a stretcher attached to a rope attached to a fire engine pulley. Nathan had been conscious but barely, and the EMTs hadn't let me talk to him. They whisked him away and Jodie got in her Bronco, drenched up to her armpits from the deep snow and not allowing any EMTs to evaluate her condition, and followed behind. Another officer had brought me back to the shop, leaving me still frantic with concern. Chester, Adal, Marion, and I had all been on edge as we waited. Fortunately, Jodie knew I'd be waiting and had called to say that everyone was okay but she'd have to give me the details later. I was relieved to see her walk through the front doors a couple of hours later.

I nodded as Baskerville jumped up to the counter and rammed his head into my arm. I responded by scratching behind his ears.

"He'd just gone out to explore the cabin?" Chester asked.

"Well, yes, kind of. He wanted to stop by the bookstore, Starry Night. He had some books he wanted to give the shop to sell. They were some of his books, first editions with his signatures, and he wanted them to have the books as a gift. He claims to love every part of Star City," Jodie said.

"That's very generous," Adal said.

"It is," Jodie said. "He was awake and out of the hotel early. He got up to Starry Night and it was closed. He realized he was too early to come in here, so he decided to see if he could go find the cabin, maybe say hello to his friends if they were there. He said he didn't realize it was a summer-only cabin. He was turning around when he hit some black ice and went over."

"It's amazing that he wasn't killed," Chester said.

"Not only was he not killed, but his only real injury is a scratch on his forehead. He was dehydrated, so they're filling him up with fluids and then sending him on his way. No sign of frostbite or hypothermia. He was well covered up by his clothes and a couple blankets in the car. He was just stuck and couldn't get out. He threw the scarf out last night when the wind was whipping down the canyon. It was a smart move. He's absolutely fine, eternally grateful to have been found."

"I bet," Chester said.

"Whose car was he driving?" I asked.

"He had rented a car when he got to Utah." She paused. "We should have checked that, but we didn't."

"I told you he didn't have a car," I said.

"I still should have checked that. Anyway. He just pre-ferred to walk up here. He likes the exercise," Jodie said. "The stack of books made him decide to use the car."

"I can't believe he's okay," I said.

"Right. Me either. Now I have to get back to the busi-ness of trying to find Lloyd's killer, but at least we don't have another victim on our hands."

"Actually," I said as I looked at Adal and Chester, "I have a couple of things I want to tell you. We got inter-rupted earlier."

"I'm listening."

So were Chester and Adal, but that was probably okay.

I'd thrown my bag behind the counter. Still with noo-dle legs from the drop of adrenaline, I walked around everyone, grabbed the bag, and lifted it up to the counter.

"These are some more articles. I asked Marion to help me find them." I handed Jodie the copies. "Howard and Donte weren't as successful as they seemed at first glance. Both of their businesses are struggling."

"Right." She took the papers and looked at each one, skimming quickly.

"You know this stuff?"

"Well, we've looked, but I'm going to take these in case we've missed anything."

I pushed up my glasses. "Thank you. And what about Creighton?" I said.

"Which part?"

Her question garnered some attention from both Chester and Adal. Chester rubbed his mustache with his knuckle as he inspected Jodie, and Adal looked like he wanted to say something but then changed his mind.

"I, uh. Well, here's what my head has put together," I said boldly. "The meeting was Lloyd's idea. He was successful, but he knew the others weren't anymore. Howard, Donte, and maybe he knew something about Creighton that you don't know yet, something big enough to lead to his fall, something you *might* have been suspecting. Anyway, maybe Lloyd wanted to show off. Though no one is admitting to having a close relationship with Lloyd back in high school, maybe he was taunted by them. They were those kinds of people."

"Despite all his failings, though, Creighton wasn't that type of person," Jodie said.

"I know." I nodded and swallowed hard. "But what if I'm the reason he invited Creighton? He obviously knew about my personal life, and maybe he wanted to point out to Creighton that he and I were no longer together. Anyway, you know what Brenda said."

"I do," Jodie said.

"Who's Brenda and what did she say?" Chester asked.

"I'll tell you later," I said.

"Lloyd had a thing for Clare ever since high school. I don't know if it was love or obsession, but"—she looked at me—"you might have a good point, Clare. I'll have to take a look at it from that angle, see if the pieces come together. It's a lot of extrapolation and guessing, but there might be something there."

"Maybe," I said.

"I think we, the police, also need to consider that the tie these people had to each other had nothing to do with their business success or lack thereof. There's another connection."

"High school?"

"In a roundabout way, maybe."

"Did you look up Eloise MacPherson?" I asked.

"Who's that?" Chester asked.

"Tell you in a minute," I said.

"Yeah. A woman named Eloise MacPherson was shot and killed one year ago in her home, a trailer outside Heber. She was a known drug dealer, and so were those suspected of killing her."

"Uh-oh."

"Hang on. There's no record of Creighton arresting a woman with that name, or even being in the area at that time. And, according to what I could find, Creighton hasn't turned in any drug evidence for over eighteen months."

"He took the drugs?"

"Not what I'm saying. I just think that he hasn't worked a drug case in that long, at least one that's bigger than kids with some weed. My guess is that Eloise was a fabrication by our séance folks. In theory they could have researched Eloise's murder and made up their own story about Creighton's being involved. I'm not sure. Honestly, Clare, it wouldn't be the first time. People try to catch or accuse cops of doing bad things all the time. Goes with the badge, I suppose, but for the most part we know how to point out evidence or the lack thereof, so those setups usually backfire."

"But why would they want to set Creighton up for anything?"

"The only reason I can think of is to divert our attention from something else, but my attention isn't on anything I can use right now anyway. Lots of unknowns."

"I guess the thing that needs the most attention is who killed Lloyd?"

"That's what I'm working on. Well, now that we've found our wayward author. Look, I gotta go."

Jodie turned and took fast, quick steps out of the shop. She hadn't changed out of her wet clothes, but they seemed to be a little dryer.

"Change clothes. You'll catch your death," I said as she went out the door and sent us a backward wave.

"Jodie!" Adal said.

She turned. "Yeah?"

"Where is he? Can we go see him?"

"Yep. He didn't even go down to Salt Lake. He's at the Star City Med Center."

"Thanks," Adal said with too friendly a smile.

"You're welcome," she said with too friendly a smile before she went through the door.

"Oh boy," I muttered.

Adal looked at Chester.

"Oh yes, go ahead. You go too, Clare," Chester said. "I've got the store, and Marion will be back later."

"Let's go," I said, not needing any further prompting.

ᥴᥩ

The drive to Star City Medical was quick and almost free of traffic.

As we sat in the otherwise-empty waiting room, I counted off the times I'd visited the small Star City hospital. I'd been a patient only once—a sprained ankle. Other than that, I'd brought three broken ankles, one broken wrist, and two dislocated shoulders over from the slopes.

"You brought them over from the slopes?" Adal asked when I told him about the shoulders.

"Yes, when I was a teenager, we all just took care of

each other out there. We didn't bother with ambulances if the person was conscious. Things have changed just over the last ten years or so, and that wouldn't be allowed anymore."

"You just put them in your car and brought them over?"

"Sometimes. There's always been a ski patrol, but there didn't used to be as many around as there are now, and there weren't as many rules, safety stuff. And, of course, we were young and thought we could handle everything ourselves. Different time even if it wasn't that long ago."

"When's the last time you were here?"

"With my grandmother," I said. My voice skipped and it surprised me

"Oh, I'm sorry."

"I will always miss my grandmother, but usually my emotions aren't quite so close to the surface. I think it's just been a highly emotional day. I'm fine, and it's always good to think about her even if it makes me a little sad sometimes."

"Chester was talking about her the other day."

"He was?"

"Yes, he has good memories and he shared a story about one of their adventures. They went to New Mexico and ended up being adopted by a Native American tribe. He laughed as he told the story. Your grandmother apparently enjoyed the entire trip."

"I remember them talking about that. At first I wondered if it was something Chester made up. Can you be adopted by a Native American tribe? But my grandmother assured us all that it was true."

"I believe so."

"Clare?" A nurse came out through some doors.

I stood in a rush. "Can we see him?"

"He'd like to see you," she said. "He's fine, but tired."

"But he's truly going to be fine?" Adal said.

"I think so," she said. "Follow me."

We walked down a wide corridor with curtains at each emergency bay opening.

"Are you going to take him to a room?" I said.

"He said he just wants to stay in the bed here, but you can talk to him," she said as she pulled back a bit on a curtain.

We went to its other side and she closed it after us.

"Clare, Adal," Nathan said with a wide smile and a Band-Aid over the injury on his forehead. "So good to see you."

"Nathan, man, you are a sight for pained eyes," Adal said.

Nathan and I looked at him and I realized he meant "sore eyes." It was rare that he got mixed up or confused regarding American phrases.

"What happened, Nathan?" I asked, wanting to hear the details myself.

"Oh hell, I was dumb and hit black ice when I ventured up that canyon. I was fascinated by the snow-covered roofs and I wanted to see what my friends' cabin looked like. I honestly don't remember the car falling off the side, but I remember waking up and thinking I was in trouble. I won't go into the details of how horrifying that was. I'm sure I'll use it all in a book anyway, and you can read and experience it firsthand."

"Go on," I said after he paused.

"After our delightful dinner, I thought a lot about Lloyd Gavin and what might have happened to him. I thought about the people involved and then I took a stroll up the hill instead of down toward the hotel. I wanted to see the bookstore we'd talked about for myself, and it was dark enough that chances were pretty good that I wouldn't be bothered by fans."

Nathan leaned to his left slightly and looked at the curtain. It was closed tight, but there was no privacy here. He signaled us to move closer.

"What about Sarah?" he said quietly.

"Sarah?" I said, just as quietly.

"Is anyone suspicious of her?"

"I'm equally not suspicious about everyone," I said. "I don't have any idea what the police think."

"Well, there we are," he said. "I was going up to talk to her yesterday morning after looking in the window the night before. I thought she'd like some of my books, and all bookstore owners like to meet me." He shrugged. "I was going to ask her some questions, see if she's evil enough to kill."

"I think that sounds reasonable," I said doubtfully.

Nathan smiled. "I'm pretty good at spotting evil. But there's more."

Adal smiled too. "Ah, now we get to the good part."

"Yes, I was building to the good part there. How'd it work?" Nathan asked.

"You've done better," I said.

Nathan shrugged one hospital-gown-clad shoulder. "Needs a little editing. All right, when I got up to the bookstore yesterday morning, I looked in the window. At first I thought no one was there, because it was completely dark inside, but just as I stepped away from the window, a pop of light showed from the back, as if someone opened a door and the space inside it was lit. I zipped to the side of the window, where I could be mostly hidden by the building, and peered in as inconspicuously as possible. Two people came out of the back room, quick-stepping it to the front door. There was really nothing for me to do except either be seen or hide. Fortunately, there was a thin space between the two buildings that I could duck into. It was so early that no one else was around to watch me, so I slipped into that space and waited. The man and the woman both came out of the shop, and from what you've described to me, Clare, the man in the cowboy hat was named Howard, and the woman was Sarah."

"Well, that's interesting," I said. "Maybe. I know they're friends, and Jodie and I saw him there later."

Nathan said, "And even more interesting is what they were saying to each other."

Adal and I looked at each other as Nathan paused for dramatic effect, and then we looked at Nathan.

He smiled again before he continued. "The man, Howard, said that she had gone too far this time, that he couldn't believe what she'd done."

"What did Sarah say?" I asked.

"She said she was sorry, and to please not tell the police. The man hurried away after that, down the hill. Passed right in front of where I was hiding but didn't see me. Sarah went back inside and after a few minutes I ditched the idea of giving her the books, hopped back into my car, and went out to look at the cabin. I might not have done that if I didn't need the time to think about things. I like to drive and think."

"Did you tell Jodie?"

Nathan sighed and shook his head. "No, I talked to her here not that long ago. I wasn't sure what to do. I wanted to tell you first. Her brother is a part of the group involved. Family always comes first. Should we tell another officer?"

"No, we can tell Jodie. We should." I pulled out my phone, but doubt bloomed and stopped me from calling her right away. Nathan was correct, family did come first. But hadn't Jodie just told me that that wasn't always the case with her, that sometimes other people, like me, come first? And hadn't she always been about the job? Yes. Except when maybe she looked the other way for a brief instant or two, and more than once those instants had been for me. "Let me think about it a minute."

"You should tell Jodie," Adal said. He had skin in this game, but I wasn't sure how much.

"I will," I said. "I just need a few minutes to think."

"See, you get what I'm saying," Nathan said.

I waved away his comment. "We should let you rest."

"Sure. But I think I'm going to ask if I can leave soon. I'll be at The Rescued Word tomorrow, I promise."

"Do as the doctors tell you," I said.

"I'm fine. I was dehydrated, but they gave me some fluids. I'm as good as new."

Over the years, I'd heard many stories about cars sliding off icy roads. A limited few of those stories had included a mountain road and a steep slope. It came with where we lived. I'd never heard of someone sustaining the little to no injury Nathan had.

"Was it horrible, those hours in the car?" I said.

Something other than joviality shaded his eyes, but he smiled again a second later. "I was scared, but I knew I wasn't hurt. I couldn't gain purchase to get myself out of there, but I could reach a couple of blankets in the backseat. I threw out the scarf and sent a prayer of sorts out

with it. I stayed warm and tried to rest. I hoped the snow
would melt enough that I could find some friction, but that
didn't happen. I did my best not to think too much about
the grave circumstances, and about the murder instead. I
have a whole new novel right here." He tapped his head.
"I think I would have been scared again if it had gone on
much longer. I'm grateful you and Jodie found me."

"It could have been so much worse," I said.

"So much."

"We'll let you rest. Adal?" I said.

"I think I'm going to stay. I'll make sure he gets back
to the hotel. Unless you need me at the shop?"

I hesitated. Should we both stay? Was it rude that I
was leaving? I didn't think so. Adal had taken on a responsibility for Nathan that was akin to my protectiveness
for my apprentice.

"No, that would be fine," I finally said. "Do you want
my car?"

"No, we'll figure it out."

"I'm okay," Nathan said. "I promise."

I turned to leave but then turned back again.

"Nathan, is there any chance you called for help last
night? I mean, used the word 'help' specifically?" I said.

"Yes, many times."

I nodded.

"Why?"

"Just curious. Get some rest."

I slipped around the curtain and left the medical center. I couldn't help wondering—had we heard him through
Donte?

Probably not. Those things weren't truly possible.

Were they?

18

I was eager to get back to work, but as I was about to turn onto Bygone, I spotted a familiar figure up the hill walking into Starry Night Books. Creighton. He wasn't in uniform, and for an instant I thought he spotted me, but his eyes didn't stay on mine. But—and even though I only had an instant to determine this—he behaved like he was trying to be sneaky. Dressed in jeans and ski coat and a John Deere cap, he didn't look like any version of Creighton that I was familiar with. He wasn't a small person, though, and only so many people walk with their shoulders and chest held like they could huff and puff and break down a door or a wall at will.

I turned off my blinker and drove up the hill, finding a parking spot a few doors down from the bookstore. I didn't have a plan after that, so a couple of minutes later when he hadn't come out yet and I began to feel ridiculous for spying, I started the car again.

And then he did exit the store. And saw me. After sending me some highly disgruntled eyes underneath the brim of his cap, he took long, quick steps to get to my car. He opened the passenger door and got in.

"Spying on me?" he asked before I could inform him that I hadn't invited him inside.

"Yes, I suppose I am," I said, and authoritatively pushed up my glasses.

"What are you looking for?"

"I'm not sure. I saw you go in and I couldn't stop myself from parking and watching."

"What do you want to know?"

"You'll answer my questions?" I said.

"I don't know, Clare. I want to know what you're trying to figure out first."

"Doesn't seem fair."

"Don't care."

I bit my bottom lip as I looked at the bookstore. "Okay, why did you go in there, in civilian clothes?"

"Last night was weird," he said.

"Yeah. You think something's up with the whole 'séance' thing?"

He huffed a laugh. "Everyone knows there was something up with the whole séance thing. But not only that. I think someone there last night had something to do with Lloyd's murder. I thought I'd play the friendly role and see what I could find out about why Eloise was brought into the picture last night."

"Sarah's the common denominator?" I said.

"No, we all are," he said, almost exactly like Nathan had. "But last night was strange and obviously staged.

Whether you believe it, or anyone believes it, Clare, I did not kill Eloise MacPherson. And I can't imagine why that was set up the way it was. Where did they get that name, and why?"

I nodded. "You know who she was?"

"Of course I do. I'm a police officer and I pay attention to what happens around here. She was a drug dealer, a bad one. I'm of the belief that other drug dealers killed her."

"Okay, but because of that act you think one of them killed Lloyd?"

"No, the séance was dumb, but I think one of them might have had something to do with Lloyd's murder, because I did some research and their businesses were struggling."

"You think they were jealous?"

"Or they tried to borrow money from Lloyd but he wouldn't give it to them. I don't have any idea, but we were all invited to the meetings. There had to be a reason."

"I know! I mean, I just gave Jodie some articles about that."

"Good. We've seen some, but it can't hurt to read whatever is out there."

"In my mind you're the biggest mystery. Why were you invited?" I said.

"That's what I was in there trying to figure out."

"As a civilian?"

"I'm a cop, Clare. I dressed as a civilian to make me less threatening, but I'm always a cop. You should know that."

"Did you learn anything?"

"I'm not sure yet, and I'm not as easy as my sister. She tells you too much."

I sighed. "I'm glad Nathan was found."

"Me too. I thought they were somehow involved with his disappearance too, and that added even more questions."

"You really do think one of them killed Lloyd, don't you?"

"Pretty sure. I just can't figure out why."

"Lloyd was killed out on the slopes. Were any of them skiing that day?"

Creighton sent me a half smile. "There is no evidence that any of them were skiing. They all have season passes, even Howard, but none of them have a gun registered in their names. That's sometimes easy to get around. And, in case you were wondering, none of them have goggle tan lines. In fact, they all claim not to have been skiing for over a month."

I nodded. As strange as he looked in his civilian clothes, it was clear the police were hard at work on figuring out who killed Lloyd. Or Creighton was making everything up, but I didn't think he would bother wasting his time doing that with me.

"Gotta go, Clare. Quit spying on people. Stay out of the way of our police work."

"I'm not in the way."

He got out of the car, shut the door a little too hard, and then hurried away. For a big guy, he could sure disappear into a small crowd easily.

I started the car, turned it around, and finally went back to work.

∞

"Dillon, hello," I said as I walked into The Rescued Word. "I'm kind of surprised you're still in town."

"I'm not allowed to leave," he said. "I'd like to. Believe me."

"I do believe you," I said. "You look tired. Are you okay?"

"I'm not sleeping well," he said. "But I suppose that's to be expected. I keep seeing Lloyd's foot in my dreams, but it doesn't have the ski boot on it."

"That's not good."

Dillon was too young to look as tired as I felt, and I was sure the dark circles under our eyes matched well.

"No, it's not." He ran his hand through his hair. "And now I have another task. I wondered . . . well, is there any chance you could come with me to the cemetery?"

"Um."

"Brenda asked me to find Lloyd's family plot and make sure everything is ready for the service tomorrow. The police haven't released Lloyd's body yet, but the family wants to go ahead and have the service."

"Sure, I'd be happy to," I said. I looked at Chester. Sympathy for the young man showed in his eyes as he nodded once. "Where's Brenda today?"

"She had a bunch of phone calls this morning and then she's spending time with Lloyd's parents. They'll be going to the cemetery later today to check on things, but . . . well, Brenda wants to make sure the family has no surprises. She's always a step or two ahead of everything, but she forgot to stop by there yesterday. She suggested I see if you could go with me."

"Okay," I said.

"You two be careful," Chester said.

"Let's go," I said.

I hadn't heard a peep from Baskerville, so I looked up to the high shelves as we left. The cat was there, eyeing the goings-on below. It seemed he didn't have any commentary to add, so we just shared a blink. He probably wondered if I was ever going to get back to my job duties. I did too.

The Star City Cemetery sat amid some rolling hills next to a mountaintop. Final resting place views were stunning no matter what the season; sides of mountains made for pretty sights if they were covered in snow, wildflowers, green grasses, or just rocks. One border of the cemetery property ran along a busy two-lane highway. When Dillon shared the Gavin family plot's location, I zoned in on where we were going and pulled into the parking lot halfway between the grave site and the small brick building where I'd been to more than a few viewings and services over the years.

"It's right there, I think," I said as I pointed.

"Let's go look first, make sure it's in good shape, and then we'll go talk to whoever's inside," he said unenthusiastically, though I saw an element of maturity I hadn't seen the night he tried to deliver the Hoovens. Maybe the days in Star City, and the circumstances, had aged him. "There will be no . . . burial tomorrow. It needs to look nice."

The cold wind wasn't unbearable, but it bit at my cheeks as we crossed the grounds. I zipped my coat up around my chin. The plot, surrounded by a low wrought-iron fence, had no gate; we just stepped over the wrought iron. It looked like both of Lloyd's grandparents on his father's side had been buried there about ten years earlier, but no other plots had been used yet, their stones marked with names and birth dates, but no death dates, even Lloyd's. I wondered when that would happen and if it was something we needed to ask the cemetery manager about.

"That's what I was worried about," Dillon said as he stepped next to Lloyd's space. "The grass is uneven and brown."

"And a little snowy, but it's winter," I said. "It would be impossible to have green grass right now. I doubt the family will expect it."

"Brenda told me she wanted it cleaned off, mowed, and green by the time she came out after visiting with his parents."

"She didn't mean that literally," I said, but that was just a guess. Even if I was wrong, it didn't matter. Her wishes could not feasibly be met. "She just wanted you to make sure that it was okay. That nothing would surprise them in a worse way than they'd already been surprised. And it looks very nice, Dillon."

"I don't know. She usually says what she means."

"Lloyd would be pleased. It's very nice," I repeated. I swallowed hard. The last thing Dillon needed was for me to get emotional. He had his own stuff to deal with.

"I hope so." He stepped back over the fence and collapsed into a sitting position.

I stepped over too and crouched next to him. "Are you okay?"

"I'm sorry. Yes, I'm fine. Well, not really, but I'm going to be okay. My knees felt weak for a second, that's all. Just give me a minute."

I stayed next to him on the cold, slightly wet ground.

"When's the last time you ate?" I said.

"This morning. It's not that . . . I'll just miss him. I can't believe all this has happened. I want to go home."

"He was a good guy, huh?" I said, shoring up my emotions.

"Very. Smart, kind, good guy."

I nodded. "Did everyone like working for him?" I felt a tiny bit awful taking advantage of the moment, but not enough to hold back.

"Sure." He shrugged.

"So, *almost* everyone, huh?" I said with a small smile.

He returned the smile. "Well, it's probably better to say that everyone liked working for him *most* of the time, but probably not every single moment."

"Sounds like he was successful. It can't all be fun and games to get as far as he got."

Dillon shrugged again.

I waited. I wasn't sure what to say, and though I didn't always follow my own rule, I knew that sometimes, particularly when you don't know what to say, you can get better answers if you're just quiet.

And this time it worked.

"He was demanding, and sometimes up and down with his anger, but mostly . . . well, he could be kind of obsessed with things."

"I'm not sure, Dillon, but I think that's somewhat typical of people who are categorized as geniuses."

"That's probably true, but some people thought he was too much. Didn't like him because of it. Some people got really angry at him."

"Well, I know we're just talking here and I know this is a big jump to a crazy conclusion, but of those people who got angry at him, any of them get too angry? Can you think of someone who might have wanted him dead? One of his employees, or maybe a competitor?"

Jodie might have rolled her eyes at me. Or maybe not. I'd ask her later if I'd done this correctly.

Dillon shook his head slowly. "Not sure. You know the typewriter things he wanted you to have?"

"Sure."

"He called us all in one Sunday just because he wanted us to go to the sale of the building together. It was an auction. He'd heard about the possibility of the typewriters, and we all had to come in to work and then go together, just in case he needed help. He did stuff like that all the time."

"Call people in on their days off?"

"Yeah. But he never took a day off. He was always working. I think it surprised him that people weren't supposed to be at work." Dillon laughed. "He just worked all the time."

"Seventeen employees?"

"Yes."

"Did Jodie ask you for all their names?" I asked.

"Yeah." He paused. "He told us all about you, you know. I think it was after Brenda learned about you. That's when we all heard about you. He was fond of you. If he'd lived by you, I bet he would have been a stalker."

"That's a stretch." And creepy. "I expect the Hoovens made him remember our friendship and his attention to detail, maybe some sort of obsession over the typewriters, took over."

"Think whatever you'd like, but he was at least obsessed from afar. Brenda and I talked about how it was a good thing you didn't live there. In fact, she and I thought it was Lloyd who planned the meetings here in town. The invitation came shortly after we all trekked out to that auction for the Hoovens. He kept saying that getting that invitation was destiny that he was supposed to bring the Hoovens out to you right away, but it was forced, you know. 'Destiny' wasn't his thing. We felt like he said that just to throw us off. He got a haircut, new glasses, started eating only vegetables. It was weird."

It was. "To your knowledge, did he ever have a girlfriend?"

"No. I thought he and Brenda might have dated, but she insists they didn't. They got along very well, though, most of the time."

"Except when they didn't?"

"No, they actually got along very well, and worked well together. Sometimes, though, they would get caught up on a project and forget about everyone else. It was a problem for . . . I shouldn't be talking about this. Forget I mentioned it. It turned out okay anyway."

I nodded. "How did Brenda feel about him wanting to give me the Hoovens?"

He looked at me, his eyebrows coming together. "Do you mean was she jealous? No, she wasn't jealous. She just wanted to get the delivery and the meetings over with. She wanted us all to get back to work."

At the same time a gust of cold air moved across the cemetery, another car pulled into the lot.

"Here she comes," he said as we both stood, straightened our coats, and started walking toward the parking lot, greeting her as she got out of her rental car.

"His parents just want me to help with everything," Brenda said to me. "They're struggling. It's understandable. They were doing okay when I left them." She looked at Dillon. "How's the family plot look?"

"Good," Dillon said. "Well, brown and wintery, but

what's there looks as good as might be expected this time of year."

"Good. So, you asked Clare to bring you out here?"

"Oh yeah, I did."

"That was very kind, Clare," Brenda said. "Thank you."

"Not a problem."

"Want to come inside with us?" she said.

"No, but if you don't have plans for dinner tonight, I'd love to take you both out. Of course, Lloyd's parents are invited, but I would understand if they didn't want to come along."

Dillon and Brenda looked at each other. Brenda shrugged, but Dillon tried to look neutral. She was his superior at work, so she was in charge here too. Made sense, but there was definitely an edge to her that I hadn't noticed when she, Jodie, and I had had barbecue.

"Sure," she said. "The service is tomorrow. You'll come?"

"Of course."

"We'll call as soon as we're done here," she said. "Thank you for the invitation."

They disappeared inside the building and I sought shelter in my car. My knees were damp from kneeling, but I didn't have the time to run home and change. I pulled out my cell phone and hit Jodie's number.

"What up?" she answered.

"I'm at the cemetery with Dillon and Brenda. They just went inside. I'm taking them to dinner, but I wondered if you guys had looked at *everyone* at Lloyd's company. There were only seventeen employees."

"Yes, we have, Clare," she said, a smile to her voice.

"They are clean as a bunch of whistles that haven't been taken out of the package yet. Except for Dillon, they were all in Nebraska at the time. We suppose Dillon was on the road."

"Suppose?"

She hesitated. "We're confirming, but he used cash for gas. He told us the locations and we're trying to track down security camera footage."

"Who uses cash for gas?"

"Someone who's given a giant wad of cash from his boss and told not to worry about spending too much as they're being told to travel safely. Oh, and Dillon mentioned that Lloyd didn't let him know he was to drive the truck out until two days before. Dillon thought Lloyd wanted to make the trip less of the inconvenience it truly was."

"That's what he said?"

"Yes."

"No company credit card?"

"The company has a few credit cards, but Dillon didn't use one. By the way, those credit cards are paid off in full every month. Lloyd's business was ridiculously successful, Clare. More money than Zeus, if you know what I mean."

"Makes me wonder about life insurance. I'm sure you looked there too."

"We've requested the paperwork, but the insurance company isn't playing nice. We'll have it soon, though, and we suspect his parents were his only beneficiaries. I'll get a judge involved if I have to."

"That might tell us—I mean you—lots."

"Yes, we're looking forward to receiving the information. Why are you going out to dinner with them?"

"I want to get to know them and, through them, Lloyd, a little better. We, I mean you, haven't found one good motive for murder yet. I'm just trying to find a reason to dislike him."

"Dillon told us he was gaga over you too. So far both he and Brenda have corroborated that fact."

"Dylan mentioned that to me. He and I hadn't spoken in years, Jodie. The typewriters were nostalgic to him, and took him back to when we were kids. I think I'd have heard from him if I was that important in his life. And in case you're wondering, I didn't kill him because he was stalking me or anything. If he had been, I would have just called you."

"I'm getting the same read."

"Want to go to dinner with us? Or want me to call you if I learn anything interesting?"

"No and no. I want you to call me no matter what. Memorize everything they say. Take notes if you can."

"That should be easy. It's a common courtesy to take notes while you're at dinner with people you don't know well."

"You know what I mean."

"Why don't you want to come?"

"I just can't," she said quietly. "I'm tailing my brother tonight, Clare. You're the only one who knows. Don't tell anyone, Seth included."

"By yourself?"

"I have no choice."

"Yes, you do. I can come with you."

"No, not tonight. I need to see if I can figure out what's going on with him and I don't want to worry about you."

"Jodie."

"Clare," she said. "Think about why I have to do this alone."

"Because you don't want any other cops to think your brother is up to no good, and because you don't want to put anyone else in harm's way, particularly me."

"Exactly. Call me after dinner. I'll have my phone off if I'm in a precarious position."

She clicked off before I could voice further protest. Brenda and Dillon exited the small building only a moment later. They both got into her car. She drove around and rolled down her window.

"Dinner now?"

"Perfect," I said as I thought about keeping my wet knees hidden under a table.

"Okay, we'll follow you," she said.

I knew just where to go.

19

I hadn't seen someone devour a pizza like Dillon did since I'd been in high school. Either he was starving or he was just a young man with a healthy need for lots of food.

I got him his own, topped with everything, and it was almost gone by the time Brenda and I each took a third piece of our vegetarian. I wasn't a shy eater, but I'd never be able to keep up with Dillon.

"What will happen to the company now?" I asked.

"It's in his will that the business continues. He was good about those things. Met with his attorney every few months or so just to make sure things were in order. He was worth too much not to take care of things."

"Who'll be in charge?" I asked.

"Her name is Dauphine Ritter," Brenda said.

"Really? I thought it would be you," I said.

"Right," she said as she looked at me. "That doesn't mean I killed him, though."

"I, uh, well, I didn't think that."

"It was just a couple of months ago I was taken out of the hierarchy," she said. "I was angry and hurt, but if you think about it logically, I would have waited until he put me back in the chain to want any harm to come to him."

"Brenda, I'm not accusing you of anything. I know you're stressed, and because of that you might say something you don't mean. You've thought about answers to questions that someone might ask, but not me."

She sighed deeply. "Yes, I am stressed, and I'm upset about Dauphine. I was the one who was to be in charge, but Lloyd got angry at me, so he made the change. He was spiteful like that sometimes."

"That's the first time I've heard that he was spiteful. Who else was he spiteful to?" I took a drink of soda, trying to remain casual.

"Oh, he was spiteful to everyone at some point or another," she said. "Even got mad at Dillon once, and it's difficult to be angry at Dillon."

I looked at Dillon.

"I was late for a delivery. I shouldn't have been late, and he called me the next day and told me to come back to work," Dillon said. "I always liked him, no matter."

"He was three minutes late," Brenda said.

"He fired you?" I said.

"Just told me to leave."

"He was a tyrant?" I said.

"No!" they said together.

"He was a good guy with a short fuse for imperfection," Brenda said. "His interpretation of perfection was important. And he was successful enough that he could behave any way he wanted to behave."

I disagreed, but now wasn't the time to say so.

"Who's Dauphine?" I said.

"His office manager," Dillon said. "She doesn't understand the company at all."

"Weren't you his right hand, left hand, everything? What did you do to make him angry?" I said to Brenda.

"There's too much of a history to put this in the proper context, but yes, I was actively involved."

I pushed my plate back a little. "We have all night."

She shook her head.

Dillon wiped his mouth with his napkin and then placed it on his plate. "Excuse me, I'll be back in a bit."

"That wasn't too obvious," Brenda said with a smile after he left the table. "He knows what happened, but he's a nice kid, wants to spare me my dignity."

"That bad?"

"It was pretty humiliating."

"Want to share? Let me rephrase. I'd really like to hear the story." I wished I could take notes.

"I need to share it with the police, Clare. I've thought about our dinner the other night and I know I wasn't up-front with your friend, Jodie, but my only excuse is that I was still in such a state of shock over Lloyd's death, no, his *murder*. It's so unreal. It's a terrible tragedy and Lloyd was more good than bad, but I should have been much more up front about the bad."

"I can call Jodie and ask her to come join us," I said.

"No, it's all right. I'll go talk to her or that other officer

tomorrow, but I'll tell you now. It started with a mis-
understanding about the typewriters he wanted you to have.
Well, those contraptions with the typewriters attached."

"Hoovens. They were part typewriter, considered the first
way to duplicate the same letter. Kind of the first computer."

"I do know that. Now, at least. At the time, I thought
the whole idea of going to an auction on a Sunday just to
buy the ridiculous-looking things was . . . well, ridiculous.
I'm afraid I was grumpy and Lloyd overheard me being
grumpy to Dauphine. I should not have done that; it was
very unprofessional. However, he took is so personally. He
thought I was calling *him* ridiculous and he was extrasen-
sitive to that sort of thing; well, sometimes. Sometimes he
had thick skin, but sometimes not. He was an unusual man,
but a very good one. Please don't think I'm trying to tarnish
his memory." Her eyes welled with tears and I could see a
pull of emotion at the corner of her mouth. "I'm sorry."

"You cared deeply for him," I said.

She sent me an impatient glare.

I clarified. "As a person, not romantically, though you
spent so much time together it would be easy to see something romantic develop. You shouldn't beat yourself up
for being human."

"You truly shouldn't mix business with pleasure, and
we didn't. But the way he handled moving the power of
the company to Dauphine was embarrassing, humiliating.
He announced it in a company meeting. You can imagine."

"Why did you keep working there?"

She pushed up her glasses. I had to force myself not
to mimic the move.

"Because before that he'd set me up to take over if
something happened to him and I thought he'd go back

to that plan. I thought maybe he'd even apologize and then put things back into place again. He didn't, or he died before he had the chance."

"You need to be brutally honest with Jodie about this. For what it's worth, I don't think you killed Lloyd, but what happened to you might help her find the real killer."

"The officer who was also listed on the invitation, Creighton, came to see me at my hotel last night. He was in civilian clothes, but he had a badge. I would only talk to him in the lobby. It was weird at first, but he seemed pretty competent and not after anything but information about Lloyd's company. I didn't tell him any more than I told your friend and you. Should I call him too?"

"Jodie will tell him," I said.

"So, who wants dessert?" Dillon asked as he slid into the booth next to Brenda. I caught their shared glance of understanding, but it was brief.

My suspicious mind wondered if maybe the entire thing had been scripted. Had Dillon's request for me to go with him to the cemetery been the beginning of an act they'd planned, something that culminated with . . . well, with what exactly?

No, I was working too hard to find someone guilty enough to have committed murder. For a moment I marveled at the police and their ability to be suspicious but not paranoid.

And then we ordered cheesecake all around.

≈

"This is crazy," I whispered. I was sunk down low in the passenger seat of a car Jodie had either rented, borrowed, or stolen. She hadn't given me a clear answer.

"Yeah, I know, but you said you wanted to join me."

I'd called her right after I got home. She was parked on Main Street, a few stores down from Bygone. Creighton had gone into the Rusted Barrel, one of our local drinking establishments, and Jodie was waiting for him to come back out. She said if I hurried down the hill from Little Blue, I could join her in the car and spy. However, I needed to get into the car without anyone noticing, including all the people walking up and down the street enjoying the Star City nightlife. Despite the fact that it had been Creighton himself who told me earlier today to stop spying on people, I didn't hesitate to set off down the hill. I'd been very sly and I didn't think anyone had seen me. The car windows were blacked out, so no one could notice how foolish we looked.

"I do want to be here, but this is still a little crazy. What's he been up to?" I said.

"Nothing much. He went home, changed clothes, went to the ATM, got some money, and came here."

"By himself?"

"Yeah, I don't know if he met anyone in there, but he didn't pick up his latest fling on the way."

"Maybe they met inside."

"When did Creighton ever meet you anywhere? He picked you up all the time."

"Not all the time, but if we were going out he'd pick me up. I was the one to initiate meeting places if that was going to happen." I stretched my neck and tried to look out farther. "You want me to go inside and see what's going on? Wait, what do you think is going on?"

"I can't be sure. Any locals inside know who he is. He's not attempting anything undercover. He couldn't pull that off in town."

"Maybe he just wanted a beer."

"When Creighton just wants a beer, what does he usually do?"

"Open his fridge."

"He's not social, but he made himself look nice and went to a bar."

"My crack detective skills tell me there's a girl in there he's trying to meet or get to know or something like that," I said.

"That's what I was thinking too, but it still doesn't fit."

"Why don't I just go in and pretend I'm looking for Seth? In fact, I bet I could call Seth and get him down here. He and Creighton seem to get along just fine."

"They do, don't they? That's weird, but for another conversation. Yeah, call Seth. . . . No, wait—is that Howard?"

Along with his wardrobe, Howard's persona had changed since high school. He moseyed up the hill with his cowboy hat in place. He looked so much like a cowboy that I imagined I could hear spurs on his boots jingle-jangling. He didn't resemble the preppy kid he'd once been.

"Call Seth," I said as I reached for the door handle. I wished that Nathan had called her to tell her what he'd overheard, but I doubted he had, and if I went into it now we might miss an opportunity. "Tell him to come meet us. Come in with him when he gets here."

I got out of the car before Jodie could speak, but she was reaching for her phone, so I took that as agreement with my sketchy plan.

"Howard, hi!" I said as I greeted him at the bar's doorway.

"Hey, Clare," he said without a smile.

"You going in?"

"I am."

"I'm supposed to meet my boyfriend and Jodie, but I'm early. Care for company?"

"Sure." He couldn't hide his hesitation, but he tried. I was probably cramping his style.

The bar was full with a typical Thursday night crowd of skiers and boarders who'd been on the slopes all day; some were still dressed in their ski gear. The air had been cold, but the sun had been bright over the past week, and even in the dim bar light I could spot a number of goggle burns.

Howard craned his neck as he looked around the narrow but deep space. His eyes landed on Creighton at the same time mine did.

"I'm meeting Creighton Wentworth," Howard said.

"We're friends," I said.

"Want to join us?"

"Sure," I said, ignoring his frown of disappointment and confidently pushing up my glasses.

He led the way to the small back table where Creighton waited.

"Hey, Clare," Creighton said with even more disappointment than I'd sensed from Howard.

"I ran into Howard on my way in. Hope you don't mind if I join you two. Seth and Jodie are on their way, but I don't want to get in *your* way, so let me know—"

"No, stay, of course," Creighton said. "I'm surprised Jodie's going out on a work night, but the more the merrier. What would you like?" He signaled a waitress over.

"Whatever you're having." I eyed his glass, still filled with some sort of dark beer.

"Really?" he said.

"Yeah."

"Well, that's a new twist. Clare drinking beer. Howard?"

Orders were placed and we fell into an uncomfortable silence. Well, uncomfortable for me and Howard; Creighton appeared somewhat amused, which irritated me. I wasn't sure why and I didn't like being the subject of his amusement.

"So," I said. "Were you guys just meeting tonight to catch up, talk about old times?"

"Creighton and I weren't friends in high school," Howard said.

"That's true," Creighton said as he took a sip of his beer.

I nodded, trying to hide the fact that I suddenly realized that Creighton had probably asked to meet Howard at the bar because he was investigating a murder and he was playing the same sort of game with Howard as he had done with Sarah. I'd gotten caught up in Jodie's escapades and suspicions.

"So, why, then?" I asked.

"I asked Howard to meet me here for a few reasons. Though we didn't know each other in high school, I wanted to get his take on why he and I would have been invited to the same meetings."

"I wish I knew," Howard said.

"No idea, then?" Creighton said. "Did we ever hang out back then? Did we ever do anything together?"

"Not that I can remember. You're older, Creighton, not part of my crowd." Howard laughed. "I remember we were kind of scared of you back then."

"Why?"

"Not only were you older and not part of our crowd, but your dad was a cop and your mom worked for the fire department. You've always been a big guy and, well, you were intimidating."

I noticed that I nodded involuntarily. Creighton looked at me over his beer.

"It's interesting that you're here, Clare," Creighton said.

"Why?"

"As I was thinking back—and it hasn't been all that easy, mind you—I had a memory. I wasn't going to bother you with that memory, but since you're here and all."

I nodded again, this time on purpose.

"Do you remember that dance we went to back when you were a senior and I'd been out of high school for a couple years?"

"We went to a couple of them."

"Right, but if you think back hard enough you might remember one that stands out from the others."

Creighton and I had gone to many things together as a couple. We'd started dating when I was a sophomore and he was a senior, and our high school was big on dances and socials and had exercised the control of having those events on campus, under the watchful (or attempted watchful) eye of parent and teacher chaperones.

"Oh! Are you talking about the one where your tires got slashed?" I said.

"That's the one."

It had been one of the smaller, more casual events, something Halloween-themed even though we were all too cool to wear costumes. I'd made the poor decision of volunteering to be on the decorating committee and I had to stay late and help clean up. Creighton had stayed and helped too. We were some of the last few people to leave the gymnasium, and had come upon Creighton's car with two of the four tires slashed.

"That was terrible," I said.

"It was," Creighton said. "Do you remember what happened after we noticed the tires?"

Again, I had to work my memory gears. "Yes! We heard voices from around the corner of the building and you ran after them."

"That's right. I never told you what I saw, though, because you were too upset by the words that had been written the car window. Remember? Someone had written 'she's too good for you' in bright red lipstick."

"I do remember that. We just thought it was some kids being stupid, taking advantage of your car being one of the last in the parking lot."

Bizarrely, the loud bar noises faded to the background and for a brief instant, I was back in that parking lot, laughing at something Creighton had said about the goofy decorations inside. I'd been a part of the goofiness, and I'd told him that they probably should have checked my artistic abilities before they let me be on the committee. But when we saw the tires and the lipsticked words, the mood changed. I got angry and scared, but Creighton just got angry. When we heard the voices, he took off after whoever was attached to them.

He'd come back a few minutes later and claimed not to have seen anyone. I did remember being upset by the words. They made me feel like I was being watched, and I didn't like that feeling at all.

"Right, but I did see something when I took off after the voices. I just didn't see enough to make me know for sure who I'd seen. I had some idea, though," Creighton said.

"Who?"

"Someone in a very preppy outfit, and that someone also had bright red hair."

We both looked at Howard.

He gave it a second before he laughed. "Well, you didn't see me, Creighton, I promise. Everyone knew your car and no one in their right mind would have slashed your tires. No, it wasn't me."

"Actually, I saw three people. The redheaded guy, another guy, and another girl who looked a lot like Sarah from the back."

Howard looked neither guilty nor impressed. "It wasn't us, Creighton. I think you might be grasping at vapory memories."

"Possibly," Creighton said as he set down his glass of beer.

I wondered the same thing. I also thought it was possible that Creighton had just made up the part about the details of the people he'd seen, just to see what Howard would do.

"However," Creighton said, "you had a thing for Clare, didn't you?"

If I wasn't sure about Howard telling the truth about not slashing the tires, I was sure now. Because he had zero skill for lying.

"No!" he said. That one word, void of anything resembling truth.

I didn't know what to say, but I wished I'd never joined Jodie in the car with the blacked-out windows.

"All right, okay, yes, but that was a long time ago. Besides, Clare, you knew," Howard said.

I didn't, but it seemed ridiculous to say that.

"Creighton, this was all a long time ago," I said.

"I know, but I wouldn't be surprised if that night, that event, had something to do with Lloyd's murder."

"How?" Howard said.

"I'm not sure."

"Look, Creighton, I didn't kill Lloyd. And, Clare, while I might have had a tiny crush on you in high school, none of any of that time has anything to do with my present-day life."

"I get that," I said.

"Okay, then what about your business, Howard? What happened to make it tank, or should I say sink, so badly?"

Creighton was hitting Howard with both barrels. I felt kind of bad for him, but I couldn't wait to hear the answer.

The straight line of Howard's mouth twitched at one corner.

"It hasn't tanked. We've run into some stumbling blocks. All businesses do. I don't know why it's any of *your* business," Howard said.

Creighton nodded slowly as he bit his bottom lip and gave his beer a thoughtful gaze. He looked up at Howard a brief moment later.

"You're trying to borrow money," Creighton said.

"How do you know . . . what business is that of yours?" Howard said.

"Well, your financials weren't really any of my business until yesterday when I looked very closely at them and then made some phone calls. From what I could gather, you've been asking for money from lots of people and places. Banks, friends, family."

"So?"

"I wonder if maybe you asked Lloyd for some help and maybe he didn't want to help you out."

"What? Creighton, I haven't thought about Lloyd for years, not until I got that stupid invitation to come back to this place—a place I don't relish returning to often." He paused as the waitress placed beers in front of me and him. This must have given him enough time to think about what he was doing. "Look, Creighton, it's easy to see where you intended to go with this, but I'm afraid I'm going to have to ask you to contact my attorney if you want to talk to me again."

He stood, turned, and left the bar.

"He didn't even try one sip," I said as I tried one myself. The beer was bitter but not terrible. "I'm sorry, I didn't even think about you questioning him. I should not have gotten in the way."

"It's okay. It was going to go how it went no matter what," he said. "I don't have anything to bring him in on and question him officially. We weren't friends in high school, so I was surprised he even agreed to come out and meet me. Sorry if that was uncomfortable."

"Uncomfortable? That was awesome," I said. "Did you really see a redhead, another guy, and a Sarah lookalike?"

"No. Well, the Sarah lookalike maybe, but not the others, and many girls had long brown hair, but I knew some of the other guys had crushes on you. It was just a police trick."

"I did not know about the other guys. I kind of wish I'd known."

Creighton laughed. "Anyway, you being here just moved things along a little more quickly, which isn't a bad thing."

"Obviously, you were trying to see if he was the killer."

"Always looking for the killer, Clare. I'm a cop. However, we're still trying to get the lay of the land so to speak. He didn't deny that he asked Lloyd for money. He kind of made it sound like he was denying it, but he wasn't. Not really. That might help us find a clue."

"You think he asked Lloyd for a loan?"

"Don't know, but it's something. Maybe." He bit his lip again and looked toward the front door. "Looks like Jodie and Seth are here." He swallowed the rest of his beer. "Good to see you, Clare. Have a nice evening."

"I'm kicking you out of your table."

"No, not at all. I have work to do." He dropped some money on the table and wove his way through the crowd, stalling only to greet Seth and Jodie.

"Hi," Seth said as he came to the table. "We scared your subject away."

He'd been working, probably reading. He wore his reading glasses, an old faded T-shirt, holey jeans, and flip-flops. His messy, curly hair was conducting a party of its own. It was cold outside, but he'd probably been in a zone when Jodie called and hadn't even thought about a coat. She'd probably made it sound like a dire emergency. I liked it when he got in a zone and had to be pulled back into the real world. One morning he almost went outside to get the mail in his underwear because the newspaper article he'd been reading had transported him to that "other place." I found the trait endearing and ridiculously attractive.

"You were looking for something?" Seth said as I

handed him my beer. He'd like it better than I did. He took a sip and raised his eyebrows in appreciation.

"Howard didn't touch that one." I nodded as I looked at Jodie.

"No, thanks," Jodie said. "We've lost him now."

"Sorry," I said.

"No, it's okay. Tell us what happened," she said as she sidled up onto a stool.

I told them what had transpired, and then I told them about my dinner with Brenda and Dillon. I finished by telling them what Nathan had overheard. He hadn't called her yet.

"Interesting," Jodie said when I'd finished.

"More than interesting?" I said.

"Everything helps. It's just that I don't think the meeting between Creighton and Howard did go the way Creighton hoped or planned it would. I'm sure he left something out because you were there."

"Really? Why?"

"Because, Claire, Creighton was invited to the meetings too. He knows more or suspects more than he's saying or would want you to know."

"Good point," I said.

"But this was great. Thanks for busting your way in with the two of them. Creighton would have just told me to go away. Speaking of which, I'm going to do that now. Gotta get the car back."

"Back to where?"

She smiled. "Just back. Talk to you tomorrow."

Once she was gone, Seth and I decided to turn the evening into a real date night. The best part was that neither of us mentioned the word "murder" once.

20

I balanced the tray of coffees on one hand and held a bag of pastries in the other. I used my elbow to push the tired-sounding buzzer and waited.

"Clare?" Adal said when he opened the door. After hesitating a beat too long, he said, "This is a lovely surprise."

"It is?"

"Of course. Come in," he said.

I felt like I'd been ignoring my apprentice. He could handle almost anything on his own, but he was still supposed to be learning stuff from me and we'd all been distracted the last few days. I decided to pick up breakfast for the shop and walk with him to work so, for a few minutes at least, just he and I could talk about things like restoring old books and repairing typewriters.

"Hello, Clare, long time, no see," a voice said from the

corner of the dark front room. Adal's apartment was small, a few rooms on the backside of a Main Street business. He'd decorated it in what I called sparse charming. He was neat and tidy to levels I could never aspire to reach, but I chalked that up to the fact that he hadn't wanted to clutter his temporary American home.

I recognized the voice. "Hey, Jodie. Sorry, guys. I didn't think . . ."

"It's okay, we're still keeping things quiet for the general public, but we know you know," Jodie said as she stood.

It was all I could do not to gasp. She looked so girly in the robe and with her hair free of its tight ponytail. I wanted to hug her and check her fingernails for polish. Instead I tried hard to hide a smile. "Won't tell a soul. Where's your Bronco?"

"Around the corner."

"You got the car back to where it belongs?"

"Yep, no problem." She looked at the tray. "One of those for me?"

"Definitely."

She took a cup, gave me a shy smile, and then turned and walked toward the back rooms I'd never seen. She stopped in front of Adal.

"I'll see myself out when I'm ready," she said. "Go ahead and go with Clare."

I should have looked away, but I was fascinated by their brief embrace and the way they made a quick kiss look like something bursting with passion. I sighed noisily. It was good to see her in the middle of something I didn't even think she really wanted, or at least wanted to the level I was witnessing.

Jodie looked at me and laughed. "Clare."

Adal pretended to be embarrassed, but he wasn't.

When he and I were out of the apartment, he took the tray of remaining coffees.

"We don't have to talk about that if you don't want to," I said.

"Good," he said, his German accent extrastrong.

"But one quick question. Have you thought about the fact that you don't have plans to stay here forever?"

"Jodie and I don't think about forever. Our moments are too full to pay attention to more than one at a time."

"While that is potentially the most romantic thing I might ever have heard, you have given it some thought and maybe a conversation or two?"

Adal laughed. "Yes."

"Good. Then enjoy the moments while you can."

"We will."

So much for time talking about repairing books and typewriters. We unlocked the front door of the shop and were greeted by Chester and Baskerville coming from the other direction. Chester was turning on lights and straightening counters.

"Nathan will be here in about an hour," Chester said. "But you have an emergency repair in the back first and we have Lloyd's service this afternoon."

"A typewriter emergency?" I said.

"Yes, we have a high school student in town who is writing a paper using only his parents' old typewriter. It's a deal he made with his teacher or something. Anyway, the carriage lock will not come unlocked. They just left, so I haven't had a chance to look at it myself. His parents aren't pleased with him for waiting until their vacation to finish his paper, but I assured them that their child was no lazier than any other high school student. The young man said you would be on the same plane as Wonder Woman, or maybe that was Catwoman, I don't know, if you got it fixed and ready to type again."

"Come on, Adal," I said. "I bet you can handle this one."

After a tired greeting from Baskerville and a coffee handoff to Chester, we hurried back to the workshop.

The Olympia SM3, with its camouflage green case, always reminded me of a sturdy military machine. The carriage and the keys could be locked in place with a small lever on the top left side of the keyboard. Adal and I both tried to move the lever, but to no avail. The machine was locked, old-time talk for modern technology's "frozen." However, everything is connected in one way or another with these old machines, so we set out to follow the trail. We lifted the case lid and peered inside. It looked like the small mechanical pieces were in place.

The last step was to turn the machine over and look at the small piece that was actually the lock, the thing that kept everything from moving when it was in the locked position.

"I think we found the problem," Adal said.

"I believe so," I said.

I reached to the shelves, grabbed some long-nosed pliers, and handed them to Adal. "Would you like to do the honors?"

"Thank you," he said.

With the pliers, he pulled on the small piece of plastic that had become wedged under the lock. It took a tug or two to remove it, but once it was out, the machine worked fine.

It looked like we were destined for superhero status.

"It was just a random piece of plastic stuck in there," I said when Chester poked his head in. "It's fixed. We can't even charge for this one."

"Excellent! I just saw Nathan park out front. He'll be right in, I'm sure."

We hurried out to greet him. Even Baskerville hadn't climbed up to his shelf yet. The cat hurried to the door when he must have sensed his new friend would be inside soon.

"I have returned with a new rental car and everything!" Nathan said when he came through the door. Baskerville let him pick him up, but demanded to be put down after a brief greeting. The cat liked the author, but enough was enough.

"You look very good," I said.

"Thank you. No worse for wear. Well, tired a little, but the doctors cleared me and told me to return to as normal a life as I was living before, so here I am."

"I always knew you'd be fine," Chester said.

Even Baskerville didn't buy that one. The cat sent Chester a tail twitch before heading up to the warmth from the rising sun.

It was good to get back to work. The Hoovens loomed along one wall, making me think of the upcoming service for Lloyd every few minutes or so, but Nathan was in good shape and tons more polite and patient than he'd been before what could have been another terrible tragedy. We opened the new box of type, happy to find it in spectacular shape, and as close to being Bridgnorth as could be, and started putting together the first printing plate for one of Nathan's poems, titled "Hearts Away."

It was a sweet poem, only sixteen lines, but when each

letter is placed one at a time into the plate, sixteen lines can be hours of work. And when all three of the people, four if you included Chester's intermittent comments and suggestions, were perfectionists, more time had to be added in.

But no one became impatient with anyone along the way. It wouldn't last, of course, but for now, perspectives had changed, and little quirks were more appealing than annoying.

Nathan had written thirty-six poems for the book and he only wanted to print on one side of each page, making the facing pages a place for people to write their own poems or sketch something the facing poem might have inspired. It was going to be a lovely book, particularly when we (he—he wanted to do this by himself, but we offered to help) bound each copy with the plain red hardboard he'd chosen.

"Aunt Clare," Marion said as she stuck her head through the doorway between the workshop and the retail area. "There's a lady with a book here to see you."

"Okay." I took off my work apron, hung it on a hook beside the doorway, sent one last glance toward Adal and Nathan, who were deep into setting up the next press plate, and then went through to the front.

"Sarah, hi," I said. "Marion, this is an old high school classmate of mine, and she owns the new bookshop up the hill. Starry Night Books. Sarah Senot."

Sarah nodded toward Marion, but they didn't shake hands. Sarah held a bag tight to her chest, and her eyes were wide and a tiny bit crazy.

"Everything okay?" I said.

"Sure, I'm . . . well, someone brought this into the shop

today. It was in the bottom of a box of other books. The second I saw it I tried to call the woman who'd brought it in, but no luck, so I came here right away."

"What is it?"

Gingerly, Sarah placed the bag on the counter. "Will you move all the rest of this stuff?" she said to Marion.

I nodded when Marion looked at me for approval, though I wasn't sure I liked Sarah's tone. We'd see how it went.

Stacks of brochures, a cup full of pencils, and some business cards were dispatched to the lower shelves, clearing the counter for the mystery item.

"This is going to curl your hair," Sarah said.

Marion laughed, but put her hand up to her mouth and then took a step backward. Sarah blinked at her.

"Well, more than it already is, I guess," Sarah said. "I know you guys know things about books. You're the first person I thought I should show this to, Clare."

Slowly, she unfolded the top of the bag and then reached inside. With all the drama that her wide eyes promised, she pulled out a book.

"*Carrie*!" Marion said.

"Not just *Carrie*, but in pristine condition, I see," I said. "May I?"

"Sure. Just be careful. Look on the title page, though," Sarah said.

I'd been to this rodeo before. I knew how to be careful with an old valuable book, but I gave her a conciliatory smile.

I lifted the cover and found the title page. "It's signed."

"Yes, and look at the dust jacket," Sarah said. "This book is perfection."

I checked the print run. "First edition, signed copy in perfect condition. This *is* amazing," I said. "You found a good one."

"No, not found. It was given to me. I don't know what to do with it," she said.

"I think trying to get ahold of the person who dropped off the box of books was the right thing to do."

"They didn't give me a valid number, or they didn't write it down correctly. It's not a working number," Sarah said.

"Well, maybe just keep the book safe for a while in case you hear from them again."

The door to the workshop opened and Nathan stepped through.

Sarah gasped and put her hand over her mouth, similar to what Marion had done a moment ago. We all looked at her.

"I'm sorry," she said. "I knew he'd been found, but I didn't know he was here."

"Oh yes," I said.

"It's okay." She smiled and tried to be casual. She looked at Nathan. "I'm such a fan. I think I'm more surprised that you're here, right in front of me, than the fact that I knew you were okay. Wait, that sounds terrible. I'm glad you're okay . . . but, well, I guess I'm a fan."

"Thank you," Nathan said as he spied the book on the counter and moved toward it with quick, long steps. "Oh my."

"I know—isn't it something?" Sarah said as she moved next to him, closer than most people would move next to someone they didn't know well, maybe even a friend.

Nathan bristled and took a step away from her. Sarah wasn't deterred and she stepped right back toward him.

"It is an amazing book," Nathan said. His eyebrows came together as he frowned down at Sarah. He was only slightly taller than her, but he'd puffed out, like an animal sensing a predator. He looked at me. "Excuse me for interrupting. Just when you have a minute, we have a question."

"I'll be right there," I said to his retreating figure.

"I can't believe I just talked to him," Sarah said. "I can't believe we just breathed the same air."

I understood starstruck behavior, but since I'd come to know Nathan on such a human level, it seemed weird.

"I'm sorry about his face. The cut, but he doesn't look like he was hurt any worse," Sarah said.

"He's okay," I said. "Really fine."

"Unbelievable." She blinked back toward the book. "Now, what do you think this is worth?"

I shrugged. "I'm not sure without doing a little research first, but I would guess at least a few thousand."

"Oh my goodness." She took a deep breath. "Clare, may I leave it with you?"

"Why?"

"You've seen my place. It's a disaster piled upon another disaster. You are used to these sorts of valuable books. You would take better care of it. Just temporarily."

"Well, okay, I suppose," I said. Even before I finished responding, I regretted my answer. I should not take care of someone else's valuable property. It wasn't even clear whose property it was, but it most certainly wasn't mine. Between worrying about the Hoovens and now the book, I doubted I'd ever sleep a worry-free night again.

"Here," Marion said as she gathered some papers and a pen from under the counter. "You can document it like a consignment, just keep the price too high to sell."

I was often impressed by my niece's quick smarts. She'd seen the need for at least a paper trail of ownership, or at least something that Sarah signed that kept The Rescued Word safe from any damages the book might incur while being here. I hoped for no damages.

"Oh. Well, okay, but I don't want you to sell it," Sarah said as Marion scooted the papers toward Sarah.

"We won't," I said.

She signed with a flurried signature that could be interpreted as just about anything, and then I signed and set the pen on the counter.

"All right, then. Thank you," she said almost breathlessly.

Marion and I looked at each other as Sarah turned and hurried out of the shop. However, she made one brief stop at a shelf of note cards.

"These are the prettiest things," she said.

"Thanks. Marion can personalize some for you if you'd like."

"Good to know. Thanks!" she said before she resumed her quick scissor steps out the door.

"She's nuts," Marion said.

"Well, she certainly seemed a little off today, but maybe she has a lot on her mind. Who knows what anyone's going through? And she got to talk to Nathan. Remember when you met all the movie stars during the film festival? You were a little nuts then too."

"No, I was way nuts. Do you want me to lock the book under here?" she asked as she peered at the small safelike compartment under the counter. Chester had recently put a new lock on it.

"Yes, please."

She put the book back inside the bag, carefully folded over the flap, and gently deposited the whole thing into the cubbyhole. She locked the door and slipped the key into a side slot, the spot only those of us at The Rescued Word knew about, though I didn't think we'd shown Adal.

"All clear?" Chester asked as he stuck his head through the doorway.

"All clear," I said.

"Nathan said you had one of his rabid fans out here."

"Sarah Senot," I said. "We now have her ridiculously valuable book held in our safe. We're not to sell it."

"Nathan mentioned the book. We'll not sell it, if that's what she wants. You and I have a funeral to attend. Nathan and Adal will continue to work on Nathan's book. Marion, just let Adal know if you need any help up here." He looked at me.

"Right," I said, sadness filling my chest. "Let's go say our good-byes to Lloyd."

Chester sent me a sad smile. "I'll drive, dear girl."

21

Late winter and early spring in Star City meant complete weather unpredictability. We might have a snowstorm in the morning that dusted blooming tulips and daffodils with snow and then cleared off the flowers by noon. Rarely did the spring snow help with the base on the slopes. Sometimes, when the blazing sun followed the snow, the runs got slippery, sometimes icy—spring snow wasn't typically some of our magical Utah powder. But sometimes we got a doozy spring storm that allowed the resorts to stay open a little longer and skiers and boarders got to hang out on the mountain as far as into the middle of the year. The latest date of skiing I remembered was June 15, but that was a very rare year.

As I looked up into the clear blue sky, slipped off my sweater, and wished I'd either put on my prescription sunglasses or gotten some of those Transitions lenses, I thought all signs pointed to a shortened season this year.

I didn't remember that Lloyd was a skier, but that was where he'd been when he was killed, skiing. I wondered if he would have preferred snow falling instead of the spectacular day we were having, but I decided that no one could be unhappy with this perfection.

I knew or recognized about half of the attendees. Brenda, Dillon, and Lloyd's parents huddled together. I expressed my sympathies again, but it had been tough. Lloyd's dad had once again remembered that junior high dance. I'd hugged them both and told them how sorry I was.

Jodie, her partner, Omar, Creighton, and his partner, Kelly, were also there, all of them in their dress uniforms, and none of them behaving as if they were searching the crowd for a killer, though I knew they were.

I was too. It was impossible not to speculate.

Howard was there, though he kept a good distance away from those of us he'd gone to high school with. I didn't see him talking to Lloyd's parents, but Chester and I arrived after he did, so I couldn't be sure he hadn't done so already.

Neither Donte nor Sarah showed up, which surprised me. I'd thought that maybe Sarah had hurried out of The Rescued Word because she needed to get ready for the funeral.

There were about twenty other attendees, but I didn't know any of them. In fact, only one of them looked familiar, as if maybe he was a local business owner, but I couldn't place which business.

I nudged Chester. "If you recognize anyone, memorize names so you can tell me later."

"Are we searching for a killer?" he whispered.

"It wouldn't hurt to pay attention."

He nodded, brushed his mustache with the back of his knuckle, and then surreptitiously scanned the crowd.

The service was brief, and sweet, and emotional. Funerals were tough even if you didn't know the person who was being dispatched. However, there was one moment that stood out to me more than the rest of them.

Lloyd and his family were Mormon, so I assumed the man presiding over the service was their ward's bishop. In the Mormon Church, the bishop is someone who lives in the neighborhood and is already a part of their house of worship, their ward. I wasn't in the know regarding most of the religion, but I knew that the bishop wasn't a position of employment, but a position in the church that required many hours of devotion—mostly to the other people in the ward—and I thought each bishop served in the position for two years.

I didn't think the current bishop would know the man Lloyd had become before he died. Lloyd had left Star City for college and had stayed away. Or so I thought. But the man giving the service seemed to know Lloyd very well, mentioning moments they'd shared over the recent years.

The bishop said that Lloyd had been a good man with a big heart, someone who'd worked hard for his accomplishments and had never forgotten his parents or where he'd come from. In fact, he'd visited Star City often.

I wondered what "often" meant and if the bishop was just trying to make him sound like a great guy. Chester called post-death accolades the Funeral Treatment. I sent him a sideways glance to see if he was sensing the Funeral

Treatment or if he thought the words were genuine. His face was neutral.

"That was lovely," Chester said after the words and a prayer were spoken.

"I need a minute," I said. "Can I meet you at the car or maybe you could talk to Jodie and Creighton a minute?"

"I'll find a way to pass the time. What are you going to do?"

"I want to talk to that guy." I nodded toward the bishop, who was now stepping over the grounds toward the parking lot.

"Oh," Chester said as his eyes followed him. "He's a Nelson if I remember correctly, but I can't place his first name."

"Thanks," I said as I took off in pursuit.

I stepped around graves and tombstones. Years ago Chester had told me I should never step on a grave if I could help it, so I did my best to stay on the perimeters.

"Mr. Nelson," I said as I waved.

"Yes?" he said as he looked over his open driver's-side door.

"Yes, hi," I said as I joined him and extended my hand. "I'm Clare Henry. I went to high school with Lloyd."

"Ah, Clare. I know your family. Your grandfather's a delight even if my father couldn't convince him to convert."

"Chester's not all that religious, but he's pretty spiritual."

Mr. Nelson laughed. "Oh, we know. I believe he's offered my father a beer or two at a number of events over the years. Dad's always declined."

I smiled. "Sounds like Chester."

"What can I do for you?"

"I went to high school with Lloyd, and I heard your kind words about him."

"He was a good man."

"I believe that. I haven't seen him since high school, though, and I wondered . . . well . . ."

Mr. Nelson squinted at me a moment, but then clarity brightened his features. "You're wondering if he really was a good guy or if I was just giving lip service to the man who'd died."

"Yes." I nodded.

"I knew him very well, Clare. He did come visit his parents often. He was an only child, you know."

"I did know that."

"Well, whenever he visited, he came to Sunday services and always asked what he could do while he was in town to help someone else. Did someone need some work done on their home, did someone need some help with groceries, many different things. He was a genuinely good man, I promise. In fact, he didn't have a bad bone in his body as far I knew. His parents didn't want me to share all those details, said that Lloyd wouldn't have wanted that sort of recognition. They just wanted a nice service."

"Was he . . . well, was he especially intense? Do you know what I mean?"

"I think I do, and I'd have to say that yes, he was a perfectionist, but when it came to doing good works, he could mellow and be less wound up maybe."

"Do you think he might have ever wanted to rub others' noses in his success?"

"No, never. I believe he was humble to the end." Mr. Nelson's (I didn't ask for his first name and he didn't offer it) mouth formed a hard line. "He might not have wanted his fellow ward members to see that side of him, though, if it did exist. When we're of my age and experience, we're already pretty aware of the world, Clare. We know everyone has good sides and bad sides, but if that sort of bad side was a part of Lloyd, I never saw even a hint of it. If it existed, he hid it well."

I nodded. "I see. Thank you. It was a lovely service."

"Thank you. Give your family my best, particularly Chester. And tell him I still don't believe the story he told me about the bear he tamed."

"Ah, that one."

"Yes, he told it to me when I was a kid." Mr. Nelson whistled. "He certainly got my imagination to spin in full speed on that one."

"He does that well."

"Have a nice day, Clare," he said before he got into his car and shut the door.

I watched him drive away.

"Well, what did your investigative skills tell you?" Jodie said as she came up behind me.

"Hi, Jodie. I don't think Lloyd sent those invitations. I don't think he put the meetings together, at least not so he could rub everyone else's face in his success."

"The bishop tell you Lloyd wasn't that kind of guy?"

"Yes."

"I would tend to believe him, based on the Lloyd we used to know."

"Me too. But who sent those invitations, and why?"

"We're working on it," Jodie said as she rubbed her chin, all hints of the early-morning girlishness I'd seen now completely gone.

"I hope so," I said. "I really hope so."

22

"Where are we going?" Chester asked.

"We're going to go talk to Donte Senot again. I went with Jodie last time, but it'll just be you and me this time."

"What are we going to talk to him about?"

"His failing business."

"That should be an easy conversation."

"He admires you."

"Ah, I see. I'm your grease for the squeaky wheel."

"Yes."

Chester laughed. "All right, I can do that." He switched the radio to a big band station.

"You know his family, don't you?" I asked as I turned down the radio a little bit.

"Sure. Hardworking folks. I knew Donte when he was a kid because he had some interest in printing, and I seem to remember you and he were friends for a brief time in high school. At least he came into the shop a time or two to see you."

"I don't think that was Donte," I said.

"Sure it was. He and a couple of other people came into see you. I can't remember who they were, but since I knew Donte's family, I knew who he was."

"High school was just over ten years ago, and I don't remember that at all. I don't think Donte and I were ever friends."

"Well, you were so smitten with Creighton that you might not have noticed the others who were smitten with you."

"Chester, I don't think that's correct."

Chester shrugged.

As I steered through a couple of curves toward the bottom of the canyon, I thought back hard to that time but still could not place those moments. I did not remember thinking or knowing anything about Howard or Donte and their feelings for me. It was high school. Maybe I just didn't notice or care what anyone else thought of me, but that's a rare high school attitude. I had Creighton, and in that stupid high school way, my boyfriend was my everything.

"What about Sarah Senot? Her name was McMasters back then. Did I know her?" I asked.

"I don't remember you knowing her, but I remember Sarah when she was younger. She came into the store all the time. She liked to write letters. She liked our pens and paper, and she was one of our first note card customers. When Nathan came back to tell me about the woman in the store who was behaving oddly, I was surprised. She might not have been a friendly girl, but she wasn't odd."

"I don't remember that either."

"So much was going on during that time in your life and everything was moving so quickly. I can see how you'd forget things. It happens."

"Huh. I'm not sure it's supposed to happen this quickly. Maybe in thirty or forty years, but not just over ten."

Chester laughed. "As you get older, my dear, you'll find you start to remember the strangest things, many of them from when you were young. I often think of our memory banks as really long tapes, and at some point the tape has to circle back around. You'll see. And you're as sharp as a katana. You'll be fine."

I looked over at him briefly, but put my eyes back on the road so I could maneuver us through the freeway's spaghetti bowl.

"That's a sword, right?" I said. "A katana?"

"See, you haven't lost a thing."

I laughed, but this sort of memory block or loss was a new experience for me. I wasn't necessarily worried, but I made a mental note to pay better attention. Of course, now I just needed to remember the mental note.

Donte's receptionist was MIA again, and when Chester sent a "yoo-hoo" down the hallway, we were greeted with only silence.

"I think I hear a press running," I said as I bent my ear toward the back.

"Let's go see," Chester said as he led the way down the hall.

I peered inside Donte's office as we passed by, finding it empty and seemingly unvisited today. The lights were off and there was a sense that the computer keyboard was still resting from the night before. The desktop was too organized.

"Hang on," I said.

Chester stopped and looked back at me.

"Maybe we're not welcome back there," I said.

Chester's eyebrows rose. "We'll ask for forgiveness."

"All right," I said, though I felt a distinct discomfort niggling in my gut.

Chester pushed open the door and we were greeted by the mechanical whish-whish of the printing press.

"Donte?" His voice carried through the space, but the only answer came from the noisy press.

"There was no one in here last time either, but the press wasn't running," I said.

"I bet there's someone on its other side. Can't hear me probably," Chester said.

We set off at a brisk pace. Whatever niggling had gotten under my skin seemed to have spread to Chester's too. I knew this quick walk; it only happened when he was in a rush to find out why he thought something was wrong.

I had a sense that we looked like the Flintstone characters bringing their foot-powered vehicles to a halt as we came around the press. We stopped and slid and maybe went backward a little too.

"Donte!" I said before I regained movement in my limbs and took off toward the man on the floor.

"Clare!" Chester said as he grabbed my arm so tightly that I slid again, and just barely stopped myself from falling.

I looked at Chester.

"Let me," he said sternly. "Stay here."

My hands went over my mouth, and my eyes went wide as I tried to understand the scene before me. I couldn't possibly be seeing a dead man, one who'd been stabbed with something I didn't even recognize but looked like some sort of handle.

"Call 911, Clare," Chester said when he was sure I was listening.

Chester moved much more carefully than I think I would have. He stepped around the body and a pool of blood to get to a spot where he could lean over and check for a pulse. He bit his bottom lip as he must have gotten confirmation that Donte was in the state he looked to be in. Dead.

Chester stood and came back to me. I found my phone and hit 911. He took the phone out of my hand as someone answered. In a much calmer voice than I'm sure I would have managed, he told them what we'd found.

"Will do," he said before he ended the call. "Come on, Clare, let's go sit down."

Chester and I had come upon a dead body once before. Twice felt extremely unlucky and a trend we needed to exorcise as soon as possible. However, the first body hadn't belonged to someone I'd known, someone I'd gone to high school with, someone I'd recently had a friendly conversation with.

Donte Senot was dead. Had been killed; the second murder of one of my classmates in less than a week's time. This was not the stuff of successful reunions.

❧

Jodie, Omar, and Kelly joined the contingent of Salt Lake City Police officers and detectives who'd arrived on scene only a few moments after the call.

It had been a flurry of uniforms, suits, and people with questions. I couldn't pay much attention to the questions, so I wasn't sure of my answers, but no one threw handcuffs on me. When Jodie asked me if I was okay, I said that I was okay, but I wasn't.

It took two cups of water that Chester gathered for me and a good hour to feel like I was almost back on an even keel. And when I did feel like I fit into my skin again, I became angry and curious.

I stood up from the bench I'd been sitting on as Jodie reentered the building through the front doors. I merged with her heavy, fast footfalls as she cruised down the hallway.

"What do you know?" I said.

"That Donte Senot was murdered and you and Chester came upon his body," she said, more reluctantly than I would have liked.

"Any clues?"

"The police have just started gathering the clues, Clare," she said. "This won't be our case. Not our jurisdiction. They're letting us stick around because everyone's pretty sure this murder is somehow tied to Lloyd's. Listen, I have to get back into the press room. We'll talk later, I'm sure. I'm sorry you had to see him that way."

I nodded. We'd made it to the pressroom door and she had her hand on the knob.

"Is Sarah okay? She wasn't at the funeral either," I said.

Jodie understood my somewhat random comment. Since we hadn't seen either Donte or Sarah, it was normal to feel concern for her.

"We know she's fine. Well, distraught, of course, but not hurt."

I nodded. "All right. I'll wait for you out front."

"No, you and Chester are going to be dismissed soon. You need to go home. I'll call you when I'm done here."

"Promise? You don't always do that when you say you will."

"I know. How about I'll call you if I'm not too busy? It might be a long night."

I nodded again. "Where's Creighton?"

She looked back down the hallway with a concerned frown, and lowered her voice. "He's being detained in Star City. He and Harold. It's the way it had to be handled."

"Oh. Of course, that makes sense. Please call me if you can."

"I will. I have to get in there, and you absolutely cannot come inside. You understand that, don't you?"

"Yes."

"Go back out front and wait for someone to tell you to go home."

"I will."

Jodie waited by the door as I retreated toward the front of the building. I was less freaked out, but it still felt like my limbs weren't attached appropriately, like they were way too fluid; they'd fall off if I didn't hold on to them tight enough.

"Clare, you okay?" Kelly, Creighton's partner, was exiting Donte's office.

"Yeah, I'm okay," I said as I peered over his shoulder and then at the bag he held. It was a plastic ziplock type of bag, but he held it so his hand covered up anything that might be inside it.

"Did you find anything that might help?" I said.

"I'm not sure. We'll see. We'll catch a clue soon. We always do."

I silently agreed with his statement and swallowed the mean words I wanted to say that had to do with the fact that they might want to hurry it along before someone else got killed. I knew the Star City Police weren't dragging their feet, but it was difficult not to feel outrage at the murders, and then project that outrage in their direction. Maybe now that the Salt Lake City Police were involved, things might go better. I kept that thought to myself too.

"I hope so," I said before I continued down the hall. But I stopped and turned again. "Creighton upset?"

Kelly's eyebrows rose. He might have thought I was concerned about Creighton's welfare. I wasn't; I just wanted to know his reaction to being "detained."

"Yes, he's upset. He wants to work the case, of course," Kelly said.

"But he's under suspicion now?"

Kelly's eyes slanted. "Excuse me, Clare, but I have to get back to work."

"Sure," I said as he went back into the office.

"Ms. Henry," an officer said as he approached. "You can't be back here, and we've told your grandfather that the two of you are free to go."

"Got it," I said as we passed each other. He made sure I didn't turn around in the other direction again.

"There you are!" Chester said with too much relief when I was back in the reception area.

"I'm sorry. I didn't mean to worry you. Let's go home, Chester."

"Yes, right away," he said. "Let's get out of here."

23

We escaped the crowded freeways of the valley and made it back up the canyon to Star City in one piece, despite my heavy foot on the accelerator. I was feeling an urgent need to get home and escape the horrors of the big city.

I debated going inside The Rescued Word with Chester to check on Adal and Nathan, and sharing the terrible news together, but Chester somehow convinced me that it would be better for him to do it alone. I dropped him off outside and texted Seth to see if he could meet me somewhere. If he couldn't get away from work, I was going to go to his office.

He had a small office down the hill and amid a Star City retail district that included a few chain restaurants and a grocery store. But Seth spent most of his time out in the field, and much of his fieldwork took him to southern Utah, so I was glad he was currently in town. I didn't wait for his answer to my text but drove directly to the office.

He responded just as I got out of the car. Just in the office. Come on over. I'll buy dinner.

"Uh-oh," he said as he removed a magnifying head-piece that had been awkwardly plopped on his head, and placed a sparkly rock on the desk. "What happened?"

I closed the door and told him.

"Clare, that's absolutely terrible," he said when I'd finished. "I'm so sorry you had to see that, and I'm sorry about your classmate."

I nodded. "I wish the police knew what was going on."

"They will."

"I hope soon."

"Me too. I'm trying to understand more of the dynamics here. Did you say you and Donte were or weren't friends in high school?" Seth asked. "What about his wife? The séance was strange, but I got a definite impression that they made a good team, if you know what I mean. Were you friends with Sarah?"

"I know what you mean. Honestly, I don't remember much about Donte, or any of them, from high school, but Chester seems to think we were sort of friends at one time. He remembers Donte, at least, coming into The Rescued Word to see me. I don't remember that at all."

"Chester's got a pretty good memory," Seth said.

"He does, but it's been just over ten years for me. I should remember too."

Seth shrugged. "Weird things are important to us when we're young. We only hold on to a few moments, prob-ably either the really good ones or the really bad ones."

"Yeah . . ."

"What?"

"I just had a thought. Want to help me do a little research?"

"I'm always up for research, the more tedious, the better."

I laughed, though it felt inappropriate. Seth sent me a supportive smile.

"It's going to be okay," he said.

"I know."

"So, what are we going to research?"

"Some high school yearbooks."

"Let's go," he said as he stood. "I can't wait to see what you looked like back then."

"Dinner first, though?" I said.

Seth smiled. "Definitely."

We headed out, but I had second thoughts about taking the time to eat, so we picked up garlic burgers from O'Malley's, where we had our first date. Even though I'd been terribly distracted at the time and I made for a horrible date (I gave myself a C-, though Seth claimed it was no lower than a B), we'd managed to still be together, so our memories of O'Malley's were now fond, though still punctuated by the owner's disapproving glares when we went into the bar together. Orin O'Malley thought I'd be better suited to one of his reformed (I think only one had reformed) felonious sons than to the new geologist in town. I had to keep proving to him that Seth and I hadn't broken up quite yet.

Armed with delicious garlicky-smelling bags, we made it up the hill and into Little Blue. Soon, we were poring over my high school yearbooks as we tried to keep greasy smudges from the food at a minimum.

"You were adorable," Seth said as he looked at my sophomore picture.

"You have to say that," I said. "I wasn't. Look at that hair. Oh my, why did it take so long for me to figure out hair conditioner? And I could have chosen better glasses. You know why I'm not smiling?"

"No."

"Braces. Big ones. I think I got them off the week after the picture was taken. Oh yeah, I remember that now. Jimmy thought it was the funniest thing. The orthodontist would not take them off early. It was traumatic."

"See what I mean? We only remember those sorts of things when prompted. You look like Marion. Or Marion looks like you."

"She's the athletic 'after' version. I'm the nonathletic 'before' version. I skied, but I wasn't athletic. She works out. I always enjoyed O'Malley's garlic burgers."

"Still, you two look lots alike."

"I'll take that as a compliment. There's no one I'd rather share my high school phase with than you."

"I'm honored."

"How about your high school days?" I asked as I caught some ketchup before it fell off a fry and landed on the marching band's picture.

"Well, I was good at math and science and baseball, and even then I was fascinated by rocks. I bet you can imagine how popular and dashing I was."

"I bet you were cute."

"Not any typical cute, mind you, but the nerdiest kind of cute."

"That's the best kind."

We smiled at each other for a couple of beats. I hadn't

known such an easy relationship before. We were friends and found each other ridiculously attractive. It was as if we'd found this new secret place to inhabit together.

Seth cleared his throat. "Back to work?"

"Right."

He turned back to the yearbook on the table in front of him. "Okay, to me it looks like Howard and Donte were friends this year. They're in a few random pictures together. Things like the homecoming game and a track meet."

"I remember them being friends, I think."

"Lloyd's not even in this book at all," Seth said.

"Not even in the individual class picture?"

"Not that I saw. Gavin, right?"

"Yeah."

I scooted closer and thumbed to the page where his picture should be. No Lloyd Gavin.

"Not pictured," I quoted from the small print at the bottom of the page. "Lloyd Gavin. I remember that he was in Chess Club. Nothing?"

Seth turned back to the name index; Lloyd's name wasn't there either. Or on the Chess Club page.

"He certainly avoided cameras," I said. "Even if you're just rolling along through high school, there were yearbook people snapping pictures at everything. I'm even in there a few times."

"You are. Three pictures. Your class picture, and one of you and Jodie." He turned to that page.

"Oh my," I said.

The photo captured two young women who hadn't grown into the women part yet. For whatever reason we both thought that we should salute the camera with small milk cartons after we'd both given ourselves milk mustaches.

Seth smiled. "Can't wait to show you some of mine."

"Where's my third picture?" I said.

Seth smiled again. "You don't remember, do you?"

"No." I shook my head. "Is it that bad?"

Seth turned to the page he'd held with his thumb. I'd forgotten my tiny step into the world of theater. I'd been Juliet for a classroom production of a scene from *Romeo and Juliet*.

"Oh," I said.

"You and Marion, almost twins," he said.

"Well, this one was after the braces came off." And someone had smoothed my hair back into a braid and put pretty girlie clothes on me. "You know what? I just remembered that it was Sarah who helped me with my hair and the dress. She and I had nothing in common, but I remember how sweet she was." I laughed. "Well, I remember how stunned she was that I wasn't going to do 'something with my hair,' so she jumped in and took over, but in a very nice way."

My voice trailed off and I felt my eyes squint. Other than her friendly helpfulness, something else had happened that day, something I thought had given me an unpleasant jolt of sorts. I couldn't remember all the pieces except that Sarah had been involved. It couldn't possibly have been something important to the murders, but a nagging in my gut told me to think hard to remember it.

"What?" Seth said a second later.

"Sarah was kind to me that day, but something tells me she and I didn't get along perfectly." I bit my lip and then shrugged. "She probably wanted me to wear makeup or some such thing that I frowned upon back in those days. As you can see, I got over that hang-up."

"Did Sarah date Donte back then?"

"I don't know exactly when they got together, but I think they were at least friends in high school."

"And this is Creighton," Seth said as his eyebrows rose at the senior picture. "I get the appeal."

"Yeah, he was definitely all that. He and I started dating right before my short stint as Juliet."

"See, you remember the important stuff," he said with a false jealous tone.

I smiled.

"I can see why he might have turned your head," Seth said. "High school jock material."

"Most definitely. And two years older. Imagine how cool I felt."

"You guys got along for a long time," Seth said, matter-of-factly. There was no jealous tone to his voice now, either real or false.

"Not really. We were intrigued by each other, but even when we got along and were friends, we never connected," I said. "I only know that because this new relationship I'm in is all about connection."

"It is, isn't it?" Seth closed the yearbook.

It looked like the research was done for the evening. Both of us read the signals the same way, and we leaned toward each other.

"Wait!" I said when our lips were only about half an inch apart. If he hadn't had a garlic burger too, I would have been horrified by my breath.

"What?" Seth said, checking his own breath.

"No. I remembered what happened between me and Sarah."

"What?"

"I need to call Jodie and then I can tell you both."

She was just pulling into the Star City Police Station when she answered, telling me first that they'd found nothing yet that could tell them who killed either Donte or Lloyd.

"Listen, Jodie. I remembered something," I said, interrupting her explanation.

"Okay."

"Back when we were sophomores, I was Juliet for English class, do you remember that?"

"Kind of."

"Sarah helped me get ready, and she said something to me that I just remembered and might not be pertinent to anything that's going on now, but you were trying to find a connection between Creighton and our classmates."

"I'm listening."

"She was nice, but then she said something that I later decided was why she *pretended* to be nice. Anyway, as she was fixing my hair, she said she heard that Creighton was going to ask me out and that he'd asked her out a couple weeks earlier and the date had been horrible. He'd been mean, she said, and she just wanted to warn me."

"Sarah wanted to warn you about Creighton being mean? Sarah might have spit in your lunch if you looked at her the wrong way back then. She was the mean one. Well, sometimes, at least."

"Right. Anyway, that might be some sort of connection. Maybe Creighton liked her. Maybe Lloyd did too, and Harold. Do you suppose Sarah is the connection, but not in the way we've been thinking?"

"And that Creighton or Harold is killing the men who he'd thought were in the way of his true love all those years ago?"

"It sounds really ridiculous if you say it that way, but there might be something there."

"When you're right, you're right, Clare. We were definitely trying to find a connection between Creighton and the others and we had nothing. That's at least a little something. Who knows? It might lead somewhere. Thanks for letting me know. I'll be talking to Creighton tonight, in about ten minutes if I'm correct."

"Has he been arrested?"

"Just detained."

"What does that mean?"

"He's here in the station, Clare, and we've asked both him and Howard to stay put. It might be more for their safety than because we suspect them, but we don't want them going anywhere."

"Right."

"I want everybody to be on their toes. We've a killer in our midst, and the fact that the two victims were in our high school class means you should be diligent too. Got it?"

I blinked and goose bumps rode up my arms. "I'll be careful. You too."

"Will do, but I have a gun. You watch your back."

We ended the call, but I began another one right away.

"Clare?" Jimmy said as he answered. "What's up?"

"Where are you?"

"At Mom and Dad's. I'm cleaning out their garage, so they have a place to put things."

"They're coming back to Star City now?"

"Yeah. Well, in three days. Oh, I forgot I wasn't supposed to tell you. Don't give me away. Act surprised when you see them."

"I can do that. Want some help?"

Jimmy hesitated. "Absolutely, but is there something you need?"

"A sister can't offer to help her brother clean out the garage without ulterior motives?"

"It would be a first."

"I have some questions."

"Bring me a Slurpee or something. I'm working up a sweat in here."

Slurpees had always been my older brother's drink of choice. It was always strange to catch him in a business suit, holding a domed icy drink as the inner part of his lips turned red or blue.

"All right. We're on the way," I said.

Seth was already cleaning up our dinner paper boats and napkins.

$$\boxed{\mathbf{24}}$$

"I was too old to pay attention," Jimmy said. "You were my little sister and while I would have fought for your honor, I was not interested in spending any time with you. At all."

My parents had purchased a house halfway between Star City and Heber almost thirty years earlier. Those were the days when their house was considered out in the woods, not part of the town. They'd purchased the large cabin because the town had announced that electrical, plumbing, and running water would be available in the area. They'd been one of a few that had jumped the gun, and they spent the first two years using a generator for their electricity, drawing water from their distant neighbor's well, and using an outhouse. They often said it was worth it because they liked the solitude of being surrounded by trees instead of buildings.

By the time Jimmy came along, all the modern amenities had been added and our closest neighbor was only about a hundred feet away, not a quarter of a mile.

It wasn't really a cabin anymore either. It was slightly larger than that, made for a family of four, though we fit tightly inside. The driveway had seen more cars than the garage, which was where my parents kept all their toys: things like four-wheelers, kayaks, trailers, and even a boat or two over the years.

They'd decided to become snowbirds and get away to Arizona during the cold and snowy Utah winters. Soon enough, they realized that they weren't meant for the snowbird life and that one of the reasons they moved to Star City in the first place was the snow, and the outdoor activities that came along with it. Jimmy and I had both known they'd figure it out.

However, I didn't know they were on their way home soon and had asked my brother to make some space in the garage for "a few things."

"Okay, do you remember when Creighton and I started dating?" I asked him as I lifted a deflated raft from one of the shelves along a side wall. Underneath, I found a lantern and a flashlight that looked like a dog had chewed off the handle.

"Of course, you were . . ." He looked at Seth. "Of course."

Seth laughed. "It's okay, Jimmy. I not the least bit threatened by their past romance."

"They were all gooey-eyed over each other," Jimmy said.

"Oh. Well, gooey-eyed. That's different," Seth said with a half smile at my brother.

They got along very well, but sometimes Seth had to remind my brother that they actually liked each other. I wouldn't say that Jimmy was a narcissist, but he leaned that way. Chester always said that Jimmy simply couldn't handle his surprise single parent gig. His wife left shortly after Marion was born. He wouldn't talk much about it, and I still didn't know all the details, but I remembered the rough times. I also saw how difficult it was to be a single father to a beautiful, intelligent, and talented young woman who'd probably be competing in the winter games someday.

"Yeah," Jimmy said. "They weren't right for each other, though. You could see that from the start."

"You could?" I asked.

"Yeah, but what gooey-eyed teenage girl would ever listen to that sort of thing from her big brother?"

"Good point. Do you remember anyone from my class other than Jodie?" I asked.

"No."

"Donte Senot, Lloyd Gavin, Howard Craig?"

"I know Lloyd's family but none of the others. And you and Lloyd were friends when you were kids, weren't you? I might only remember him because of his recent murder. I can't believe there's been another one, but no, I don't remember Donte or Howard."

Seth and I had filled him in on the recent tragedies. Jimmy worked a lot, so he missed out on many current events, but he had heard about Lloyd.

"You remember the dance?"

"Of course, you stole my thunder with your gracious go-to-his-house-instead-of-the-dance move. I'd just made the baseball team, but you were the star that week."

"Sorry."

"Clare, I'm kidding. Kind of. I mean, you did steal my thunder, but that was an awesome thing. It got talked about. The baseball got talked about the next week."

"Lloyd didn't want pity. I hope it didn't come off that way."

"No. Just cool."

I put my hands on my hips and sighed. "Where are all the pictures? The ones from when I was in high school?"

"Probably in your room, under the bed. That's what Mom did with the pictures. Separated them, boxed them, and slipped them in each of our rooms."

"Do you mind?" I asked.

"I didn't think you'd even lift the raft and pretend to help, and you did bring the Slurpee. You are dismissed."

"Come on, Seth," I said.

They probably didn't think I caught their shared shrug, but I did.

My room was the one at the back corner of the wide "cabin." My parents' room was on the other side, and Jimmy's was in the front corner on the same side as mine. Seth had been to the house with me a few times as I'd checked to make sure nothing had flooded or had been set aflame, as well as make sure no wild animals had found their way inside and set up a housekeeping or hibernation spot. We'd found a curious moose out back once, but he'd kept his distance as we watched him from the back deck doors.

My room didn't look much like mine anymore. The bed was still there, but any posters I'd put on the walls were gone along with the old quilt I'd used since I was a little girl. It was threadbare by the time my mother found the perfect opportunity to throw it out when I wasn't looking. I was still thinking about forgiving her, but I wasn't sure I ever would.

I reached under the bed and pulled out two long boxes, placing them on the bed and lifting the lids.

"Wow, did you organize any of these?" Seth asked.

"No, Mom did. She loves organizing photos. She's not a fan of leaving things on the computer. Even with the digital age, she prints out pictures and organizes all the time. It's just what she does."

"An enviable obsession."

"I know. Okay, I'm trying to find some pictures from a sophomore winter dance I went to with Creighton."

"Everything's labeled. Should be easy."

Seconds later we found my sophomore year, and then the subset folder that contained the dance pictures. I dumped the folder on the bed and spread them out.

"You two made a great-looking couple, I must admit," Seth said.

"Right. Okay, I'm looking for something specific here," I said. "Sarah. She'll look just like she does now, but even prettier and younger, of course."

"This one?" Seth handed me the picture.

"No, but she looks good there. Dang, she was—is—pretty."

We kept looking.

"Here," he said as he handed me another picture.

"That's the one! And I did remember correctly. She and Howard went to the dance together. Look."

"That's Howard?" Seth said. "With all that red hair?"

"Yes, he's gone gray way prematurely, but he used to have the brightest red hair."

"It's not just the hair."

"Yeah, he was preppy, buttoned up, no wrinkles. I'm sure his head never saw a cowboy hat until he moved to Wyoming."

Seth appraised the picture and then squinted at me. "You know, even I went to a few dances, with friends. I didn't really date anyone. This might just be a friendship thing. They weren't dating people and they hung out in the same crowd, so they went together. It happens, and it doesn't usually mean very much."

"I agree, but I think I need to tell Jodie about it. And then we need to scour those yearbooks for signs that Sarah might have been closer to Howard, or maybe Lloyd."

"So, you think maybe this is a jealousy thing on Creighton's part?"

"I have a hard time believing that," I said. "But we're at least finding more connections. We had over two hundred people in our class; they came from here and surrounding small towns; we weren't a small class. There's a reason someone invited those specific people to some meetings, and it's difficult not to think it had something to do with something that happened back then."

"I agree, but I do think it would be strange for someone like Creighton to hold a brokenhearted grudge all these years later, unless it was about you."

I half rolled my eyes.

"No, seriously, Clare. He was crazy about you, there's no refuting that. From all indications, there's nothing at all to think that he felt that way about anyone else."

"Actually, Creighton wouldn't hold a brokenhearted grudge about anyone, but he's up to something, Seth. Or at least Jodie thinks so," I said.

"Well, I don't know what good it will do, but do you want to give her a call, or should we run this picture down to the police station and give it to her in person, and maybe have the chance to ask if there's anything new?" Seth said with a conspiratorial smile.

"I could kiss you for that idea," I said.

And then I did.

↶

"Howard and Sarah are standing next to each other in a picture from a high school dance. I don't think that means much of anything. I'm sorry, Clare, but thanks for wanting to help us out," Jodie said as she frowned at the picture. In fact, her face had been in a perpetual frown ever since Seth and I walked into her office. Well, the frown was probably there before, but it got deeper when she saw us.

"I know, but there's a connection here," I said.

"I agree," Jodie said, "but if we started using pictures from high school dances, we'd be going in many different directions. Maybe these murders are because of something from high school, but we still need more."

Seth and I both inspected her a long moment.

"That was the first time all these people came together. You know something else?" I said.

"I don't, Clare. I just think we might have exhausted that angle. Creighton said he never had one moment's interest in Sarah. In fact, he said that he didn't even really remember going to school with her."

I pointed at the picture. "And yet we were all at this dance together. I was there with Creighton. And just last night he accused Howard and someone who looked like Sarah of slashing his tires."

"He made that up to see if he could get anything out of Howard. He said it didn't work."

"I've had funny memory moments the past couple of days. Not like I'm losing it really, but realized I forgot stuff. Maybe he forgot."

Jodie looked back and forth between Seth and me. "He wouldn't have forgotten that, Clare. It was all about you back then. That might be something *you're* forgetting. There was no Sarah in his life. No Lloyd, no Howard or Donte. There's a connection, I'm sure, but we still don't know what it was. I think we have to move the high school connection to the back burner. There has to be something else."

I handed her the picture. "Take this. Show it to Creighton and Howard. See what they say."

Jodie hesitated but took the picture. "All right."

"Where are they—Howard and Creighton?"

"Howard's back at his hotel and Creighton is home. There was no reason to hold either of them, but I've got officers watching them both for their protection as well as to make sure they don't skip town."

"How's Sarah?" I asked.

"A mess. They had no kids, but she has some family in Salt Lake City. I didn't know her or Donte's families. I had to ask her to tell me who to call for her. It's rough."

"Any leads at all, Jodie?" Seth asked.

"Nothing substantial. There were many sets of fingerprints in the press room at Donte's building, and we'll have to eliminate employees, past and present. We're hoping that might give us something, but we'll have to see."

"Can we go grab you some food, coffee, something?" I said when I couldn't think of any other questions to ask.

"No, I'm leaving in a minute too. Just finishing up things here."

Her dismissal was uncharacteristically gentle and she sent us a forced smile as we waved from the doorway.

"Do you want to go talk to Creighton?" Seth asked when we were out of Jodie's earshot.

"I don't know."

"If you want to talk to him, I'll take you there. I'll wait outside too if you'd like, but I want him to know I'm there. Well, that you aren't alone. Want to?"

I thought about it all the way out to the car.

"No," I said as he turned the key. "I don't know what I'd say and I don't know what he's really told Jodie. He might be lying, he might not, but I'm not the one to figure that out. Thank you, though."

"No problem. Home, then?"

"That's the best idea of the night."

25

"We're still hanging on to it for her?" Chester said as he straightened. He'd been leaning over and peering into the compartment under the counter.

"I had a moment of unguarded weakness," I said.

"I'd say," Chester said. "Well, we'll just keep it locked up until things settle, I guess, and then make sure she gets it back. I don't really understand why she brought it to us."

"She said for safekeeping, but I'm with you, I don't understand very much myself. We're not friends really, and she knows what we do here at the shop. I was going to call her today and ask, but now . . ."

"Of course," Chester said. "I suppose it's okay to keep it for a while."

"I'd consider buying it from her," Nathan said. "Believe it or not, I'm not much of a book collector, but that would be a true treasure, and one any horror writer would happily own. I'll ask her if I think it's appropriate."

Chester and I both nodded our agreement.

The front door swung open. Janise and Evan Davenport were back, but this time with a much different demeanor. Janise led the way forward, and she sent me a small smile that I read to mean that we weren't going to dislike this visit as much as we might have disliked the last one.

"Hello there!" Chester said cheerily.

"Hi," Janise said as she and Evan reached the counter.

"Hi," Evan said with a sheepish smile. He looked at his wife and then back at Chester and me. "I'm so sorry about my behavior."

"Not a problem," I said.

"Not at all," Chester said.

"I was under much more stress than I thought. Of course I was upset about my mother's death and the fact that I'd destroyed her beloved typewriter, but still. I'm sorry. We're on our way home, and I didn't want your last impression of me to be bratty behavior."

"Oh, we know all about that sort of thing," Chester said. "Truly, not a problem at all."

"Thank you," Evan said.

"Oh, the Splendid folks," Nathan said.

"Yes, that's . . . Wait," Janise said as she took a good look at Nathan. "Wait, you aren't? Well, there's no hat and scarf, but you aren't Nathan Grimes, are you?"

"At your service." He extended his hand.

"Nice to meet you," Janise said. "Evan, it's Nathan Grimes."

"I see that. My goodness, what a pleasure." He almost

forgot to shake Nathan's extended hand, but Janise tapped him on the shoulder. "We heard you were in town, and then lost, and then found. We're glad you were found."

"Me too. I'm sorry about your recent tragedy. Please. Will you wait here a moment?" Nathan said.

We all looked around at each other as Nathan disappeared to the workshop. A moment later, he brought out his Splendid, which he'd brought with him again.

"Clare and Chester told me about your recent tragedy. I know this isn't your mother's, but I would love for you to have it," Nathan said as he held the typewriter toward Evan.

Chester and I were stunned speechless for a moment. Even Baskerville's whiskers twitched in shock. Evan didn't know what to say either, and Janise had to blink hard to get rid of a few tears.

"I couldn't," Evan finally muttered.

"Yes, you could, and I insist that you must," Nathan said.

"I've never been given something so wonderful," Evan said.

"Well, I'm glad you think so. I did write one of my bestselling novels on it."

"Oh my. Well, thank you," Evan said.

"Thank you," Janise said.

"My pleasure. Now, if you'll excuse me, I need to get back to work. Have a lovely day," Nathan said before he turned and went back to the workshop again.

"I'm . . . I still don't know what to say," Evan said.

"I think you should just enjoy the typewriter," Chester said. "Use it. Make it as special to you as your mother's was to her."

"I will. Definitely."

Evan and Janise looked at each other.

"So you got your book?" I interjected before they could protest again. "The one from Starry Nights up the street."

"Oh no, we've been back a couple of times, but the shop has always been closed, and when we've looked in the windows, it's a terrible mess, papers everywhere. Bad timing, I guess. We hadn't paid for the book already, so no financial loss, and I think we can get it shipped to us, but I was really hoping to see it before I paid for it," Evan said.

I thought hard back to when Sarah told me that Evan and Janise had picked up their book. Had I misheard her? She'd been in the bookstore every time I'd been there. Evan and Janise must have chosen strange times to stop by, but the place had been messy, always in different ways, but definitely . . .

"Clare?" Chester said.

"Oh, sorry," I said, realizing I'd made a perplexed noise. "She's had a terrible tragedy. I'm sure the shop will be closed for a while." I bit my lip. I'd already gotten myself too involved with Sarah's valuable copy of *Carrie*; I didn't need to get any deeper into her business. But I couldn't help wondering why she'd lied about the book being picked up. Why would she? Why would it matter enough for her to lie? "How about you give me your address? I'll check on it and see if we can get it to you."

"That's above and beyond," Janise said.

Chester made a noise that sounded like he agreed with Janise. And Baskerville sent me a tiny warning meow. I was stepping too far.

"Gracious," Janise said as she looked at Baskerville. "Is that cat okay?"

"Yes, Baskerville just likes to chat sometimes."

Chester smiled at the cat as Janise wrote down their address. They thanked us all and apologized again. With the piece of paper with their address tucked into my pocket, I watched them leave and then looked back at Chester.

"I'll be right back."

"Where are you going?" Chester said.

"Up to Starry Night Books," I said.

"It will be closed," Chester said. "And Sarah won't be there."

"I know, but I have to go up there," I said. "I just need to see something, maybe just through the window. I'll be right back."

"Either Nathan or Adal is going with you. One second, and I'll grab them."

A few seconds later, Nathan came back out with Chester.

"Let's go," Nathan said.

"Okay, but it's broad daylight and the streets are busy. Don't wear your scarf."

"Good plan."

We set off at a quick clip.

"What's going on, Clare? Why are we in such a hurry? Surely, Sarah won't be there," Nathan said as he double-stepped once so that our footfalls matched.

"I don't know, Nathan. Something about the shop. Evan and Janise made me think more about Sarah's strange behavior, which caused me to remember something, sort of. You know how you're minding your own business and something happens, someone says something or you see something and you remember back to something you didn't notice when you saw it at the time, but your sub-conscious suddenly makes it come back to the forefront?"

"Sure. Mostly, that happens to me as I'm falling asleep. It's why I keep a notebook and pen by my bed."

"Right. Well . . . well, I'm remembering some pieces of something. I saw something in there and I think it's important."

"What?"

"Some pieces of paper."

"That's slightly vague. It is a bookshop."

"I know."

We dodged some pedestrian and car traffic.

"That was very generous to give them your typewriter," I said.

"Not really. Actually, I have quite a few of the exact same model. That one has a sometimes sticky *R* key. It would have been more generous if I'd given them my favorite one, but it's at home."

"Still, very kind."

We made it to the bookshop in record time, not surprised to find the door locked and the lights off.

I stepped up onto the stoop and peered inside. The messes I'd seen before looked to be more under control, but I couldn't competently judge based only on the neat and tidy counter and the lack of random stacks and boxes here and there. Where had I seen what I was remembering?

"The back room," I said aloud.

"What's that?"

"I think I saw it in the back room."

"Well, what are the chances that what you saw is still there?" Nathan asked.

"Normally, I would think the chances would be nil, but I have to check."

"I don't understand, Clare."

I jiggled the doorknob.

"Locked, huh?" Nathan said.

"Yes, but if one of us had a paper clip, I think we could get in. It's an old door and an old lock."

Nathan laughed.

I looked at him. "I'm not kidding, Nathan. I want to get inside. If I had something that would work, I'd try."

Nathan blinked. "That doesn't sound like the mild-mannered typewriter repair person I've come to know."

"At the moment, I'm the Star City High School grad who's recently lost two of her classmates, and who has regrets for not being a better friend to one of them."

"I see," he said. "Well, step aside, then."

Without a moment's hesitation, I moved back and let Nathan into the space. He looked back at me. "Are *you* sure?"

"I'm sure, but you're the one breaking in. I'll take the blame, but you could get in trouble too. Are *you* sure?"

"Oh yes, of course I'm sure. This is excellent research. There was a séance in here. Perhaps there are still spirits hanging around. I can use their communications for a future book."

"Whatever you need to tell yourself," I said.

I watched his back as he miraculously produced a paper clip from his pocket, but no one was paying us any attention, their focus either up or down the hill.

"Easy as pie," he said as the lock clicked and he turned the knob. The hinges squeaked a creepy welcome as he pushed the door open. "See, perfect."

For the record, there's a big difference between wanting

to break into someplace and actually doing it. Once we were inside the frigid shop, probably cold from the furnace being turned down, my conscience kicked in big.

"This is horrible," I said.

Nathan shrugged. "We aren't here to do any damage, and the entire world could have been watching us. It's daylight out there. We weren't too sneaky, which should count for something, right?"

"Yeah, I doubt it," I said. "We should get out of here."

"Or we could take a quick look around," Nathan said. "Quick."

"Quick," I said a moment later.

He let me lead the way as we headed toward the back of the shop. I looked over the counter and saw only a clean floor. Not even one stray paperback. Even the shelves underneath looked to have been organized.

"There's a room back here," I said when we reached the door. "If this one's locked we're not going in."

Nathan nodded.

But the door wasn't locked. We pushed through and I found a switch on the wall to my left.

"This place is spotless now," I said.

Nathan sniffed. "Smell that?"

I sniffed too. "Citrus?"

"Yeah, strong."

"Maybe a cleaning product."

The room was neat and organized, the boxes of books on the shelves in a tight formation. The shelves that held books without boxes were also neat and organized. The small table that served as a desk was minimalistic with only one notebook and one pen at the ready. For an instant, I was jealous of the organization, and then I wondered how in the world Sarah had pulled it together. Hadn't this shop been a total mess just a few days before?

I glanced into the garbage can.

"She even emptied the garbage," I said as I looked at Nathan.

"You sound disappointed."

"I am. I think what I saw was in the garbage."

"I'm sorry, but good grief, that smell is strong," Nathan said.

"We need to get out of here anyway. Let's go." I guided us out of the room.

I flipped off the switch, but as I pulled the door closed, I was interrupted.

"Police. Hands up!"

I knew the voice. The person attached to the voice knew me. Nevertheless, Nathan threw both hands into the air.

"Clare?" Jodie said as she flipped off the flashlight that had blinded Nathan and me.

"Oh, crap," I said.

"Dammit, Clare. You're kidding, right?" Jodie said.

"I'm sorry," I said.

"My fault," Nathan said.

"I bet," Jodie said. She sighed heavily. "All right, let's go."

"Are we being arrested?" I said.

"Get in the Bronco, both of you. We'll talk at the station."

The good news was that she let me call Chester as we were on our way down the hill to let him know we wouldn't be back as soon as we'd thought.

Unfortunately, the truly bad news was still to come.

26

"But you don't know what you saw?" Jodie asked.

"There was so much stuff in there that day, Jodie, so I can't be sure. But I just couldn't stop myself from going up there and then trying to get in. Nathan tried to stop me."

"I did not," Nathan said. He had been delighted to be taken to the police station. He thought that breaking and entering into a bookstore just might sell more books.

Jodie hadn't arrested us. As she'd steered the Bronco down the hill, she called the security company that monitored, with hidden wires, Starry Night, and told them the alarm had been tripped but that there was no sign of anyone breaking and entering.

When she ended the call, Nathan had asked, "If I used a paper clip to jimmy the lock, does that mean I only entered illegally but didn't break in?"

She had sent him some of her unhappy eyes via the rearview mirror. He hadn't seem fazed.

"Anyway, Clare," Jodie said from across the interview room table. "You can't remember what you saw, but you were compelled to go find it?"

"That's the only explanation I have," I said. "I think it was something important, it must have been, but it's still partially buried in my subconscious or something."

I wasn't lying, but it sure sounded like I was.

"A book?" Jodie said.

"Maybe," I said. "What else could it be?"

Jodie's partner, Omar, knocked once and then leaned into the room.

"Jodie, do you need any paperwork on these two?" he asked.

"No, I'm going to let them go. It was a mistake. The door was unlocked and they thought the store was open for business. That's all." Again she sent some angry eyes to Nathan. This time he kept quiet.

"Okay, I'm out of here, then. Call me if you need me to come back later," Omar said.

"Will do. Thanks," she said.

"Are you in charge?" I said as the door closed.

She shrugged and said, "All right, the two of you. Seriously, I can't believe I have to say this, but don't do that sort of thing. Call me. Clare, if you really felt like there was something inside there to see, you should have called me. I have some connections, you know. I could have had the alarm disarmed."

I nodded. "But are you in charge?"

"I am. For the time being," she said. "Creighton would

be the one in charge, but he's home being watched by another officer."

"That's cool that you're in charge."

"Clare," she said.

"It is cool, but yes, I hear what you're saying."

Jodie sighed. "All right, I'm going to take you both back up to The Rescued Word and we're not going to speak of this ever again."

e⁓

Chester and Adal weren't amused by my adventure with Nathan. However, after Jodie left, Chester became distracted by the Hoovens, and Adal and Nathan did some page design work on Nathan's book.

I helped a couple of customers, but my mind was completely distracted. What had I thought I'd seen? Was it something in the garbage can? Was it a book?

"Clare, come look!" Chester said from the workshop doorway just as I was flipping the sign on the door to CLOSED. "It's extraordinary."

I hurried to the back.

"I just used my last sheet. Grab some of the scratch paper," Chester said as he stood by the Hoovens.

I gathered some of the green paper from the corner of my desk and brought it to Chester as he, Nathan, and Adal crowded around the Hoovens. He'd pulled the middle machine away from the wall; it now seemed less dusty than the others.

"Here," I said as I handed him a piece of paper.

"Now watch," he said.

He threaded the paper through the paper feed and about an inch up on the carriage roll. He flipped a switch and the machine started to rumble and shake. He pushed a button and the paper moved upward as the keys struck it. The piano player roll also moved as an arm read the pattern that was being translated by the keys.

It was like watching something appear out of thin air, a magic trick, something old and outdated but new to our eyes.

Once the printing stopped, both Adal and Nathan applauded and Chester grabbed the paper and gave it to me.

I read aloud. "April 19, 1960. Dear Kind Friend and Loyal Fan. Thanks for your congratulations on my Oscar. It was nice hearing from you; it was nice hearing from them. But I appreciate your support. Thanks again. Bob Hope."

I paused.

"What?" I said. "This machine belonged to the comedian and actor Bob Hope?"

"We can't be sure, of course," Chester said. "But I think so. If that's the case, he must have sent out this form thank-you letter to some fans."

"Oh my," I said.

Chester smiled and brushed the back of his mustache with his knuckle. "How about that?"

"How did you do this?"

"The machine is in great shape. We have ribbons galore. I loaded one up, dusted the old guy off, plugged it in, and this happened. I can't wait to see what might happen with the other two."

"A working Hooven. That Bob Hope owned. Holy moly," I said. The machines were awesome enough. This new development was almost unbelievable.

"Yep," Chester said.

Even non-typewriter folks would be intrigued by this. Chester and I both decided we would show Lloyd's parents the Hoovens as soon as it seemed appropriate, but in the meantime, Adal would take it upon himself to clean them up, plug them all in, and see what magic they had waiting for us to discover. I still didn't feel right about keeping them, but it was impossible not to enjoy them while they were in our possession.

With Baskerville bringing his full authoritative attitude to the front as he bade Adal, Nathan, and me good night with a growly meow, I locked the front door right after he and Chester disappeared behind the workshop door.

I drove Adal and Nathan to their current homes: Adal's apartment and the hotel. I thought about asking Nathan if he wanted to stay on my couch just because, but the idea felt uncomfortable, so I didn't.

I called Seth but had to leave him a message. I didn't remember what his plans for the day or evening had been, but I knew he'd call later.

I drove up the hill toward Little Blue, and my attention turned once again toward Starry Nights Bookstore as I passed by it. Pedestrians traveled both up and down the street and I had a car both in front of and behind me, so I couldn't keep my eyes on the shop the whole time. For an instant, I thought I saw someone I recognized standing against the wall next to the shop. Was that Creighton? But when I was able to focus there again, I didn't see him. I didn't see anyone mixing with the pedestrians who looked like him.

He was at home being watched, according to Jodie. I was sure I'd imagined him outside the bookstore. I grabbed my phone to let Jodie know about the hallucination anyway. She would want to know, wouldn't she? However, I couldn't bring myself to press the SEND button. She would want to know if I was sure, but the reaction I'd get if I told her what I *thought* I'd seen didn't seem worth the effort. I'd already given her enough trouble for the day. I'd tell her tomorrow.

It looked like dinner would be some cheese and crackers and something on television, preferably something mindless. Actually, maybe just some crackers with the TV. I didn't think I had any cheese. Dinner would be crackers and water until I heard from Seth, just in case we could still manage a real dinner together.

As I sat on the couch with the plate of crackers and a glass of water, I tipped over my bag that I'd put there. A green piece of paper fell out.

I put the first cracker in my mouth and grabbed the Bob Hope letter I'd somehow managed to take with me. I unfolded it and read the words from a long time before. I wasn't transported, but I was definitely impressed. I didn't know much about Bob Hope and his Oscar, but Chester did, and that . . .

The next cracker stopped halfway to my mouth.

"Oh!" I said aloud as I carelessly lifted the plate toward the coffee table, missing my landing and sending it and my sparse dinner to the floor. I ignored the mess as I pulled my phone out of my pocket. "Jodie! Meet me at Starry Nights Books, right away," I said, recording a message. She'd get it soon enough. She didn't go long without checking her messages.

I didn't remember if I locked the door or shut it all the way as I hurried out of the house. With the paper clutched in my hand, I hurried down the hill. It was dark and cold, but there wasn't as much pedestrian traffic, so I was able to move at a quick clip.

I peered inside the dark shop and then stepped up to the stoop. I didn't expect the door to be unlocked, but the knob turned easily and the door swung open with the now-familiar squeak. Jodie must not have locked it. I wondered if I'd set off the alarms again, but I didn't care.

I just needed to see one thing. One small thing. I looked around and behind me; again, no one paid me any attention.

"Hello?" I said after I went into the dark shop and closed the door behind me. I held up my cell phone with the flashlight app turned on.

No one answered, so I stepped forward and then took quick steps toward the back room. I didn't even think about announcing myself as I opened that door.

But I should have.

Sarah was sitting in the chair behind the table. She lifted her head from her arms and sniffed.

"Oh, Sarah, I'm so sorry to disturb you!" I said. "The door was open and I thought maybe I heard someone back here. I thought I'd check." I switched off my phone.

The only light was a small desk lamp that gave the room more shadows than illumination. However, half of Sarah's face was lit with a sallow yellow glow. She'd been crying; her eyes were puffy and smudged with ruined mascara. Her hair was a wild neglected nest.

"Clare? What are you doing here?"

"I . . . The door was unlocked."

She blinked and nodded as if I was making sense.

"Are you okay, Sarah?" I asked as I took a step forward. I glanced in the still-empty garbage can, now sure that

I'd seen the thing that had been trying to make its way up to my subconscious. I knew the can would still be empty, but I also thought that the object I'd seen there hadn't gotten all the way thrown away. It was still in this office somewhere. I was sure. Well, at least ninety percent sure.

"No, I haven't been okay in a long time."

"I'm so sorry about Donte," I said as I stepped closer.

"I'll be all right eventually."

As she said the words, I saw the item again. In her grip. If we'd been in a movie, some sort of discovery music would have played in conjunction with her hand wadding up the invitation and pulling her hand off the desk.

"That's the invitation, isn't it?" I said.

"I don't know what you're talking about."

"The invitation. You're holding it."

For a moment she just glared at me. I wanted to demand that she show it to me, prove that I was right about what she held, but we were silent as we stared at each other for what seemed like a long time. She made the next move.

The room was small. We were basically a desk away from each other as she came around. I didn't have a lot of time to think about what I was doing, but her move felt threatening. In a split second I decided to fight, not flee. I don't know why.

As she came at me, I stood strong and put my focus on her hand. Somehow, even though her move toward me was forceful, I grabbed her hand and the item she held as she knocked me to the floor. I had too much adrenaline to feel any immediate pain.

It was the invitation to the meetings. She'd used the ugly green paper. I doubted many places sold such ugly paper, but it was possible that it had come from somewhere other than The Rescued Word.

Doubtful. I still didn't know what it meant, the invitation being in her grip, and why she was denying it. It might have been just the invitation Donte threw away, but I didn't think so. I didn't think Sarah would be so physical if that was it. She could have used it as an excuse, and maybe neither of us would have ended up hurt.

I shrugged her off and then shoved her backward. Somehow I did the moves with such strength that she stumbled back and into the desk.

"Ouch!" she said.

I swallowed the apology that reflexed at my throat. "Keep your hands off me, Sarah!"

She straightened again, but seemed tamed. "I'm sorry, Clare, but that's not your property."

"It was in the trash a few days ago. Trash is anyone's property." I made that part up, but I said it with authority. "What's it doing here anyway?"

Sarah shook her head and looked at the floor.

I stepped to the wall. I flipped the switch for the overhead light. The brightness made us both squint, but I managed to get a much better look at the paper. It was an early version of the invitation, I guessed, one with a mistake having been crossed out with red pen. Creighton's name had been spelled incorrectly.

My quick and un-thought-through conclusion was that Sarah and Donte had planned the meetings, but why? And why had it been such a secret who'd done the planning?

I couldn't formulate a question quickly enough for Sarah's need to speak, apparently.

"I meant to get rid of that," she said. "But I just couldn't. I just . . . I don't know why, but I couldn't."

I looked at her and nodded.

She was certain I was onto her, I could tell by the way shame slumped her shoulders and kept her eyes away from mine. I just hoped she'd continue and I could continue to play along successfully. None of this moment meant much of anything to me. Yet.

"I heard it was your niece who found Lloyd's boot. If she hadn't, the police wouldn't even have thought to look for his body, and I could have taken care of them all without anyone figuring it out, at least for long enough to let me get away."

"So you . . . why did you kill Lloyd and your husband?" I couldn't even believe I was asking that question. It seemed unreal.

She nodded once, her eyes flashing only briefly to mine. "It was bound to fall apart after the boot, I guess. Was it Chester?"

"What do you mean?"

"Was it him that told you I came in for the paper that day? After the boot, I knew they'd find me once they saw the invitation. I thought it might take them a few days to track down where I got it, but there's only one Rescued Word, you know? I got rid of Donte's, but there was nothing I could do about Lloyd's, Howard's, or Creighton's."

"No," I said, being honest for the first time since finding her in her back room. "No, I saw it in your trash can earlier and I finally recognized it as something from the shop. It was all a fluke really. No one else had easy access to their invitation, but you're right, if we'd seen it we would have known that paper."

She gave one ironic laugh. "You Henrys, I tell ya. Wait. Earlier? Earlier when? When did you see it?"

"Why did you kill them, Sarah? I don't understand," I said.

She blinked as if she couldn't believe I didn't understand. "They failed me, Clare, you know that!"

"No, I don't. How in the world did all those men fail you?"

"My husband's business was tanking. We were going to have to live off whatever this bookshop brought in. Can you imagine? We'd have had to put a cot out front to have a place to sleep. And the rest of them denied me what I was due."

"What was due to you?"

"For goodness' sake, Clare, they should have loved me, worshipped me. I was the one, the girl every boy should have wanted. Donte did, but, God, he was a disaster. He only got lucky to make the money he made. I knew it was only a matter of time before he squandered it away. Howard was only interested in getting out of town without any ties to anyone. I could have made him so successful, Clare, I could have."

I nodded, morbidly interested in her confession. She was more than a narcissist; she was a narcissistic killer. Who wouldn't be intrigued by that? Scared too, but I still hoped she continued.

She did. "And Lloyd was too afraid of me to pay me any attention. He was such a nerd, but even back then, Clare, I knew the nerds would be the successful ones. He was so smart." She smiled wryly. "Except that day last week that he let me lead him out to the backcountry to ski. What a fool. He was so easy that day."

Poor Lloyd. "Creighton?"

"Oh yeah, him. He loved you back then. What an idiot. I tried to get him from you. I tried to get you to dump him too. Remember *Romeo and Juliet*? I tried to make you think less of him. Remember?"

"I do." Now.

"You haven't done anything outside that typewriter shop and you dumped him anyway. If he'd been with me, I would have made him so much more than a police officer. Good grief, how in the world do you people make a living at that shop anyway?"

I shrugged, but she wasn't truly looking for *my* financials.

"After Lloyd's body was found, why did you go ahead and kill Donte? Why didn't you just get away? Leave town. I don't know."

"With what? We had nothing—the last of our money went into paying a couple months' rent on this place and letting me acquire some inventory. Used books—that's what it came down to. I needed his insurance money." She rubbed her finger under her nose. "The thing is, I can still contact Donte, though. He's on the other side and he's mad as a rabid dog right now, but he'll cool down and I'll be able to talk to him."

"That séance stuff isn't real."

"Of course it is."

"You were still going to kill Creighton and Howard?" I asked.

"Maybe, or I was going to get one of them to fall in love with me. I tried to tell Howard he and I belonged together. I even thought he'd tell the police about that after Donte was killed, but he must not have."

"They didn't want you back then," I said. "What makes you think they would have wanted you now?"

Those were some mean words, but I couldn't stop myself from saying them. However, saying them to a deranged, narcissistic killer probably wasn't the best idea I'd ever had. Sarah lunged again, with a jump move and a swinging fist thrown in for good measure.

One second I was upright, the next flat on my back with stars in front of my eyes and a strange disconnected sense of all-over pain.

In the next instant, Sarah was on top of me, straddling me with one arm lifted in the air. She must have held something that she was going to hit me with. I wanted to brace for it, but I didn't know how; she had my arms pinned at my sides. I closed my starry eyes as I lay on the floor in Starry Night.

But the blow never came. Instead I heard other loud noises and a loud male voice.

"Clare, are you okay?"

I sat up woozily and saw Creighton at the door, holding Sarah's hands behind her back.

"I think so," I said.

"Call 911. I need to get her subdued. We need help," Creighton said.

I did as he said. After I found my phone, which I could do only after the stars cleared a little more.

27

I *had* seen Creighton looking in Starry Night Books' window as I was driving home. He'd escaped his police officer babysitter because he couldn't let go of the idea that Sarah was somehow involved in the murders that had occurred. He was looking for her, and then he watched for her from across the street. He'd been three steps behind me when I went inside the shop, his curiosity about what I was up to greater than his desire to stop me from exploring and asking a few questions. I hadn't noticed him at all. He was good at being covert.

"Why did you think Sarah was involved?" Jodie asked.

We were in the office that Jodie and Creighton shared with four other officers, but we were the only three in there at the moment.

"She'd been too friendly to me," Creighton said. "It was weird and uncomfortable. And the séance, Eloise

MacPherson. I had no doubt it was a story she put together, though I had no idea why. Now I know she was just diverting attention. It didn't mean much to me until Donte was killed. By then I knew his business was suffering and that they'd laid off most of their employees. Not many other people would have had access to the building. I had no clue as to the motives for her killing, however. She's one delusional mess."

"Howard never entered your mind?" Jodie asked.

"Sure he did, but I could tell he wasn't a killer by his behavior at the bar."

Jodie sent her brother a sideways look. "Yeah, I thought the same after Donte's murder. Howard just didn't act like a killer. But neither did Sarah, really. We should have seen that she wasn't operating on all cylinders. She'd come unhinged."

"How did Howard not act like a killer?" I said.

Jodie shrugged. "There was no underlying current of panic to him. That's the best I can tell you, Clare. Psychopaths can lie, innocent people can behave in a guilty manner, but that underlying current is what you look for."

"A cop thing?" I asked.

"Probably."

"You know Sarah came into The Rescued Word to show me a book. *Carrie*. She was off then, but I didn't know to attribute her strangeness to having killed her husband."

"She was trying to establish an alibi but wasn't good at it. The book and the time she spent cleaning the store," Creighton said. "That's what she told me on the way down here. She thought you'd figured it all out when you confronted her."

"I hadn't. I just remembered seeing the green paper in her trash. It didn't register at the time I saw it, but I also saw the word 'invitation' on it. If I'd just put it all together the next day or so . . ."

"It was too much. The stress of Lloyd's death jumbled us all up a bit, and then when Nathan went missing, we looked away from the murder, or, as in my case, tried to make the two events be related."

"You mean"—I swallowed hard, because my question was going to sound critical, but I had to ask it—"if Nathan hadn't gone missing, Donte might not have been murdered?"

Creighton said. "Not all of us were distracted, and her plans were all about murder."

For a moment Jodie didn't make eye contact with either Creighton or me, but she was neither angry nor ashamed. I couldn't read her; it was rare that I couldn't read her.

I asked, "The gun she killed Lloyd with?"

"Not registered anywhere. An old .22 that had been in her family," Creighton said. "The financial troubles she and Donte were having sent her over the edge. She became obsessed with those of us who, in her mind, had wronged her."

"She was a mess," Jodie said, a thread of sympathy to her words.

"I'm sorry, Clare," Creighton said. "I thought I could get in there before she tried to hurt you, but I needed to get her whole confession." He held up the small recording device that he'd put at the right angle under the door to record what we'd said. Yep, he was good at being covert.

"I'm okay," I said as I repositioned the ice pack on my chin.

"Clare!" Chester said as he came through the doorway. "What in the world?"

He rushed to me and tilted my chin up with his finger. "Creighton, Jodie, what happened?"

"I'm okay," I said.

Chester sent both Jodie and Creighton a look that told them he was yet again tired of their shenanigans. They were both a little scared of him, but they kept their firm police officer faces this time.

"Clare!" Seth said as he, Adal, Nathan, and Marion also came through the door.

It was getting crowded.

Jodie, still the one in charge, it seemed, gave everyone a summary of what had happened, and how Creighton had actually saved me, though I'd been the one to solve the murder, all because of a piece of ugly green paper.

As we were all leaving, I heard Seth thank Creighton for his heroics. Creighton told Seth he was sorry he hadn't gotten to me sooner. Was it possible that we all might be friends someday? A ping of pain hit my jaw and I decided I'd think about that later.

Marion and Nathan walked out with Chester, and Jodie walked with me to Seth's car after telling Creighton to have a seat and wait for her. We walked a bit behind the others so we could talk privately.

"You think Creighton's not telling the truth?" I said.

"He's telling the truth about Sarah," she said.

"But there's still something else?"

"I'm sure he's up to something, Clare, and he escaped the officer observing him. That's not good, even if he helped you."

"Tell me what he's up to."

"Not now, but let's just say Eloise MacPherson's death is more of a mystery than Creighton wants us to think."

"Sarah made up the séance, right?"

"Of course, but still . . ."

"I want to hear more."

"I'll let you know if I can let you know. Hey, I'm sorry you were hurt, but you really did solve the murders. You called me, but next time, you need to wait for me."

"I understand. I really do. So, Dillon and Brenda can go back to Nebraska? They'll be glad," I said.

"Yes, to leave the beauty of our mountains and starry skies for Nebraska is everyone's dream," Jodie said.

I tried not to smile because it hurt too much.

"Take care of yourself, Clare," Jodie said.

"You too." I motioned with my head toward the station. Adal was also inside, waiting for Jodie.

"Will do," she said.

"Jodie, did you have *any* idea that Sarah was the killer?" I asked.

"I suspected everybody, but . . . Well, I just should have remembered high school personalities more. Sure, we've grown up, but Sarah hasn't changed all that much. Image, money, those things are still important to her. I didn't realize how important or how she hadn't matured past that yet, apparently."

"Maybe none of us really changes," I said.

Jodie blinked at me. "Maybe. Maybe not."

A flash of light behind the station's doors caught my attention. Creighton stood there, looking out, watching us—or watching something. When he saw me see him, he turned away and walked back inside. I wondered what was going to happen to him now.

I was sure Jodie would tell me. Tomorrow. Or the next day.

"Maybe he's a good cop, just like everyone always thought he would be," I said.

"Maybe. Good night, Clare." She turned and walked toward the station.

I walked toward Nathan, Chester, Seth, and Marion as Sarah's words rang in my head. She had mocked me for never doing anything with my career other than working at The Rescued Word.

"She who gets the last mock . . . ," I said under my breath as I walked toward the people who made my life almost too perfect to care.

It didn't matter that in high school I'd never been voted "most likely" to do anything. I had succeeded. I loved my job, my friends, my family. It was good to live and work amid good, kind people, some of whom also rescued words. It was very good.

Maybe, even, it was the best.

Afterword

I made up the letter from Bob Hope. However, it was based on a letter I found online that'd he'd written to Colonel Tom Parker. I also discovered that Mr. Hope might have owned one of the original Hoovens. Maybe my fictional letter wasn't too much of a stretch. Thanks for the memories, Mr. Hope.

Ready to find
your next great read?

Let us help.

Visit prh.com/nextread